Breaking Arrows

Books by Luis Figueredo

Breaking Arrows
Dime

Breaking Arrows

Luis Figueredo

SPEAKING VOLUMES, LLC
NAPLES, FLORIDA
2022

Breaking Arrows

ISBN 978-1-64540-796-6

In memory of my Leonberger Swayze
and my Mastiff Sammie, two loyal friends
whose constant love and companionship
will be forever remembered.

Acknowledgments

To Tiger Hobia and Jeremiah Hobia, the Meekos of the Kialegee Tribal Town who have never stopped fighting for their tribal members and who inspired me to write this story. To Moises Grayson and Shane Rolls for your friendship, wonderful advice, and guidance. And to my family for your love, support and understanding that even when I was physically around, sometimes I was mentally elsewhere, trying to come up with twists for the story.

Chapter One

WETUMKA, OKLAHOMA

Samuel Tiger was eight years old and the younger of two Indian boys who decided to beat the sweltering Oklahoma heat by going for a swim in C.C. pond. The tribe's elders repeatedly warned the town's children to stay away from the abandoned pond about a mile north of town, but the pull of the cool water in parched and suffocating temperatures was too much to resist.

The pond was overgrown with weeds. The rusting remains of cars covered in leaves and moss that had been abandoned over several decades were littered throughout the grounds. Copperheads and pygmy rattlesnakes burrowed in the twisted and rotting remains. The boys slipped through a gap in the rusted barbed wire fence, threading haphazardly past the crumbling walls of separate outbuildings reclaimed by nature towards the pond.

Near the pond's edge the raised back-end of a submerged 1957 Chevelle with its reddish color broke through the muddy water and the slippery surface served as a launching point. Samuel threw himself headfirst into the pond, eager to feel a reprieve from the intolerable heat. He splashed around and called to Jacob to jump in after him. But Jacob had second thoughts and elected to just watch Samuel jump and splash in the warm pond water. Each time Samuel lost his footing on the algae-covered rocks, his head slipped under the black water. The third time he slipped, he stopped having fun. Samuel looked for a spot along the edge where he could climb out. He didn't remember the embankment being as steep as it now appeared from the water. On his last attempt to escape the murky water, he slipped, hitting the dark liquid face first and plunging into darkness. After a few seconds he panicked, moving his arms and legs frantically. His legs and arms kicked up stirred mud and his throat and lungs burned with the bitter taste of brackish water. Samuel screamed for Jacob to pull him out.

Jacob, only ten and small for his age, almost fell into the water himself when he tried reaching for his friend. Samuel's screams for help were soon relegated to a queue of bubbles as his tired arms and legs struggled to keep his head above water. The rumble of silty and dark liquid began to envelop Samuel, and his small lungs ached. Jacob desperately looked for anything that he could use to shorten the distance between them. He spotted a long tree branch and inched it toward Samuel's hands. Groping as if by instinct, Samuel's small hands reached for the branch until they found it. Slowly Jacob pulled Samuel from the darkness of C.C. pond.

It was five days later when Samuel complained of headaches and a stiff neck. His symptoms rapidly worsened. By the time they transported him to Saint Francis Hospital in Tulsa, Samuel was suffering from a high fever, vomiting and hallucinations. During the hours between sunset and sunrise, Samuel slipped in and out of consciousness. In the final conscious minutes of his life, he locked his eyes on the tribal elders gathered around his hospital bed. He heard their singing; beautiful songs in his native Creek language. Even while doing her best to maintain a cheerful tone Samuel's mother's face was white with fright. He didn't have to look into her red sunken eyes to know that he was on the last leg of his journey. The tribal members continued to chant and pray, stealing anxious glances at Samuel. His mother took his small hand and placed it inside of her own. Samuel looked up at her and smiled faintly. He was trying to say goodbye.

At dawn, when the faint gray light of morning leaked through the window, Samuel Tiger was gone.

*****

SAMUEL'S MOTHER SCREAMED a painful, piercing cry and collapsed in a chair, plunging into her own bottomless darkness. She was too emotionally distraught to concentrate on the voices behind her. Samuel's doctor was trying to explain to Jeremiah Tiger, Samuel's grandfather and the chief of the Kialegee Tribe that Samuel's death resulted from an infection most likely caused by a deadly amoeba known as Naegleria fowleri. A tiny single-celled organism with a ravenous attraction to the human brain.

"The amoeba travels up the nose to the brain, where it causes inflammation of the lining of the brain and spinal cord. Then it attacks the central nervous system and destroys brain tissue. This condition is called primary amoebic meningoencephalitis, and it is almost always fatal," Doctor Gupta said.

Jeremiah clenched and unclenched his fists.

"How did my grandson come in contact with that . . . amoeba?" He asked with a hint of impatience in his voice.

Doctor Gupta, who headed up the neurological practice at Saint Francis hospital frowned and shook her head. "The most logical explanation is that Samuel went swimming in contaminated water."

"Is that the only way he could have caught this?"

Doctor Gupta nodded. "Yes, I'm afraid so. This is an extremely rare condition. The amoeba lives in the mud in warm stagnant water in lakes and ponds. Samuel must have gone swimming in a contaminated lake or pond, and the amoeba probably entered through his nasal passage and made its way to his brain..."

Jeremiah's skin prickled with sharp needles. He glanced over at the mirror and eyed his fractured reflection; his long silver hair pulled back tight in a ponytail, his bronze skin and his eyes so dark they were almost black.

He let out a slow deep sigh before speaking in a low voice. "There's no place for our kids to swim so some of them wander off to the old Concentration Camp outside of our town. There's a small pond there."

Doctor Gupta quickly scrawled a note. "Concentration camp?" she repeated slowly, wondering if she had heard him correctly.

"There is an old-World War II prisoner of war camp outside of town. It once held German prisoners, but it was closed and abandoned right after the end of the war. There's a basin that was used as a reservoir when the camp was open."

"And," the Doctor asked, prodding Jeremiah. "You think Samuel may have gone swimming in this abandoned reservoir?"

Jeremiah's face tightened. He suddenly felt the weight of his Tribe's problems tugging at him with each word, so kept his answers short. "Yep."

"There's nowhere else Samuel could have gone swimming?" The Doctor asked, just to be sure. Jeremiah was becoming agitated.

"No, like I said, there is nowhere else," the Chief said and then the guilt came. The Doctor was saying something, but Jeremiah wasn't listening. His mind was overwrought with regret and the voice of his conscience blamed him for his grandson's death.

Like all Kialegee, Jeremiah grew up learning the oral history and traditions of his tribe from the tribal elders. There was a time when the Kialegee had been the most feared warriors of all the Creek Tribes. In the 1700s until the infamous "Trail of Tears" that forced the eastern tribes to abandon their homes and move westward to Oklahoma, the Muscogee Creek and the other sixty-five tribal towns that made up the Creek Confederacy all respected the Kialegee. In times of war, the Kialegee led the Creek war parties into battle. They were the fiercest warriors of the Creek Confederacy. Even though those days were long behind them, the Kialegee were a proud people ever mindful of their place in history. But the abuses over the years had worn down their psyche to a point where they seemed resigned to living a desolate existence and accepting the few scraps of charity that the Bureau of Indian Affairs and the Muscogee Creek gave them.

The Kialegee eventually lost all their lands in a string of treaties with the United States. The treaties were supposed to set aside reservation lands for all Creek Indians. But the Muscogee Creek Nation with the help of the Bureau of Indian Affairs claimed ownership and dominion over all Creek lands in Oklahoma. Since that time the Muscogee Creek Nation grew wealthy and powerful from oil and gas leases and casinos, and the Kialegee barely survived. As Chief of the Kialegee, Jeremiah was unwavering in his commitment to improve the living conditions for his members. After Samuel's death, he recognized that he would have to change his tactics if he was going to make sure that no other innocent child suffered the same fate as his grandson.

Chapter Two

Samuel Tiger's death went unnoticed. No one outside of Indian country mourned him. The State Center for Disease Control made only a half-hearted attempt to investigate the cause of death, and only the Wetumka Herald reported it. Nikki Slayer, a lawyer in the Tulsa County Public Defender's office, found it undeniably repulsive how little the State of Oklahoma seemed to care about an Indian boy's death.

At forty-five years old, Nikki was too old, tainted and countrified to say anything other than what was on her mind. While her sassy twang took some of the bite out of her harsh and opinionated manner, there was no middle ground for Nikki. She graduated from Tulsa Law School twenty-one years ago, and she had been fighting for the underdog ever since. One case and one cause after another. She was passionate about Indian rights and volunteered her time when she was able to help Oklahoma tribes that didn't have the resources to hire a tribal attorney.

She had spent the last three years doing free legal work for the Kialegee Tribe. When Nikki first laid eyes on the two peeling and soot stained double wide office trailers connected by a wooden walkway off an unmaintained road and a sagging tin fence that passed itself off as the Kialegee Tribal headquarters, she knew then she would never leave them.

Jeremiah was standing outside smoking a cigarette when Nikki arrived at the headquarters for the Business Committee meeting. Her eyes watered as she hugged Jeremiah. She didn't mention Samuel because she knew he wasn't ready to talk about his grandson. Instead, it was a quick and silent embrace.

Nikki took a step back. "So, an emergency Business Committee meeting, what brought this on?"

Frown lines creased Jeremiah's forehead. "I don't see any reason in putting off what needs to be done."

Nikki gave Jeremiah a curious look. "And what would that be?"

"I think this time they might listen to you about the casino," he said as he lit a fresh cigarette off the embers of an old one.

"Really?" Nikki said, sounding surprised. Every time Nikki suggested to the Business Committee that they build a casino on a parcel of allotted Indian land in Broken Arrow, a bleak mood settled over them all. The Business Committee fretted over opening a casino only ten miles from the MCN's flagship casino, "The River Spirit." On each occasion, more than one took pains to express deep-seated concerns that the MCN might respond harshly and punish the Kialegee Tribe for trying to compete with their gambling operations. However, there was something around Jeremiah's eyes; a fire behind the sadness. Something that said this time he would make sure that the Business Committee put the Kialegee's needs ahead of any fears of reprisal.

"Won't be easy. But some on the committee are starting to realize that there is absolutely no other way," Jeremiah said.

"What about the Second Chief?" Nikki asked.

Jeremiah shook his head. "Nora will never go against the MCN."

Nikki nodded. "Is she still pissed off that she lost to you by three votes?"

"What do you think?"

Nikki nodded thoughtfully. "I think Nora believes that if she continues to oppose the casino, the MCN will fund her campaign and she can finally beat you."

Nora had been consolidating support by building a web of disgruntled tribal members to help her take control of the tribe from the minute she lost the election. She was capable and shrewd. A woman of presence with strong and square, jutting features. She was adept at spinning lies and had some tribal members convinced that only with the support of the MCN could the Kialegee prosper. Jeremiah and his trusted confidant, Juanita Yargee, who sat on the Business Committee with him, saw her for what she was: an ignorant blowhard.

"Is the Business Committee already inside?" Nikki asked.

"Everyone but Roley."

Nikki frowned. "It would be nice to have him in there if we're going to discuss the casino. You could always count on his support."

"I couldn't reach him."

Nikki followed Jeremiah down the claustrophobic hallway lined with gun-metal filing cabinets towards the only room large enough to hold meetings. The room smelled of coffee and stale tobacco. In the center was a wooden table, where three other Business Committee members were already seated. When Jeremiah entered the room Juanita and Cora Jimboy stood up and greeted their Chief. Nora sitting on one end of the table didn't rise, instead she glared at Jeremiah and gave him an almost imperceptible nod.

Jeremiah took his seat at the far end of the table, directly opposite from Nora. It could be seen as a power play, but the truth was simpler. He disliked Nora and preferred to maintain physical distance whenever possible.

After a few introductory remarks, Jeremiah turned to the subject of the land in Broken Arrow.

"I asked you here because we need to revisit the idea of building a casino in Broken Arrow. I've asked Nikki to once again explain why we should develop the Broken Arrow land."

Nikki pulled six pieces of paper from her folder and passed them around the table. It was the same summary she had passed out at previous committee meetings when the subject of the casino came up. She made it a habit to bring the folder whenever she attended a tribal meeting since the subject occasionally came up.

Nikki pointed to the last paragraph with her pen. "Let me start by cutting to the most important piece of information on this paper. If the tribe builds a casino on the Broken Arrow property, it will generate fifty million a year for the tribe."

Nora frowned at the piece of paper. The very idea of a casino in Broken Arrow was preposterous. "The MCN will never let us build a casino there," she said in a biting tone. She viewed the entire enterprise as rather hopeless. Once the casino project got set into motion, the MCN and the people with true power in Oklahoma would line up against them."

"If you have any thoughts on another way, Nora, I'd love to hear it," Jeremiah said. Typically, that was enough to shut Nora up. She excelled at tearing down the efforts of others but rarely offered anything constructive. This time, though she wasn't so easily silenced.

"Pissing off the MCN isn't going to move our tribe forward. That's my thought. You're just stepping into a rattlesnake den."

"You need to make a decision on what's best for the Kialegee without being afraid of upsetting the MCN," Nikki responded.

Nikki could feel Nora's eyes drilling into her. "Of course the MCN won't like a little competition, but you don't need their permission to develop your land."

Jeremiah agreed with Nikki. He spent a few moments watching Nikki argue for the casino and stand steadfast in the face of withering criticism. He admired her resolve and passion. If Nikki had a glaring weakness it was with restraint; she always spoke her mind, consequences be damned. When Nikki accused the Muscogee Nation of stealing the Kialegee's land and making sure that the Kialegee remained a poor and vulnerable tribe, Jeremiah could see that Nikki was grating and scraping on old wounds and shot her a look that said, "Ease up they're on our side."

Cora and Juanita seem to awaken from their stupor and the room became a melee of nervous and belligerent chatter.

Nikki listened to the same debate the Business Committee had at every meeting when she raised the issue of building a casino in Broken Arrow. She could practically predict, verbatim, who would say what. A sardonic bark from Nora, a gleam of thoughtfulness mixed with trepidation from Cora and Juanita's full support.

Clearing his throat, Jeremiah said, "What Nikki is trying to say is that we need to develop our own businesses so we can take care of our members. Wetumka is too small to offer our tribe any real economic development opportunities. Broken Arrow is the fastest growing and wealthiest community in the state."

"Also, the most powerful, Nora scoffed. "They will never allow us to build a casino there. And what about the MCN?"

Jeremiah's expression turned sour. The Kialegee Tribe's leadership was composed of simple and honest people conditioned over the years to put the Muscogee Creek Nation's interests ahead of their own. The Kialegee leaders made it a practice of soliciting the MCN's advice before making decisions. To Jeremiah, it always felt like the Kialegee was asking for permission.

For most of the Creek Confederacy's history, the Kialegee were celebrated for being fierce warriors who fought vigorously to defend Creek lands. Now, the Kialegee were a conquered people; an afterthought looked down upon by other Creeks. Jeremiah wondered how his younger tribal members would respond to real adversity that couldn't be handled by posting a negative comment on Facebook or Twitter. When the MCN retaliated, he wasn't sure if they would stand together or run and point fingers at each other.

"The Kialegee need to stop worrying about the MCN. They have housing and programs for their elderly. What do the Kialegee have? Muscogee children have a youth center and a swimming pool for their kids to swim in and we have nothing but a rotten cesspool that is poisoning our children," he said, his voice rising with anger.

Jeremiah looked around at the faces of the members of the Business Committee. They were all relatives and close friends that he had known since childhood. All the Chief had to do was flash them a withering stare, and all but Nora would remain silent.

"The land in Broken Arrow belongs to a Kialegee Tribal member. If we want to develop the land to benefit our tribe, we should be able to do it without asking the Muscogee for permission," he said.

The chill in the Chief's mood was obvious. It was the same chill that recently occurred every time he thought about his grandson or someone dared to mention him. Jeremiah was different from Nikki. There were no animated hand gestures or thespian-like facial contortions when he made his point. They did, however, share a few qualities. Each possessed a deep-seated desire to help the Kialegee Tribe, and both had a deep distrust for the motives of the Bureau of Indian Affairs and the MCN.

"If we decide to develop a casino in Broken Arrow, I will sit with the Muscogee Chief. Dialogue is good but not capitulation," Jeremiah stressed to his committee.

The three women on the committee sat with downcast eyes, but with grim expressions. After an uncomfortable silence Jeremiah turned to Nikki and said, "Thank you, Nikki. The members of the committee and I will continue to discuss the casino opportunity and we will let you know." However, when the time came to put the question to a vote, Jeremiah knew if he insisted on moving forward, all but one would cast aside their personal opinions and support him.

Nikki stood and nodded when Jeremiah offered to walk her out to her car. They heard the rancor from the committee as soon as the door shut behind them.

Jeremiah lit a cigarette and casually told Nikki to be patient. "The committee will come around. They just need a little more time to weigh everything," he said.

Nikki let out an exasperated breath. One of the increasingly frustrating aspects of representing the Kialegee Tribe was what she called their "Ostrich Mentality." Every time there was a problem, the tribe preferred to bury its head in the sand.

Nikki didn't mask her emotions or worry about political protocol when she and the Chief were alone. "Hell, Jeremiah," she muttered, shaking her head, "we can play the 'What if' game forever. But at some point, you are going to have to pull the trigger," she said with genuine fury. "So why not now?"

Jeremiah took a long pull on his cigarette as he tried to digest the challenge in front of his tribe. Slowly, he began to nod. "It won't be easy."

"Nothing worthwhile ever is," Nikki sighed. "The Bureau and the Muscogee will throw every roadblock at you they can to get you to give up . . . Remember, it's about business and exercising control. None of it is personal," Nikki said.

Jeremiah smiled inwardly. "That's where you're wrong," he thought, It's all personal. Jeremiah took a deep breath and then said, "Prepare the resolution authorizing the casino."

Nikki took a drag from Jeremiah's cigarette. "You'll have it in the morning."

"So, what do we do next?" Jeremiah asked.

Nikki's face twisted in thought. She seemed to be rolling a particular thought over in her mind. "Dode who runs the IT department for the

Chickasaw Nation told me about this lawyer, Pierce Evangelista, that she met out of Miami, Florida."

Jeremiah's eyes widened. "Miami, Florida? Are you sure a lawyer from Miami would be the best choice to represent our interests?"

Nikki smiled wryly. "Yep, he's represented tribes all over the country. He successfully represented a tribe in the Pacific Northwest on a controversial casino project and he was the lawyer that represented that poor Wisconsin Tribe a while back that had some iron ore on its rez. He convinced several countries to let the tribe sell its ore as part of some international consortium and now that tribe's rolling in money."

Jeremiah's eyes squinted deep in thought. He said nothing at first and then slowly nodded. "I remember hearing something about that."

Jeremiah appeared to be measuring Nikki. "Why can't you just handle this for us?"

Nikki shrugged. "My specialty is defending people accused of committing crimes. I'm not cut out to do this kind of work. The tribe will need someone with experience negotiating multi-million-dollar financing deals. Someone who can bring the Kialegee Tribe credibility the instant the tribe goes out into the marketplace to look for investors. This will get really complicated and we need someone on our side who can negotiate for the tribe and help them structure project financing on the most favorable terms," Nikki answered. She paused, suddenly staggered by the thought of the millions of dollars that the tribe would need to borrow to build a casino.

"We're going to need a specialist, a heavy hitter. And someone not from around here. After Dode told me about him, I googled him and from based on everything I learned . . . he's the real deal."

Jeremiah took one last puff and stubbed it against the sole of his boot. "He sounds expensive."

Nikki made a pensive face. "You're right. But my momma always said if you don't ask, you don't get." Before Jeremiah could utter a single word, Nikki said. "I'll send you his contact information."

When Nikki got into the car, Jeremiah could have sworn he saw on her face the hint of a smirk.

Jeremiah liked Nikki. More importantly, he trusted her. She was wickedly funny, with a salty tongue and loyal to the Kialegee. Plus, she could guzzle whisky and play poker with the best of them.

As he watched Nikki drive away, a frown creased Jeremiah's well-lined brow. This was not a path his tribe would normally take. He could only guess what kind of pressure was going to be put on his tribal members. The Kialegee were good, honest people doing the best they could to exist, and now they were about to step into a high-stakes drama. Jeremiah suspected that the road ahead would undoubtedly be more treacherous than his imagination could do justice to. Given his lack of alternatives, Jeremiah decided he would rather go down fighting than stand by and watch his tribe wither away. At that moment, Jeremiah decided. He would not call the lawyer. Instead, he made up his mind to fly to Miami and ask for his help in person.

Chapter Three

MIAMI

Jeremiah Tiger stepped off the elevator on the 52nd floor. The entrance to the downtown office was so lavish that Jeremiah instantly second guessed his decision to come to Miami. The polished marble floors, coffered ceilings and rich millwork were unlike anything he had ever seen. But it was the floor to ceiling windows that commanded the room and his attention. The endless view of Biscayne Bay on one side and the Miami skyline below him on the other was a constant reminder of how high up he was. Jeremiah wasn't comfortable standing in the middle of all this opulence, but most of all he wasn't comfortable being 600 feet up. After Jeremiah asked the receptionist for Mr. Evangelista, he walked over to the corner far away from the windows to wait. He stood by a potted plant with his back to the wall, hoping to be as inconspicuous as possible.

Jeremiah didn't have to wait long. Pierce was dressed in a navy blue pinstriped Brioni suit, a white Eton shirt with French cuffs, a slate blue tie and plain toe oxford shoes. Pierce's eyes swept the imposing space as he walked over. The move was reflexive in nature. As he drew close, he extended his hand.

"Chief Tiger...I'm Pierce Evangelista. It's an honor to meet you."

Jeremiah took his hand. "Thank you for agreeing to meet with me on such short notice."

Pierce flashed a perfect set of white teeth and a surprisingly warm smile.

"It's my pleasure. Are you in Miami on other business?" Pierce asked as he escorted the Chief to his office, past cubicles filled with women manning the phones and pecking away at keyboards.

Jeremiah shook his head. "No, I came all this way to see you. If I am going to ask a man for his help, I figure I need to make an effort to go see him and ask in person."

Pierce's tone suddenly took on a somber note. "I was very sorry to learn about your grandson."

Jeremiah shot Pierce a surprised look.

"If the Chief of an Oklahoma Tribe is traveling all the way to Miami to see me, I'm going to do my research and find out why," Pierce replied.

Jeremiah wasn't comfortable talking about what happened to his grandson Samuel, so he just nodded.

Pierce suspected that the Chief's reason for coming to Miami and Samuel's death were connected in some way. "Chief Tiger," Pierce began.

"Please call me Jeremiah," his voice was scratchy.

Pierce nodded. "Why don't you tell me what I can do to help you," he said in a sympathetic tone.

Jeremiah let out a long, slow breath. One brought on by his angst and uncertainty about the path he was about to put his tribe on.

"We are a poor tribe and I believe that we have some land in a Tulsa suburb...good land that can be developed so we can bring some economic development to our tribe."

Pierce studied Jeremiah. He wondered why Jeremiah phrased the last sentence that he "believed that they had some land."

Pierce was unreadable as Jeremiah continued to make his pitch regarding developing a casino on a parcel of land in one of the most affluent and influential neighborhoods in all of Tulsa County. He didn't need a briefing to know that any attempt by the Kialegee Tribe to develop Indian gaming on that land would encounter fierce opposition. His experience with Indian casinos had shown him that to the very top of the political food chain, a tribe's rights were not important. What mattered was staying in power and the votes to keep them there.

"When you said that you believe that you own the land, is this something that you're not completely sure about?"

Jeremiah shrugged. "The land belongs to a member of the Kialegee Tribe...its allotted land. It was given to his family under the general allotment act passed by Congress . . ."

"Yes, I'm familiar with the Dawes Act," Pierce interrupted. "It was passed in the late 1800s when the U.S. split up the Creek Reservation."

The act was supposed to help Indians assimilate by doing away with communal ownership of land, by giving each member of the tribe ownership to one hundred and sixty acres. Critics of the act, however, saw it as a thinly veiled attempt by powerful oil companies to steal the mineral rights to lands rich in oil from poor uneducated Indians. And that was exactly what happened.

Pierce squinted in thought while his secretary appeared with two cups of coffee. "So how can I help you and the Kialegee Tribe?"

Jeremiah drank his coffee. "We'd like to hire you to help us get the financing for the casino," Jeremiah said.

By the time Jeremiah finished his sentence, Pierce had already thought of six reasons why it would be extremely difficult to build a casino on that property and was busy putting the finishing touches on number seven of his mental list. His brain was experiencing what an art dealer goes through when examining a reproduction of a well-known original. At first glance from a distance everything looks fine, but upon closer inspection all the mistakes and missed details begin to come to the surface.

"Jeremiah," Pierce took a deep breath and let it out slowly. "Getting financing for your project is something I can help you with, but I need to know that if I commit to work on this, you're jumping in the foxhole with me. So, I need you to answer a question for me. You could have developed this land into a casino a long time ago, why now?"

Jeremiah appeared to consider his next words carefully. "It's not what I want. But it's something I now realize I have to do to save my tribe."

Pierce studied the Kialegee Chief for signs that the Chief's decision to come to Miami and ask for his help might have been an impulsive reaction to his grandson's death. "There will be blowback." Pierce warned him. "And it could be significant. No one will want you there."

Jeremiah didn't flinch or act surprised as Pierce laid out scenarios of those that would pressure the tribe to abandon the project and what would happen if the tribe refused. The battle lines and pitfalls appeared to be already clear in Jeremiah's mind.

Based on his prior dealings with wealthy tribes, Pierce suspected that the MCN would not sit back and allow the Kialegee to compete with them without a fight. The MCN consisted of seventy-eight thousand tribal members and owned seven casinos in Northeastern Oklahoma, but their crown jewel, the River Spirit Casino was only a few miles away from the Kialegee land. Pierce had heard rumors about the Muscogee Nation's Chief. He ruled the Muscogee Nation with an iron fist and no one on the Nation's National Council ever dared to question him or any of the heavily inflated contracts he doled out to his friends doing business with the Nation.

"What about the Chief of the Muscogee Nation? Have you given any thought to how he will react?" Pierce asked.

Jeremiah stared off into space and shook his head. "He won't like it."

"Yeah, he won't . . .," Pierce frowned before turning his attention to the other groups that he suspected would oppose the Kialegee. There were also the Bureau of Indian Affairs and the National Indian Gaming Commission to consider. The Bureau and Gaming Commission regulated Indian casinos, and both agencies genuflected to the powerful gaming tribes like the Muscogee Creek Nation. Regardless of the Kialegee's legal rights to develop their property, Pierce's instincts told him that the Creek Nation would pressure both agencies to withhold approvals. He'd seen it before. With the right combination of political pressure and under the table payoffs, they would bring the Kialegee project to a standstill.

Finally, there was the State of Oklahoma and the influential Broken Arrow Bible thumping community to contend with. They put up with the Creek and Cherokee Tribes much like Americans, which tolerated the Russians during the Cold War. But there was a protocol to be followed. Unspoken rules, and one of them was that the Indians would not put up a casino or smoke shop in an affluent white neighborhood. As long as the Indians knew their place and didn't upset the balance, Indian Tribes could earn money selling cigarettes and operating gaming facilities. However, the small Kialegee Tribal Town was on the cusp of crossing the proverbial line and threatening the delicate balance by building an Indian casino in the heart of the most affluent white community in all of Oklahoma.

Pierce let his eyes linger on Jeremiah, but his stoic demeanor made him difficult to read. "Let me make a suggestion," Pierce said. "Why don't we both think about everything we discussed here today and meet tomorrow around 7.30 am for breakfast at your hotel. At that time, we can decide whether to move forward together. Does that sound fair?"

Jeremiah stood, extending his hand. "It does. I'll see you tomorrow and thank you."

Pierce waited a few minutes after Jeremiah was gone before picking up the dossier prepared by his associate, Noah Grayson, on the Kialegee Tribal Town. From what he read, most of the tribe was unemployed and those lucky enough to have jobs earned minimum wage. The tribe received very few federal subsidies and suffered from very high rates of alcoholism and opioid addiction.

Noah called Pierce's assistant and asked if he could come up to see him.

"Is he alone?" Noah asked as he walked towards Pierce's office. The assistant was on the phone but gave him a nod and motioned towards the door. Noah knocked before entering.

"How did it go with the Chief?" Noah said, making himself comfortable on the couch.

Pierce replayed parts of his earlier conversation with Jeremiah in his mind, reading between the lines. "I'll know more in the morning."

Noah seemed eager to skip ahead to the point where Pierce agreed to represent the Kialegee. "They could really use our help."

Pierce nodded. "They could. But we have to be sure that they're fully committed and are ready for the firestorm that will come. His decision to build a casino could be an emotional response to his grandson's death."

"Meaning?"

"Meaning that we have to think of the people and institutions that we are going to approach to finance the project. If we recommend this project, we must be sure that the Kialegee will stay in the trenches with us and not have a change of heart when their neighbors and the rest of Oklahoma treats them like a pariah," Pierce said.

Noah shrugged. "Every deal has risks."

Pierce gave a subtle nod, confirming Noah's point. "They do. And most investors can tolerate risks associated with approvals getting held up in red tape or having to challenge a regulatory ruling. But cutting and running is not acceptable."

Noah rationalized away any obstacles. "And if they're willing to go the distance. What then?"

"That's a big if," Pierce said, shifting his gaze to the detailed information compiled in the dossier. He was satisfied that Jeremiah understood the blowback the Kialegee would suffer. He thought about the dark circles beneath Jeremiah's eyes that served as additional evidence that the Chief was not taking this decision lightly.

"After I talk to Jeremiah in the morning, I'll let you know what I decide."

Chapter Four

Jeremiah should have gone to bed hours ago. He should have ignored the small bottles of scotch in the hotel's minibar. But after five years as chief of the Kialegee Tribe, the weight of their struggles and now the death of his grandson had become a heavy burden. Instead, he hovered over the small bar, wondering and struggling with pangs of guilt until he finally surrendered to its pull. The more Jeremiah drank, the more helpless and utterly disgusted with himself he felt. Samuel's death gave him clarity, and he'd stopped ignoring the little voice in his head that told him every step he had taken until now had been wrong.

But there were still factors that could not be ignored as a raging storm of conflicting emotions battled inside him. The Kialegee Tribe had very little, and to ask them to put it at risk was still a decision that couldn't be taken lightly. He questioned whether his insatiable need to make Samuel's death count for something was affecting his judgement. Jeremiah had no reason to doubt what Pierce had told him earlier in the day. He knew there would be a heavy price to pay. Once the Kialegee went public with their decision to build a casino in Broken Arrow, they would become a target. The few tribal members who had jobs working for the MCN or the local office of the BIA in Muskogee would lose them. The federal grants administered by the MCN for the local tribes including the Kialegee would get held up and the Kialegee tribal members would be turned away from the health care clinic run by MCN.

Jeremiah looked up at the Miami moon with a healthy dose of self-loathing. He suspected he had always known the simple embarrassing truth that the BIA was not there to help the Kialegee but to maintain the status quo. His tribe had chosen him to be its leader but each time he didn't question the BIA when it protected the MCN's agenda and treated the Kialegee like children or worse, interlopers, Jeremiah failed them. Until recently, Jeremiah fell into the same trap as the other Kialegee chiefs before him. He tried to work with the BIA. Now, five years later, he found himself with Samuel's blood on his hands. Jeremiah's mind bounced back and forth between overwhelming despair and rage. He was through with rationalizing and making excuses for the BIA's bureaucracy and actions. Every time they turned down a Kialegee request for help, the BIA treated the Kialegee as if it had forgotten its place in the natural order of things.

After meeting Pierce, he knew that the tribe needed someone like him if they were going to get past the Oklahoma power brokers and BIA gatekeepers. It would take someone like him to navigate Washington's bureaucracy and cut through the red tape. Someone well connected in the investment banking community that could help a small Indian tribe, like the Kialegee, garner the credibility that they would need to borrow the millions that would be required to develop the casino. Jeremiah had no personal experience to draw on when it came to assessing Pierce Evangelista's capabilities. All he had known was what Nikki had told him, but after meeting him, his instincts told him he was the right choice.

Jeremiah took the small bottle of whisky and brought it to his lips and emptied it with two large gulps. It went back smoothly and bit his throat with a mellow burning sensation. He sat in the darkened room quietly emptying the small bottles. He didn't care which bottle he grabbed, liquor was liquor at this point, and they would all be empty before the night was done. He decided they would help him forget about yesterday and tomorrow and his pain and obligations for one night. When he had finished with the miniature bottles, Jeremiah moved on to the beer in the small fridge and by the time he was done with the two small bottles of wine, Jeremiah fell into a deep slumber propped up against the closet door.

*****

IT WAS ALMOST eight in the morning by the time Jeremiah called Pierce to tell him he would be late for their breakfast meeting. He claimed he wasn't feeling well, moaned something about eating bad sea food the night before. Pierce checked his watch when he spotted Jeremiah walking through the hotel lobby. Jeremiah moved slowly and deliberately. Each step looked like it required more effort than he could spare. Before Jeremiah could apologize, Pierce smiled ever so slightly and handed him two aspirin and a cup of coffee.

Jeremiah took a deep breath and nodded. "Thanks."

Pierce could see Jeremiah was hungover and in no mood to eat. "Why don't we skip breakfast and talk on the way to the airport?" He suggested.

Jeremiah nodded and took several sips of coffee as he waited for the caffeine to jump start his thought process. During their first meeting, Pierce had asked Jeremiah to consider the risks and toxic consequences that could result from trying to develop a casino project in Broken Arrow. Once the Tribe went public with its decision, the blowback could devastate a small tribe like the Kialegee much like an F-5 tornado cutting a path through a trailer park.

Pierce knew better than anyone that sheer desire was not enough. His grasp of the big picture was second to none, and he suspected that an Indian casino project in the middle of Oklahoma's bible belt could get messy.

He waited for Jeremiah to slide into the front seat of the car. Once he was inside, Pierce climbed into the Mercedes-Benz S65, closed the door and looked at Jeremiah.

"Have you given more thought to what we talked about?" He asked Jeremiah.

Jeremiah squinted and massaged his forehead. "We're already in the middle of a damn battle. It's time the Kialegee start acting like it."

Pierce considered his reply as he pulled the gearshift into drive and took his foot off the brake. Pierce had a simple rule before he agreed to represent a client. He laid out all the risks, costs and worst-case scenarios, including those outcomes where they didn't succeed. Once he was satisfied that the client understood the pros and cons as well as possible collateral damage that could occur, Pierce would decide whether to take the case.

That Jeremiah used the word battle to describe the Kialegee current circumstances told Pierce what he needed to know. He could see Jeremiah's burning desire to break free from meager government handouts that the tribe needed to survive. Pierce allowed some time for the aspirin's effects to kick in. He drove silently taking several back streets through Coral Gables to the airport expecting Interstate-95 to be gridlocked during Miami's morning rush hour.

Pierce pulled the car in front of the airline terminal and looked at his watch. They still had a few minutes. "If I'm going to represent you, I need you to understand, once we pull the pin on the grenade there's no putting it back in."

Jeremiah shook his head and then in a resigned tone said, "We never discussed your fee."

Pierce smiled benevolently. He knew that the Kialegee Tribe didn't have any money. "If I take the case, you can pay me when we get the casino open . . . But I have to warn you. I'm not cheap."

Jeremiah glanced at Pierce sideways, not sure what to make of his gesture. He assumed that Pierce would insist on being paid out of the money he raised. "I'm a little confused...Yesterday, you told me that the people of Oklahoma would burn us at the stake and the BIA would tie us up in red-tape if we tried to go through with the casino."

"I did," Pierce nodded. "Politics is a rough business."

"So, why would you take this project on a contingency when there's a chance that after the dust settles, we won't be able to pay you?" Jeremiah asked in a skeptical tone.

"Because I believe I can get this casino open." Pierce said with the look of a man who had been down this road before.

"Raising project financing is much more difficult when a portion of the proceeds are used to pay legal fees. The way to instill confidence is for investors and lenders to see that I'm also willing to take a risk. And for me to do that, I need to be sure that you fully understand what lies ahead and what I expect of you . . . This isn't going to be a skirmish, it's a war of attrition," Pierce stressed and paused long enough to be convinced that Jeremiah understood before he continued. "People will attack you from every direction. Folks you thought were friends will stab you in the back and the media will persecute you mercilessly. They will try to wear you down and break your spirit. And you won't be able to fight back... Not without pushing those people who haven't made up their minds whether to support or oppose the casino over to the other side...You will have to take all their personal attacks and turn the other cheek. Can you do that?" Pierce leaned back in his seat and waited for Jeremiah's response.

A scowl appeared on Jeremiah's leathered face. The idea of the Kialegee continuing to serve as everyone's punching bag didn't sit well with him. "My tribe is poor. If we don't succeed, we'll still be poor. You and the investors are the ones taking all the risks . . . We'll do whatever we have to. You have my word that the Kialegee are committed and ready for whatever it takes," Jeremiah said confidently.

Pierce studied his face for a moment. "Chief, that's what I was hoping to hear," Pierce said as he extended his right hand. "We have some challenges ahead of us."

There was a flicker of hope in Jeremiah's eyes when he shook Pierce's hand.

"So, what now?"

"I need to meet with the Business Committee."

"When can you come to Wetumka?" Jeremiah asked.

"I can be there next week."

Jeremiah nodded and got out of the car.

"Chief, one more thing," Pierce said.

Jeremiah turned around and leaned in.

"Just so we're clear, when the dust settles, the Kialegee will have a casino and I expect to be well paid for my services."

Jeremiah flashed Pierce a satisfied smile before turning and walking towards the airport terminal.

Chapter Five

KIALEGEE TRIBAL HEADQUARTERS
WETUMKA, OKLAHOMA

"Why did he have to look like Superman?" Payton Tiger mumbled as she studied the man walking next to her father. All she knew was that he was some "big deal." A lawyer from Miami who was supposed to fix everything; at least that's what her father, Jeremiah, told the Business Committee. She was sitting on the wooden stairs leading up to the Tribal Headquarters, her five-year-old Siberian Husky-German Shepherd mix, Kal, beside her.

The sun cast its warm rays on the steps. Kal craned his neck at the sound of Payton's voice and looked up at her, one of his eyes blue and the other brown.

"So, you don't think he looks like Superman?" Payton giggled to herself.

"Look again," she gestured at Kal. "He's got superhero muscles and a strong chin," Payton smiled as she rubbed Kal's head.

Payton loved comic books. When she was a kid, comic books had been her escape from her life on the reservation. In them, she found people with secret identities and superpowers, who protected those who were different and fought on the side of all that was good and right. She was different too. Every television program, magazine and social media website reminded her how different she was because she was a poor little Indian girl. Payton hated being different. When she was a kid she fantasized about a life off the reservation. She used to look at the super-heroes in her comic books and daydream that someday she would meet one, and he would sweep her off her feet. She could even imagine the panel art: an entire page with a handsome dimpled-chin superhero with athletic muscles protruding through his uniform carrying her in his arms.

Payton slid her own tortoise-shell sunglasses up her nose as the Chief and his guest walked across the parking lot towards the entrance. She raised her head, seeing if she got a sense of her father. When her nephew Samuel died, Payton sensed a crack in her father's armor, and she began to worry.

"You okay, Pops?" She asked, as her father and the stranger made their way past her to the entrance of the tribal headquarters.

The question everyone in the Kialegee Tribe was thinking, but only Payton dared to ask.

Jeremiah was peering at her, his face conflicted by his feelings. He was always happy to see his youngest daughter. But she was not welcome on tribal lands.

"I'm all right," he said, the words so familiar he didn't have to think about them.

Jeremiah eyed Payton's clothes and gave her a disapproving look. She was dressed in cutoff jeans and a T-shirt.

Payton was a controversial figure in the Kialegee Tribe but the only thing that all the Kialegee Tribal members could agree upon was that she was a beauty. She was just an inch shorter than her father who stood six feet tall and her long black lustrous hair fell halfway to her waist. She drew men into her orbit without having to bat an eyelash or flash a smile. Her almond-shaped eyes gave men a dreamy feeling; her lips were thick and full, and her cheekbones turned up to the sky.

Jeremiah did a quick double take over his shoulder and started to say something, but before he could get the words out Payton stood up and cut him off.

"I know I'm leaving. I just wanted to make sure you were all right."

Pierce briefly locked eyes with Payton and smiled while he ran his hand gently over Kal's head.

Payton shot Pierce a disapproving look. "Don't do that," Payton warned him. "He doesn't like strangers."

Kal made a sound and pushed his head up under Pierce's hand, wagging his tail. Pierce grinned, his blue eyes glistened in the Oklahoma sun. "We'll I guess we're not strangers," he said with amusement.

Payton blinked. Her sable eyes framed by long dark lashes looked at Pierce with a calculating expression.

"You better go," Jeremiah frowned. His frown was understandable.

Payton smiled, her gaze lifting from Pierce. She managed to hide the worry she'd been feeling.

"Okay, Pops," she nodded. "Kal come," Payton commanded and walked away before Pierce could introduce himself.

*****

WHEN PIERCE AND JEREMIAH entered the tribal headquarters, the other Business Committee members were just settling in. Nikki was the first to notice them and strode towards Pierce with her hand outstretched. Pierce spent the first hour of the meeting laying out the legal argument that relied on the Creek Confederacy's history, treaty rights and ultimately the Kialegee Tribal Town's rights to open a casino on Indian land in Broken Arrow, seventy miles away from the Tribe's headquarters in Wetumka. He explained to the Business Committee that to develop the casino it wasn't enough for the land to be Indian land owned by a Kialegee Tribal member. The Muscogee Creek Nation would try to protect their turf and argue that they alone could assert jurisdiction over the Creek Confederacy's former reservation and the Bureau of Indian Affairs, and the National Indian Gaming Commission would support their claim. Pierce laid out the steps that he and the tribe needed to accomplish in order to build the casino.

Nora sat across from Pierce and appraised him. She had the wrinkled eyes of a smoker and the intensity of her stare was a tool she often used to unnerve people, even her fellow committee members. It didn't take Pierce long to figure out where everyone stood. As for Nora, her expression and constant interruptions which mixed the truth with lies to keep the other business committee members off balance told Pierce everything he needed to know.

"Under the law, the tribe has to file a notice of intent to game no later than 120 days before they open. We're going to hire an ethnohistorian to prepare a report that documents the tribe's rights to exert jurisdiction," Pierce explained.

"What's an ethno-historian?" Juanita asked.

"An ethno-historian is a person who specializes in studying the historical records of cultures. In this case it would be someone well versed in the history of the Creek Indians. The ethno-historian will examine historical documents such as treaties and the journals of those present at the treaty signings. He or she will look at maps, folklore, myths, oral traditions, music, and paintings, anything really that will help give a detailed history of the tribe's history and culture."

Nikki nodded. "We can use the report to further reinforce the Kialegee tribe's right to exert jurisdiction over the land."

Nora rolled her eyes and shook her head "I hope y'all realize that this is going to stir up a hornet's nest with the MCN." She looked at Pierce with disdain. As far as Nora was concerned, he was an outsider who didn't understand the way things were done in Indian country.

"How would you feel if someone trespassed on your property and set up camp in your backyard?" Nora barked at Pierce.

Pierce took a sip of his lukewarm coffee. He had no desire to get into a pissing contest. Having said that, if he didn't answer the Second Chief's question, the Business Committee might think the MCN had rights to object to what the Kialegee did on their land.

"I wouldn't like it because as you said, they would be trespassing on my property. But that's not the case here. The KTT own the land in Broken Arrow. The MCN don't have the right to tell the Kialegee what they can do on their property just like the Kialegee has no right to tell them what they can do on the land where the River Spirit is located. As for backyard, Broken Arrow is more than a 40-minute drive from MCN headquarters in Okmulgee."

Nora remained silent, but the vein in her neck pulsed as she stared at Pierce.

Jeremiah suppressed a smile.

Pierce kept talking. "As I was saying, the ethno-historian will provide the tribe with a report that supports their claim to exert jurisdiction."

"But we own the land. Why do we need a report that says what we already know?" Cora Jimboy, the longest sitting member of the Business committee, asked.

"Being able to assert jurisdiction which is a requirement for opening a casino requires more than just owning the land. The tribe must have a historical connection to the land. That's where the ethno-historian can help us." Nikki said.

"In addition to the historical connection the tribe must demonstrate that they currently exercise jurisdiction over the land. For example, you could open a small office on the property and have some tribal meetings there."

After listing ten or so additional examples of what the tribe could do to demonstrate jurisdiction, Pierce said, "You don't need to do all of them, but I suggest you do a few. That will meet the NIGC's require-ments."

"We have that old house. We can turn it into a satellite tribal office," Juanita offered.

Nikki agreed. "All we'd have to do is open it twice a week." Nikki turned to Pierce. Would that be enough?"

Nora's nostrils flared with anger.

"As long as you post office hours on the door. It will make it easier for the NIGC to verify that there is an office. Should the NIGC claim that they sent someone by the house, and no one was there the posted office hours will help," Pierce said.

"You mentioned putting up signs," Cora said, starting to sound inter-ested.

Pierce nodded. "The signs serve to put everyone on notice that the land belongs to the Kialegee Tribal Town."

"The NIGC will see through that," Nora laughed.

"It doesn't matter," Pierce smiled without actually giving ground. "The NIGC has issued land opinions that list what tribes can do to assert jurisdiction. The examples I gave you are the ones listed in those opin-ions. If the Kialegee open an office and post signs and does a couple more things to establish a presence, the tribe will be fine."

"What happens if we do all that and the NIGC still turns us down?" Cora asked.

Pierce was aware that the big gaming tribes like the MCN funded the NIGC and in turn the NIGC acted as their watchdog and protected their turf. He suspected that the NIGC would put up roadblocks.

"We appeal," Pierce said simply.

"How long will that take?" Juanita asked.

"It depends on how long it would take the Department of Justice to prepare their case. They would need to hire an expert to rebut our expert.

It could take two years to get to trial. In the meantime, the Kialegee casino is open and making money."

It was Juanita's turn to laugh.

Nora didn't seem to be listening anymore. Her eyes stared blankly at Pierce and then at Jeremiah. The realization that she had underestimated Jeremiah came like a kick to the stomach. It was clear to her now; Jeremiah and his lawyer were not interested in asking the NIGC for permission to open a casino. They would get open and fight off any attempts to close them down. Meanwhile, the tribe would make millions and build a war chest to keep fighting.

"Do you think we can win?" Cora asked.

Cora's question snapped Nora out of her trance. She looked at Cora like she was a slow child. "Hell Cora, what do you think he's going to say?"

Pierce and his legal team had already started researching governmental archives for historical documents and narratives about the Creek confederacy and were busy dissecting every relevant governmental treaty with the Creeks. His team spent the last week contacting ethnohistorians and archeologists at several prominent universities to build a case for the Kialegee to legally build a casino on the Broken Arrow land.

"I think it's very likely," Pierce responded calmly.

Nora's face twisted in a frown. "I've heard all I needed to hear," Nora grunted as she stood up and headed for the door.

A broad smile spread across Jeremiah's face.

*****

Pierce shook each Business Committee member's hand. The three women turned as one to gaze at Pierce as he left the room. Jeremiah waited for the door to close and then turned to Nikki, "What do you think?"

"He's smart. And appears to be every bit as good as everything I heard about him."

Cora agreed. "He seems to be very knowledgeable."

Juanita nodded.

Nikki then snickered, "And it doesn't hurt that he's easy on the eyes."

Cora gave a subtle nod, and Juanita just giggled.

Jeremiah frowned and turned to Nikki. "Make sure you behave at dinner."

Nikki shrugged her shoulders in a way that suggested that she wasn't making any promises and said, "I guess I'll have to stay away from Tequila."

Chapter Six

OKMULGEE, OKLAHOMA

The Moccasin Telegraph was alive and well. By late afternoon, the same day that Pierce laid out his strategy to the Kialegee Business Committee, news of the meeting and details of Pierce's plan had already reached George Beaver, the Principal Chief of the Muscogee Creek Nation. The Chief was in the middle of a difficult reelection campaign and news of the Kialegee going into the heart of Muscogee lands and building a casino would be a lightning rod he could not afford.

George Beaver had a proverbial walk-in closet overflowing with affairs, pissed off mistresses, financial payoffs and kickbacks, but for some inexplicable reason the National Council and the tribal members turned a blind eye to it. But standing by and doing nothing while some upstart tribe trespassed onto MCN lands would be unforgivable and cost him the election. George was a believer that information was power, and he went to great lengths to keep enough members of the tribal towns employed by the MCN to make sure he had reliable informants.

The MCN Chief was a big man, broad chested with an enormous gut that made his belt line disappear. George liked food and drink too much. He befriended everyone, or at least he pretended to. He slapped backs, shook hands and said hello to everyone. When he visited the tribal elders, George spoke in the Creek's native tongue and criticized the younger generation for not learning the Creek customs and traditions. When he courted the younger Indian vote, George spoke English and advocated the need to modernize the Creek Nation and bring it into the twenty-first century. He had a talent for looking someone in the eye and pinpointing the exact half-truths to convince them he was on their side.

George sent word for Jeremiah to meet him at the MCN headquarters in Okmulgee. Word that the chief of the MCN had summoned him seemed to both unsettle and irritate Jeremiah. Jeremiah arrived at George Beaver's office at the appointed time, but George made him wait for almost thirty minutes before he had him brought in. When Jeremiah was finally shown into the Chief's office, George's brow furrowed like that of a disappointed father looking at a disobedient child. His creatively tailored suit complimented by French cuffs and fancy links did little to spruce up the unkempt man wearing them.

"Have a seat," George gestured to the chair on the other side of his massive oak desk without bothering to reach across to shake Jeremiah's hand. There was a smile on his face, but it was obvious he was irritated.

Jeremiah slid the chair forward and stood. He preferred to look George in the eyes. "So, what's so important that you needed to see me right away?" Jeremiah asked, even though he suspected that the Second Chief had tipped George off.

George eased into his chair without saying a word. It had never been his style to confront something head on. He preferred to plot and scheme and ultimately cut your legs off before you even realized he had been there. But this problem was one that didn't have the luxury of time. He needed to get control of this rumor before it spread like an airborne virus among the Creek Indians.

After an uncomfortable silence, George Beaver spoke in a tone that left no doubt that the MCN were in charge.

"Would you mind telling me why the Kialegee Tribe would want to build a casino so close to ours?"

Jeremiah stared at him with a look that said do I really have to explain this to you. "The land in Broken Arrow belongs to a Kialegee Tribal member, and we have the right to exercise jurisdiction over the property."

George gave Jeremiah a slight nod and said, "The property owner has dual citizenship. They are also Muscogee, as are all tribal town members."

Jeremiah's jaw tightened. "That doesn't make it Muscogee lands. We share jurisdiction over all Creek lands. The Treaties gave the land to all Creek Indians, not just the MCN," Jeremiah snapped defiantly before catching himself. Part of him wanted to tell George to go fuck himself but he realized that it wasn't smart to make an enemy out of the MCN so instead he held his ground and calmly said, "Dual membership doesn't prevent the Kialegee from exercising jurisdiction and developing the land."

George's face took on a wolfish smile. "I don't think the BIA and the NIGC are going to agree unless I tell them to. As far as they are concerned all the Creek land in Tulsa county is governed by the MCN."

Jeremiah never cared for the Chief of the MCN. "Shit, George. You didn't have to ask me to come all the way to Okmulgee to tell me you are going to fight me. I already know that." Jeremiah said.

George Beaver looked out the window and slowly turned his gaze back onto Jeremiah.

"I don't want to fight you Jeremiah. We should work this out between us instead of running to the BIA and having outsiders tell us how to handle our business. We are two sovereign nations and we should act like it." he said.

"And why would you want to do that when you have the BIA and NIGC in your pocket?"

"Because I agree that you should be able to develop your land. I'd prefer if you didn't build a casino, but I understand why you would want to put one there."

Jeremiah gave him a skeptical look and took a seat across from him. "If that's the case, what do you propose?"

"That you hold off on any plans to build the casino until after the election."

"Why would I do that?"

George knew that if the Kialegee moved forward with the casino during his campaign, he would not be reelected. The race was very tight. He couldn't afford any hiccups. Even if he tried to get out in front and denounced the Kialegee, his opponent would paint him as weak for failing to keep the smaller tribal town in line. He needed the Kialegee to disappear.

"If you hold off and keep a lid on things until after the election, I will support you. But, if you move ahead now, stopping the casino will become the central issue of everyone's campaign. Every candidate for Chief and National Council will have a mandate to crush you."

Jeremiah didn't respond, instead he stared through George with his black eyes. George didn't look away but in the silent battle of wills it was George that felt compelled to start speaking again. "Jeremiah, you know how Creek Indians think. If you make me look weak, I have no chance of being re-elected."

Jeremiah knew that there was nothing George wouldn't say to get what he wanted. "Even if we wait three months until after the election the MCN will still want you to stop us."

George tried to smile, but it came off as more of a grimace. "I'll be termed out."

"Meaning?"

"Meaning that I can't run for Chief again. If this doesn't become a political issue, I can come out in support of the Kialegee before opposition to the casino gets any real momentum. As Chief of the MCN, once I support you, the BIA and NIGC will get in line."

Jeremiah leaned back in his chair and tried to work through what was happening. "So that's your proposal? If we wait until November, you'll come out in support of our casino?"

There was more than a flicker of greed in George's eyes. "It's a big political lift on my part, but like I said we are in a position to help each other out."

Jeremiah didn't respond. He waited for the other shoe to drop. With George there was always another shoe.

"If the Kialegee hold off so that I don't have to deal with any political landmines and you agree to give my wife a five-year consulting contract after the casino opens, we can do business."

"How much is that going to cost my tribe?

"Half of one percent."

"That's too much."

"I'm handing you a casino."

Jeremiah knew no matter who won the election, they would fight the casino. He frowned as he thought about the old saying, "the devil you know is better than the devil you don't." He also figured it would take Pierce at least two months to put together the casino financing. There was a chance that they wouldn't be ready before November.

"I'll tell you what I'm willing to do," he paused. "When your second term is up, you can ask the Business Committee to become the tribe's governmental affairs consultant. I will remind the Business Committee how you supported the Kialegee efforts to build the casino, but that's all I'm willing to do. Otherwise, I'll move forward now and take my chances."

George didn't immediately speak. He had undoubtedly gone over this meeting in his head and had a mental list of best and worst-case scenarios. Jeremiah's offer was somewhere on the lower end of

George's list, but acceptable. George could also see that Jeremiah was dug in.

George nodded and reached across the desk to shake Jeremiah's hand. "We have a deal."

Chapter Seven

BROKEN ARROW, OKLAHOMA

The Bible Belt ran hard through Broken Arrow, Oklahoma. The Tulsa County suburb was home to ninety-six churches from a dozen strains of Christianity. Most of the folks that lived in Broken Arrow were Christians, or they claimed to be. At first glance, the people of Broken Arrow appeared to be a pleasant blend of southerners and westerners. With just under one hundred thousand people, Broken Arrow was the largest and most affluent bedroom community in Tulsa. While Main Street kept the charm and red brick buildings of an earlier time when Tulsa was an oil town, most of Broken Arrow consisted of master-planned communities, large gated estate homes, restaurants and a sprinkling of golf courses. Despite the urban sprawl, it was still reminiscent of a different time. A time before the "me-first generation and wave of self-esteem parenting subculture" took hold on America. People were friendly and spoke to strangers and to each other. Kids played on front lawns and the high school football team was still a source of pride.

Broken Arrow like much of the greater Tulsa area was once part of the Cherokee, Creek and Osage reservations. When the three Indian Nations were forcibly relocated from the south-eastern states to make room for white expansion, the United States government gave them land in northeastern Oklahoma as compensation. Over time, the Indian allotments in and around Tulsa disappeared. The Bureau of Indian Affairs was supposed to act as stewards. When people later discovered that Oklahoma land was rich in oil and natural gas, Senator George Stigler passed an act in Congress that exempted five Oklahoma tribes from the laws that require Congressional approval to purchase Indian lands. In Oklahoma, after the Stigler Act, all that was required was the approval of the local county court judge. In most cases, shrewd oil companies purchased land or leased the mineral rights for a fraction of its value from Indians, and in other cases white settlers and businesses simply squatted on their land. The remaining Indian lands that were still sprinkled throughout the greater Tulsa area were easy to spot. Development would abruptly come to a stop and start again a few hundred feet down the same road. Outside of Broken Arrow, one might find a smoke shop on a small parcel of Indian land.

In Broken Arrow, as if by some unwritten rule, most of the smoke shops and Indian businesses were outside of the city's boundaries. It looked as if they had been banished to Tulsa. The Cherokee Hard Rock Casino was situated in Tulsa just over the Broken Arrow line, and the Muscogee Creek River Spirit casino was miles away. The citizens of Broken Arrow had strong opinions about keeping Indian businesses, riffraff, gamblers and their mischief away from the better folks.

On Thursday nights the Main Street Tavern on South Main Street was a popular landing spot for locals who had grown up in Broken Arrow. Over the past few years Broken Arrow had morphed from an insignificant town nestled up against the east of greater Tulsa to the fastest growing suburb in Oklahoma. When the rest of the country was experiencing an economic downturn, Tulsa and Broken Arrow became a hub for cancer treatment, occupational therapy and specialized clinics and hospitals. Healthcare professionals migrated like the settlers in colonial America for the promise of a better life and settled in Broken Arrow in such numbers that the once sleepy town that numbered less than two thousand residents in the 1970s had exploded overnight into an endless panorama of manicured lawns. The old brick building which was now home to the Main Street Tavern used to be the old Missouri, Kansas, and Texas Railway Company building that dated back to the early nineteen hundreds. Now, the tavern was where the real Broken Arrow locals came to eat red meat, drink booze and hear gossip. The bar ran a good thirty feet, taking up a third of the restaurant. In the back room there were booths and tables. However, most of the customers huddled around the bar and virtually every conversation focused on Oklahoma Sooners football. Occasionally the stoic man approaching the hostess' podium with his companions enjoyed watching the revelry and listening to the animated conversations, but tonight he had no choice but to focus on a more critical topic of conversation.

"Table for three tonight?" Asked the hostess.

Jeremiah nodded. The place was loud, but Jeremiah liked to go there whenever he visited Tulsa.

"I can seat you in the back room where it's quiet and you can hear yourselves talk if you'd like. It's nice to have you back," the woman smiled warmly like she meant it.

Pierce gestured to Nikki to walk ahead of him as they followed Jeremiah and the young woman to the table.

The three had barely seated themselves before Payton Tiger came walking across the bar in cowboy boots, tight faded jeans and a snug pink shirt that grew tighter around her buxom breasts. She held a glass of single malt scotch in one hand and her purse in the other. Her eyes were brilliant and hard, looking too large for her face and too intense, as if battle hardened by a tragic secret that wasn't much of a secret in her hometown. There was a general stir as Payton stepped through the crowd. Practically every man stopped what he was doing and watched her move across the room.

When she got to their table—she lifted her drink to toss it off in one swallow. Payton pursed her lips as she deliberately held the abominable liquid in her mouth for a long moment, ignoring its burning as she stared into the resplendent blue eyes of the stranger sitting across the table from her father. Then she swallowed and cocked a malicious eyebrow at her father.

At that very moment, Pierce rose from his chair.

Half in her cups, she looked Pierce up and down taking measure of him and ignoring his outstretched hand. "Ah, yes, the superhero that's going to perform some miracle to help the Kialegee Tribe and save the day," she said, smiling to take some sting out of her words.

Jeremiah's eyes immediately narrowed.

Pierce smiled politely at her remark. He didn't see himself as a savior. However, he believed in causes and, as he worked his way up his law firm's ranks, he had a say in what clients he represented. Pierce only took cases where he could commit to a cause in which he truly believed. Without taking his eyes off Payton, Pierce placed his hand on Jeremiah's shoulder as if to say that there was no need to get upset. His eyes stared into Payton, searching her amber orbs intently. There was keen intelligence in his glance, curiously no irritation, and something else, something unexpected that knocked Payton off her center.

He had an unshakable confidence that said that he was a powerful man who knew exactly what he wanted and exactly how to get it. Not a fictional superhero from her comic books.

The silence stretched out long enough that Nikki could no longer endure it. She gave Payton a stern look. "The Kialegee don't need a miracle. The Tribe needs to be treated equally under the law, and Pierce is here to help."

The courage that the scotch had given her was gone and Payton stood awkwardly looking like a brooding child waiting for and wanting desperately to get her father's attention.

Sensing her discomfort, Pierce beckoned Payton to join them for dinner. It surprised her that he knew her name. A look of dread instantly replaced her initial surprise as she fretted on exactly how much Pierce knew about her.

Payton took a deep breath. Her instincts said Run! She started to shake her head, but before she could say no, Pierce had moved behind her. As he did, he pulled out her chair.

Payton's mouth went dry. She turned back towards her father and then looked around as if nothing was playing out like she had pictured. "I think it would be better if I didn't. I'm sure my dad wants to discuss business."

A half-second of silence, "Sit down, Payton," Jeremiah ordered.

Pierce smiled at Payton. His blue eyes twinkled.

Payton hesitated. Before she could say anything else Pierce gently nudged the chair forward and gestured to their waitress to bring her another drink.

Jeremiah crossed his arms. A hint of a scowl settled on his face. He loved his daughter and couldn't begrudge her anything, but her lifestyle choices brought shame to the Kialegee tribe. Wherever she went there were still prying eyes. In the time it took her to make her way from across the bar to the table where they were sitting, Jeremiah counted three people who took her picture with their cell phones. The tribal elders had shunned her. A decision that Jeremiah reluctantly agreed with and one he was grateful his wife had not been alive to see.

As forms of rebellion went, Payton's cut Jeremiah deep. He would have much preferred something like alcohol or drugs but dwelling on Payton's mistakes was a waste of time, and he had a more important issue to deal with. It wouldn't matter that the Kialegee Tribe had shunned Payton. A casino project in Broken Arrow would bring with it its own brand of notoriety and some opportunistic reporter would seize upon Payton's disreputable past as a chance to sell more newspapers by painting her and the Kialegee Tribe as pagan interlopers and a threat to their Christian values. There was a glint of sympathy in Jeremiah's eyes that bordered on pity. Payton had suffered long enough. The decision to build the casino was the tribe's and if he couldn't keep ideological evangelists and politicians bent on stopping the casino from making his daughter a target, he would make sure she did not face them alone. The Business Committee and tribal elders had decided that they would bring Payton back to the tribe before they moved forward with the casino so they could protect her.

Jeremiah leaned forward; his eyes fixed on Payton. "It's time for your punishment to end. Tomorrow morning you're going to come to the tribal headquarters and apologize to the elders."

"Fine." Payton said begrudgingly as she took a gulp of scotch and thought of ways to change the subject.

"There's one more condition."

Payton ignored his last comment. "Whatever you say pops. Let's just do this later," she shot back and reached for the breadbasket.

Payton leaned in Nikki's direction. "Is butter a carb? I'm trying to lose three pounds."

Nikki wasn't amused. Disappointment played across her face.

Jeremiah's eyes flashed with anger. "Enough," he said, the volume of his voice rising noticeably.

Payton froze.

"Chief, she was just playing—" Nikki instinctively came to Payton's defense like she'd been doing ever since they first met, but Jeremiah spoke over her.

"You are going to stop all your foolishness and work with Nikki and Pierce on the casino project. You will do whatever they tell you to do. Do you understand me?" Jeremiah snapped, struggling to keep his voice low enough not to be heard by the people rubbernecking at the nearby tables. His eyes bore through Payton in a way that suggested he was unwilling to accept anything less.

Payton gave a contrite nod. "Yes, sir."

"We're going to need to staff the satellite office on the Broken Arrow property. So, you can work there a couple days a week," Nikki said, trying to ease the tension.

"Fine," Payton said, looking increasingly miserable.

Pierce picked up the narrative as he handed Payton his cellphone. "Do you mind putting your number in my contacts so I can call you later this week," Pierce smiled. "I promise that the work you will be doing won't be mindless busy work. I could really use your help."

Payton was captivated by how he made her feel needed and his deep blue eyes.

Mid-way through dinner, Jeremiah received a telephone call from Juanita. She started off apologizing for interrupting and followed that up with the news that the state medical examiner closed the investigation on the cause of Samuel Tiger's death, conducting no tests of the water in C.C. Pond or making conclusive findings about how Samuel contracted primary amoebic meningoencephalitis. Doctor Gupta was sure that Samuel came in contact with the amoeba Naegleria fowleri from swimming in contaminated water. But the official report made no such finding. Jeremiah leaned back. He could feel his blood beginning to boil at the complete lack of regard that the State had for the Kialegee Tribe.

Everyone could see that something was wrong. "What happened?" Nikki asked.

Jeremiah let out a long breath, barely able to believe the news. "The medical examiner closed the investigation into the cause of Samuel's death making no findings."

Nikki's face twisted into a frown. She seemed to read Jeremiah's thoughts. *If Samuel had been white instead of Kialegee, there would have been no loose ends. There would have been answers and measures taken to make sure that no other child died from exposure to Naegleria fowleri.*

Jeremiah checked his watch. It wouldn't be much longer before the members learned of the State's decision. The State's complete disregard for the Tribe and the wellbeing of their children would either unify the Kialegee and strengthen their resolve for the casino or tear them apart.

A knowing groan escaped Nikki's lips. "Nora will use this to stir the pot and try to convince the tribal members that the only way to deal with the state is with the help of the MCN. In exchange, George will require us to abandon all thoughts of a casino."

"I'm not thinking of the casino," Jeremiah said.

"Well, you need to. Samuel was the reason the Business Committee said yes to the casino—"

"I know," Jeremiah snapped.

The intensity of his anger surprised Nikki, but she wasn't the target. Jeremiah was angry with himself.

"Chief, I realize that this is a tribal matter, but if I may I'd like to offer an observation." Pierce said, sensing Jeremiah's angst.

Jeremiah's face was expressionless. "You're our lawyer. Go ahead."

Pierce didn't know Jeremiah well enough to predict how he would react to a situation like this. He decided it was important for Jeremiah to maintain his clarity and commitment and not be sidetracked by setbacks and obstacles that based on his experience were only just beginning.

"The MCN has political influence with the state because it has casino revenues that it can deploy. The money that the Kialegee will make from a casino will give them the financial resources to make political contributions and retain lobbyists. The Kialegee can have the same access that the MCN enjoys. To sacrifice the casino for getting the MCN's help serves no purpose."

Jeremiah took a sip of water as he considered Pierce's point.

"Even if the state reopens the investigation what will that really accomplish?" Pierce asked.

"We deserve answers," Jeremiah replied.

"You already have them. The state can only confirm what you already know and that won't give you any greater closure," Pierce said.

Samuel intruded into Jeremiah's thoughts. This time whispering in his ear. *Pop-pop, there's only one way to make sure more kids don't end up like me.*

Nikki interjected. "If Nora gets her way, the KTT will always be dependent on the MCN."

Jeremiah's expression turned thoughtful. "Nora won't get her way. The Business Committee and most of the elders will see through her. What she'll do is rile up some members," he said.

Jeremiah wasn't sure what he would find when he got to the tribal headquarters, but he had a premonition that whatever it was, it would be too much for Juanita and the rest of the Business Committee to handle without him.

Jeremiah stood, a sincere expression of concern on his face. "I'm sorry to cut dinner short but I need to get back. Tribal business."

Nikki stood and grabbed her coat. "I'll follow you."

Payton looked across the table at her dad. She worried all the tribe's problems were too much for one man to contend with and it would put him in an early grave. But she knew that tribal business meant she had to stay away.

"Don't worry about your lawyer. I'll run him back to his hotel," she said.

Jeremiah nodded as he rushed for the door, but Payton was sure he wasn't listening.

Chapter Eight

Payton's jeep was parked a block away from the restaurant. She'd had a lot to drink, but Pierce sensed that she would put up a fight if he suggested to her that he drive. So instead he baited her. He placed a gentle hand on her shoulder and said, "If I can tell you something about you that most people don't know, you let me drive."

Payton gave him a sideways glance. "And when you misfire what do I get?"

Pierce reached into his wallet. "One hundred dollars says I'll get it right."

Payton studied Pierce for a moment and said, "Okay, you're on."

Pierce cocked his head back and looked her up and down. "You love comic books."

Payton half-rolled her eyes. "Pulheese! That's not much of a secret."

Pierce's blue eyes focused on her briefly for a second time before he said, "Your favorite superhero is Superman." Pierce extended his right-hand palm up.

Payton's eyes squinted. "Not so fast. That was a lucky guess."

"No rule against guessing," Pierce grinned. "But if it makes you feel any better. That wasn't a guess."

"Bull shit."

"Your dog's name is Kal. Kal-El was superman's name on Krypton."

"Fine." Payton nodded and tossed the keys at him. "But I still think you guessed."

"No," Pierce shook his head. "The small superman tattoo on your left ankle told me what I needed to know. If I had told you that Nicolas Cage was your favorite actor, that would have been a guess."

Payton slid past Pierce towards the door and whispered, "And you would have been right."

He's the biggest superman fan in Hollywood."

She carefully lifted herself into the passenger's seat. Pierce slipped into the vehicle and pulled out. Payton looked unreservedly at Pierce as he gripped the wheel and navigated the streets of her South Tulsa neighborhood. His black hair had a few wisps of gray coming in along the sides. She found the tiny crow's feet along his eyes when he squinted to get a better look at the street signs sexy. Payton had no proof that he had mental scars to go with the small scar just above his right eyebrow, but there had to be. She took off her non-prescription glasses that she wore to alter her appearance to get a better look at him.

Payton called out the next turn and he veered left onto South Oswego Avenue. "There the house on the right," Payton said, pointing to a large neoclassical limestone façade modeled after an 18th-century mansion.

"Very nice," Pierce commented as he rolled into a circular driveway ornamented with mature trees and exquisitely landscaped grounds.

"Thanks?" Payton remarked feigning gratitude, "But I don't live in the house. I rent out a small cottage in the back of the property."

"So, what's your deal, Clark? Are you delusional in thinking you can make a difference or are you so tired of fucking your wife you'll do anything, even take up lost causes to be anywhere other than home?"

Pierce ignored the question, but he couldn't overlook the malignant glee in Payton's voice.

"I can respect your misandrist attitude, but for us to work together, I need you to realize that I'm not your enemy."

"What kind of attitude? I don't know that word."

"A misandrist is someone who dislikes men."

She fell silent for a minute as she considered Pierce's comment. "So, you think I'm a lesbian?" Payton said, sounding a bit surprised.

"I wasn't commenting on your sexual preference. It doesn't matter to me if you're gay, straight or bi. It's none of my business. What I care about is helping your father and your tribe and I can do without your attitude."

"The Kialegee are not my tribe," she snapped defensively.

Pierce locked eyes with Payton. It occurred to him that being shunned by the tribe and her family left her feeling isolated and vulnerable. He considered his next words more carefully given the situation. "I understand that this is being forced on you. I can talk to your father if you prefer not to work on the project."

"Don't do that. I don't want to be involved. I admit that. But this is not his fault."

She broke off and stared out the window. "I'm the one that fucked up. He's just trying to help, but the tribe will never forgive me."

"You don't know that." He said in a tone that suggested that she could be underestimating the tribe's willingness to leave the past where it belongs and move forward.

Payton's eyes narrowed. "You can't say that without knowing all the facts."

Pierce stretched his back. "So why don't you tell me? I have all night."

Payton considered his request and swore under her breath. "Fine, you're going to find out sooner or later."

She fixed her gaze on the window behind him, seeming to use the blank slate to form her thoughts. "I wasn't happy living on the rez. I wanted more out of life. I moved to L.A. when I was seventeen." Payton cast her eyes down. "The little money I had didn't last as long as I hoped for. I thought I'd find an acting job before it ran out."

Payton chewed her lip for a moment. "When the money ran out, I got desperate. I tried looking for a job but being a minor and living on the streets didn't leave me with a lot of options."

"Why didn't you just go back home?"

Payton shook her head. "That didn't seem like an option. Little Indian girl running back home to the rez with her tail tucked between her legs because she couldn't hack it in the white man's world."

"This guy I was hanging out with was trying to make it in the adult film industry and talked me into giving it a try. I got a fake driver's license, and took the name India Summer. Before I could blink, I had starred in eleven adult films and made a decent amount of money and got off the streets," she said, speaking on autopilot.

Pierce studied her, slightly surprised by her honesty. "So, what happened? Why did you stop?"

Payton's eyes became unfocused as she dredged up a buried memory. "Because I wasn't the girl in those videos. I fooled myself into thinking I was acting. Those men weren't fucking me they were fucking India Summer . . . each time I took off my clothes and had sex in front of the camera, the line between me and India grew fainter."

She shook her head as if trying to shake loose a dark memory. "I switched agents several times because they all tried to force me into sleeping with them. When I refused, they gave my jobs to other girls. It wasn't like I could report them for sexual harassment."

Payton stopped for a moment; her mind went back to Pierce's earlier comment.

"I don't hate men. I just don't trust them. And, I'm not a lesbian. I'm not even bisexual. When I first started, those scenes where I had to kiss women and let them go down on me were the hardest ones to get through," she said. The slight slur of her words undercutting the acid in her tone.

Her jaw hung slack. "My life spiraled out of control. Soon, I didn't care anymore whether I was having sex with a man or woman." Payton took a moment. The memory of the details brought a slightly embarrassed grimace to her face.

"I knew that if I didn't get out right then. I never would."

Pierce nodded intently.

"After I stopped, I couldn't pay my rent, and I didn't want to go back to living on the streets, so I came back home." Payton took a deep breath and let it out slowly. "When I got back, my family and friends wouldn't talk to me."

Her eyes turned misty but there were no tears. "Worst of all, was what it did to my dad." All she could feel was guilt for what she had done. "When I got back home. I wore my hair in a ponytail, put on glasses and wore very little make up trying to change my looks but it didn't matter, India was an internet sensation on hundreds of porn sites. They recognized me a lot more than I thought they would here in Oklahoma."

The insults she received from strangers still rang in her ears. "Those sanctimonious assholes . . ." she said.

Pierce didn't immediately respond. Instead, he stared past Payton through the window behind her. "India Summer. You couldn't think of a better name?"

Payton wasn't sure if that was meant as a joke and flashed a nervous smile. "So, your first thought was that I should have had a better name?"

Pierce nodded. His relaxed manner suggested that he wasn't surprised and that he didn't care about her past.

Payton instantly became suspicious. "If you knew, why didn't you say something?"

"It's not a topic that naturally comes up in conversation," Pierce said, settling into the conversation since Payton was no longer lashing out.

Payton paused for a moment, confused by Pierce's reaction. "It's not something I enjoy talking about, but I figured you needed to know. I don't want my working with you to hurt the casino. Trust me, that's my only reason for telling you."

"You didn't commit a crime. So, what you did before shouldn't matter to anyone." Pierce's tone made it clear he thought Payton's concerns were needless. He refocused on Payton's face in time to meet her widening eyes.

Payton inched closer and looked at Pierce with more than a casual interest. A giggle was followed by a sly smile. "This is usually the time when the guy makes his move."

Pierce laughed, leaned into Payton and kissed her on the cheek. "You should go get some sleep. The elders are expecting to see you first thing in the morning."

Chapter Nine

GLENPOOL, OKLAHOMA

Jeremiah looked through the window and out at the white landscape from a corner booth of the International House of Pancakes. Three fresh inches of snow had fallen overnight. He'd gotten a call at 5 AM from George Beaver asking him to meet. George's swearing in ceremony was two days away. Jeremiah kept his word and waited for thirty days after George had been re-elected before breaking ground on the Broken Arrow site.

When George entered the restaurant, there was a flurry of activity. A buxom blonde waitress, who was George's favorite, hugged him. The general manager rushed over to shake his hand. He said hello to a couple as he passed them.

"Good morning, Jean. Easy on the bacon, Pete." George had a gift for remembering people's names. He lumbered towards the booth in the corner where Jeremiah was sitting. At six feet three, he had to be at least 300 pounds, though no one knew for sure.

George began the elaborate task of stuffing his massive body into the booth opposite Jeremiah and gestured to the waitress to bring him a cup of coffee. After taking a long sip, he let out a sigh. "This casino of yours is bringing down a lot of heat on me."

Jeremiah looked out at the traffic building on Highway 117 as the morning rush hour got underway. "Well, you knew there was going to me some push back."

George nodded and took another sip. "Not like this."

Jeremiah knew that U.S. Congressman Patrick Murphy, whose district included Broken Arrow publicly, had challenged the Kialegee's right to occupy the land. He led an opposition that within a matter of days of the Kialegee breaking ground included the entire Oklahoma congressional delegation, the Governor and the Attorney General.

Jeremiah nodded solemnly. "Most of the opposition to the casino will dissolve once you come out in support."

"You overestimate what my support could do," George protested halfheartedly.

Jeremiah gave George a skeptical look. "You sang a different tune when you asked me to hold off plans to move forward with the casino until after your election."

"A lot has happened since you broke ground on the casino. I never figured on the congressman," George said.

Jeremiah nodded thoughtfully. "Murphy admits that the site is Indian land. He's basing his entire opposition on the notion that all Indian land in Tulsa County is under the exclusive jurisdiction of the MCN, and only the MCN has a right to build a casino. He's painted himself into a corner. When you announce that the MCN supports the casino, he's done."

"Maybe, but I have had dealings with Murphy and he's up for reelection next year. He won't give up his bully pulpit that easily."

"George, the attacks are taking a toll on my tribal members. All I'm asking is for you to honor your commitment."

George grimaced. "I can't throw the MCN into the middle of this. The local church groups and a group calling themselves the Broken Arrow Citizens Against Neighborhood Gaming won't stop just because I say you can be there."

Jeremiah stopped drinking coffee and folded his hands in front of him on the table trying to quell the anger growing in the pit of his stomach.

"This is national news now and Washington is getting a lot of pressure from the public and the Oklahoma congressional delegation to shut you down. Even the Broken Arrow Mayor is weighing in claiming your casino is less than two miles from a site that the city had under consideration for a future elementary school," George repeated incredulously.

George leaned over and said, "I owed you at least this much. I wanted to tell you in person, Chief-to-Chief, that when I'm sworn in the day after tomorrow, I will come out against your casino."

Jeremiah made no attempt to hide his disgust. Without the MCN's support, the attacks on the Kialegee would steadily increase. The newspapers, TV, radio and the internet all painted the Kialegee as trespassers and that was weighing heavily on the tribal members. Once the MCN joined the opposition, Jeremiah wondered how long before his tribe came apart.

"We agreed," Jeremiah responded, lowering his voice further as the waitress stopped at a nearby table, "to stand together on this."

George frowned. "I feel for you and your tribal members," George started, struggling to sound solemn. "But I can't put your tribe's needs ahead of the MCN's. The State of Oklahoma offered us a very favorable settlement in our tobacco lawsuit. They agreed to reduce their claim of unpaid cigarette taxes from thirty-six million to four million dollars if we oppose the casino. I can't turn my back on thirty-two million dollars," George stressed, trying to sound reasonable.

Jeremiah clenched and then flexed his hand in agitation. "Of course, you can. You gave your word as a chief . . . I should have known better than to trust you."

George decided to let the comment pass. "I didn't expect you to understand but, in my world, concessions have to be made to preserve relationships. What the Kialegee are doing is crossing lines and upsetting a whole lot of people."

Jeremiah's patience was threadbare. "Thirty years ago, the MCN did exactly what the Kialegee are trying to do. When the MCN started construction on its first casino, the State of Oklahoma fought you at every step."

George sat up and said, "That was thirty years ago. Back then we had nothing to lose. You're not looking at the big picture. The MCN has a lot of business with the State of Oklahoma . . ."

"You're the one not looking at the big picture," Jeremiah cut him off. "If you don't support the Kialegee and the Governor stops the casino, you're setting a dangerous precedent."

George squinted at Jeremiah with curious eyes.

"You would be letting opposition groups dictate to Indians what they can and cannot do on Indian lands," Jeremiah said.

George adopted an uncomfortable expression and shifted in his seat. "I think you're reaching."

Jeremiah grunted with disdain. "It starts with this casino. If a neighborhood group can stop the casino because they don't want it; what's next?" If you empower them by letting them believe they can dictate to Indians what they can do on their land, they'll be no stopping them. If we've learned anything about white people, it's that all it takes is giving them a small foothold before everything goes to shit for us. Are you willing to take that risk?"

George seemed to soak in Jeremiah's point for a second and then said, "Perhaps we can reach an agreement with the Governor where she would support a Kialegee casino in another location in exchange for the Kialegee abandoning the Broken Arrow site."

"A win-win; where everyone walks away happy," Jeremiah said sarcastically.

George nodded. "It's possible. We have some restricted land near Keystone Lake. I may be able to persuade my council to lease the Kialegee the land if you agree to abandon the Broken Arrow project."

"I don't think so," Jeremiah clasped his hands together. His mood had been darkening.

"Why not? What's your problem with Keystone Lake?"

"If it was a good location, you would already have a casino there."

George looked at the floor for a long moment and then said, "Broken Arrow will never happen. I'm offering you an opportunity to walk away with something."

Jeremiah frowned. "When did you start thinking like the white man? Offering us a worthless trinket to go away."

"Careful."

"You had no intention of supporting our casino project, did you?"

George waved his hand as if shooing a fly from his face. "Nothing could be further from the truth. But there are political realities that come into play that can't be ignored."

Jeremiah let out a small laugh. "Spoken like a true politician."

George let out a tired sigh. It was his way of releasing pressure, so he didn't blow. "We're all big boys here. Take the deal or don't take it. I wanted to tell you face to face that the MCN would oppose the casino because you didn't come to us first and ask for permission."

Jeremiah glared at George. "We don't need your permission!" Spittle flew from his mouth.

George's face flushed with anger. "You forget your place. I'm still your chief."

Jeremiah slid out of the booth and stood, "A chief that goes back on his word is no chief."

Chapter Ten

CONSTRUCTION SITE
BROKEN ARROW, OKLAHOMA

David Johnson was a prime candidate for an ulcer. The sixty-two-year-old never lost his temper. He internalized stress by shoving it down into the pit of his stomach, where he fed it with black coffee and a steady supply of Pepcid antacid tablets. On an average day he went through a half a bottle of antacid a day. He was overseeing the smallest construction budget he had worked on in twenty years and he was under strict orders; there could be no construction delays or change orders. If there was a problem, David had to find a solution without adding to the project's bottom line.

Conventional financing sources such as banks and hedge funds would not invest in the Kialegee project with so much political opposition and controversy. Federal law-controlled rates of return on investments for Indian casinos and investors were subject to background checks, and sources of funds had to be verified. This decimated the investor pool and required the already creative Pierce to have to be more imaginative in securing the project financing. Pierce managed to weave together a group of Miami Beach developers and doctors, but the investors understood the risks and capped their investment at fifty million. Pierce and David often talked late into the night about bricks and mortar and steel and concrete and ways to save money and preserve the razor thin line item in the budget labeled "Contingency."

Normally a fifty-million-dollar construction job would not be big enough to get the President of Lone Wolf Construction Services Inc's attention. David Johnson focused on massive billion-dollar casino resort projects in Las Vegas, Singapore and Macau. The margins on a small construction project like the Kialegee's Red Creek casino were not appealing enough for a company like Lone Wolf Construction and David was at a stage in his life where he would rather breed Arabian horses on his Georgia farm than inspect concrete footings. If anyone other than Pierce had called David and asked him to oversee the construction project, he would have immediately declined.

Pierce had helped David by recommending Lone Wolf Construction to his clients. Several of those projects were very profitable and personally made David a small fortune. Pierce was also Lone Wolf Construction's legal counsel on a high-profile construction defect case and saved the company millions in potential liability. So, when Pierce called and asked David for a personal favor, David couldn't say no.

*****

David entered the construction site through a gate on the back side of the property to avoid the reporters camping out next to the main entrance to the site. The gate along the front of the property had been closed for a week now. The construction site had been vandalized twice, and the Broken Arrow police refused to do anything. He had no choice but to dip into his contingency fund and hire additional security around the clock. Until recently, most people that lingered by the fence did little more than yell a few obscenities when he pulled into the parking lot.

After the Chief of the MCN opposed the Kialegee Casino in a live press conference, things changed. Protests in front of the site became a common occurrence, and the press began running stories that accused the Kialegee of building an illegal casino. The articles blasted the BIA, NIGC and Justice Department for failing to act against the Kialegee and the project. David could feel trouble in the wind. The numbers in front of the construction site swelled and the mood just outside the fence was combustible. He chewed on the end of a Dominican cigar while he looked over at the beehive of activity on the other side of the fence.

David could feel the tension building. As a precaution, he posted an additional security guard by the front entrance to keep anyone who didn't belong there from trespassing.

Jay Konigsberg, a civil engineer based in Tulsa, opened the door to the construction trailer and entered the room. David had hired Jay because he had a reputation as steady, honest and he had worked as an engineer for the City of Broken Arrow before joining the private sector. Even though it was only a little after ten in the morning, Jay looked like he'd already been through a hard day. When David asked him if he'd made any progress with the city on hooking up to the city's water and sewer connections the uncomfortable look on Jay's face told him what he needed to know.

Of all the challenges David was facing, getting utilities to the property was by far his biggest. The transformer was already on site, so the building had electricity, but the city refused to allow David access to the city's water supply and sewer system. It was a predictable tactic, but an illegal one. Jay dropped down in one of the side chairs next to David's desk and blurted out, "I'm afraid that the city will never allow us to connect to the water and sewer lines. They think they can stop the project if you can't get access to water."

David wore the stern look of someone who had been down this road before. "That won't stop the project. All they're doing is exposing the city to a lot of liability. We'll solve the water issue and let our lawyer deal with the city."

"I've never seen anything this outrageous in all my years," Jay said, not bothering to hide his frustration.

David unfolded a map and spread it out on his desk. He drew circles on the map marking locations. When he was finished, he handed the map to Jay.

The frown lines on David's forehead deepened. "I'll tell you one thing. Broken Arrow is going to be a lot poorer when our lawyer is done suing them."

David sipped his coffee while Jay studied the map. He and Pierce had been plotting for the last few days an alternative approach. They had decided that they could draw water from the aquifer that existed below the property and manage the waste on site, but it wasn't an ideal solution. Pierce wanted Jay to take one last pass at the city. If they refused, they would go with their Plan B.

David took one last gulp of his coffee before edging toward the door. Follow me," he gestured to Jay.

"Where are we going?"

"To fix our problem," David shot back.

David stepped out from the construction trailer with an unlit cigar in his left hand and weaved across the parking lot. Jay followed him like a child who had forgotten how fast his pace was. It was a blustery, cold day. The wind swirled around them nipping at their ears. The shell of the two-story structure that looked like a massive barn was complete and most of the crew was working inside. With the exception of the drinking and wastewater hiccup, David had managed to keep the construction on budget and on schedule. When they got close to the building, the distinct banging of hammers, low grade buzz of power tools and country music playing in the background became audible.

A sudden gust of wind cut through David and he flinched and buried his chin into his chest until it passed.

"Jesus," David swore under his breath.

A crew member standing outside on the broad porch taking a cigarette break smirked. "Colder than a witch's tit today."

David nodded and peered over to the other side of the fence. He wondered why the weather wasn't keeping them away.

The ranks of protestors who opposed the casino swelled to over a hundred and caused the fence to sway whenever they leaned against it. David had worked on his fair share of controversial projects. The ability to use digital tools to rapidly amass large numbers of protesters with a common goal not only intensified protests, but it made them much more dangerous. The internet transformed local issues into social movements. And with it came people who believed that mayhem, looting and destruction were acceptable tactics.

The sight of David and Jay standing by the side of the building closest to the fence predictably prompted hisses and quickly escalated to people leaping up and down in their places and shouting at the tops of their voices to stop the construction. "*Shut it down, shut it down*," the crowd chanted in unison. A repulsive frenzy of hatred and malice seemed to flow through the entire group like an electric current.

David retreated a few steps to make sure he was out of range in case one of the misguided souls hurled something other than an insult at him.

They were busy marking the ground where David wanted the test wells dug when a protestor held out a hangman's noose and screamed, "We got plans for you, you fucking Indian lovers."

Jay shifted his weight uncomfortably from one foot to the other. David remained surprisingly calm. His eyes narrowed slightly. Other than reaching into his jacket pocket and fishing out an antacid tablet, he showed no signs of inner distress.

"When you finish digging the test wells, let's pull some water samples and see what we're working with. Once we know the flow rate, we can figure out how many more wells we're going to need to supply the casino."

"Yes, sir."

David squinted for a moment and pointed to an area just outside of the building but close to where the kitchen was going to be located. "Let's put a concrete pad there for the water tank."

David was counting on using the water in the tank to boost the water pressure to make sure that the casino had an adequate flow rate.

When they were finished marking the drilling locations, David and Jay stalked around to the back of the building, past the emergency generators and a clearing where the service road was planned. They stopped at a field overrun by thick tall brush too dense for a human to move through.

From where they were now standing, the sound of the protestors was relegated to low ambient noise.

"Let's get a hog-brush and clear about a half-acre," David said, with a wave of his hand. "I want to dig a trench large and deep enough to accommodate five 2,500-gallon tanks. That's where we'll hold the casino's waste."

"Standard sewage tanks?"

David chewed on the end of his cigar. "I'll get you the dimensions on the tanks."

Jay's face twisted in thought. "That should work but you're going to be pumping out those tanks a couple of times a week."

"Closer to every other day just to be on the safe side."

David's eyes moved back in the direction of the construction trailer. "Now for the hard part."

Jay shot him a confused look. "Hard part? Isn't this hard enough?"

"The hard part is telling my client I need more money. We'll need a small water treatment plant to treat the water we're going to be pumping up out of those wells if people are going to be drinking it," David said before heading back to give Pierce the news.

Chapter Eleven

OKLAHOMA ATTORNEY GENERAL'S OFFICE
OKLAHOMA CITY

The corner office that Attorney General Scott Masters coveted was the most impressive of all in Oklahoma. It was no secret Scott wanted to be the next Governor of Oklahoma. Two years after graduating from the University of Tulsa School of Law, Scott Masters was elected to the Oklahoma House of Representatives. After winning a seat in the State Senate, Masters successfully sponsored a bill designed to give churches greater power and undermine the separation of church and state. For Scott Masters, there was no middle ground - there was God's way and the wrong way. Small in stature but large on ego, Scott Masters was passionate about two things, the law and the lord's work. He was a Deacon at the First Baptist Christian Church in Broken Arrow. He talked to God when he prayed and believed his deep understanding of the Christian faith made him a gatekeeper of sorts, responsible for keeping the decadence of the secular world as far away from good Christian people as possible.

Scott Masters continued to read the draft lawsuit against the Kialegee Tribe. The complaint sought both declaratory and injunctive relief as it was the Attorney General's objective to bring the casino construction to an immediate halt. The team of attorneys that collaborated on the research and writing of the draft complaint sat quietly in Masters' office, watching him flip through the pages. He decided to not only sue the Kialegee Tribe; he sued every tribal officer. Masters wanted to scare them and send a message to every tribe in Oklahoma, that he would use every weapon in his arsenal to stop the expansion of Indian gaming. The

State of Oklahoma's complaint asserted that the casino was unlawful because the land was under the exclusive jurisdiction of the Muscogee Creek Nation. The 1866 treaty which established the boundaries of the Creek reservation in Oklahoma gave the land to the Muscogee. The state painted the Kialegee as nothing more than a band of Indians with no treaty rights.

The Attorney General sought to sue the Kialegee Tribal officials individually under the legal theory that tribal sovereignty did not prevent a lawsuit against tribal officials who acted outside their authority.

In Masters' mind, he suspected that he was reaching by attempting to drag the Kialegee Business Committee members into the lawsuit, but he didn't care. He wanted to hit them squarely between the eyes with a sledgehammer and the best way he could think of to do it was to prosecute every one of them.

The State of Oklahoma's final argument contended that the Broken Arrow parcel was right in the middle of a residential neighborhood, schools and churches and the citizens of Broken Arrow would be irreparably injured if gambling was allowed to occur.

When Masters finished the last page, he leaned back and removed his reading glasses.

"What do you think, sir?" One of the assistant attorneys asked him.

Masters looked at lawyers gathered in his office and karate-chopped the air with his hand. "What I want is to pull down their pants and spank their asses until their butt cheeks are fire engine red. I want to make an example of the Kialegee and send a message to the entire Indian community that Oklahoma will not tolerate lawlessness."

Masters handed the complaint to his deputy. There were a few arguments he might have framed differently, but it was good enough.

The Chief Judge of the U.S. District Court in Tulsa, a George W. Bush appointee, would preside over the case. While Master's and Chief

Judge Walter T. Fennell's interests were not always aligned, on matters regarding gaming and Indian rights they were both on the same page.

Checking his watch, he said, "I want this lawsuit filed today."

"Yes, sir."

"Leak a copy of the complaint to our friends at the Tulsa World as soon as you file it with the Clerk of the District Court. I want this lawsuit to be front page news in tomorrow morning's Tulsa World."

"What about a press conference?"

Nodding, he said, "Yes, but wait until tomorrow afternoon. Let the story get some legs under it. By then, the lawsuit should be the only thing anybody's talking about. Then we'll have our press conference."

The Attorney General wanted to break the will of the Kialegee by overwhelming them. He had a look of intense concentration on his face as he played out the press conference in his mind. He imagined himself standing in an elevated position, flanked by his legal team. Several pastors, city officials and community leaders ensconced behind them and the grounds filled with reporters, television cameras and hundreds of supporters.

"I don't want to have the press conference in the State Capitol. I want it at ground zero. The Church of Battle Creek is just up the street from the construction site. Get in touch with the church and every pastor in Broken Arrow and tell them to have their congregations there." Masters had a determined expression. "I want to give the Kialegee a taste of what they're up against."

Chapter Twelve

MIAMI

Noah Grayson stormed past Pierce's secretary before she could stop him. Once inside, he closed the glass door and approached his boss. He had a definite air of confidence about him that most of his peers construed as cocky. Noah was less than two years removed from passing the bar exam, but he had been fighting legal battles long before he went to law school. He began reading legal briefs about the same time most children his age were busy with little league baseball games and scout meetings.

When Pierce hired Noah, he didn't know much about him other than he graduated in the top one percent of his class at the University of Miami Law school. Pierce was familiar with the Grayson name. They were a prominent South Florida family whose philanthropic contributions were often lead stories in the "Celebrity News and Gossip" section of the Miami Herald.

After a few days in the office, it was hard not to notice the chip on Noah's shoulder the size of a sack of potatoes.

Noah stood quietly by the edge of Pierce's desk until he put the phone back in the cradle. David Johnson had just finished telling Pierce that the on-site water wells and sewage tanks would cost less than the trenching and underground piping required to connect to the city's water supply and sewer but the savings would not be nearly enough and they would need more money to pay for the water purification system required to treat the gallons of water per day that the casino would require.

"Did you read this garbage?" Noah unloaded as he slid the complaint across Pierce's desk towards him.

"Yes, I read it this morning."

"This is bullshit. The state has no standing to sue. What law has the Kialegee Tribe broken? Last I checked you have to have an actual casino operation and not the possibility of one to violate a law that regulates gaming. All we've done is build a building. There's no law against building a building. This lawsuit was filed prematurely." Noah got it all out in one breath.

Pierce watched and listened to his young protégé work himself up. It didn't take much to set him off. He'd grown up obscenely rich but when he was eleven, he had a front-row seat to the trial that stripped his family of their fortune and him of his birthright. The trial made national news, complete with allegations of both jury and witness tampering. The legal battle over the Grayson tobacco empire in the United States District *Court* was a textbook case of greed and mismanagement.

For months leading up to the trial and after the jury verdict, the Grayson family was a popular topic of conversation. When the appeals were exhausted Vidal Espinosa had seized control of the family's fortune and their company. Noah developed an unbridled passion for defending the underdog against the Vidal Espinosa's of the world. That's what made Noah Grayson tick. But it was this passion that also made him prone to impulsive decisions.

On the surface Pierce agreed with much of what he said, except Noah paid little attention to the attorney general's attempt to include Jeremiah and the members of the Business Committee in the lawsuit.

"Anything else?" Pierce asked in a tone that suggested that Noah was missing something.

Noah thought for a moment. His eyes shining with an arrogant light that Pierce was familiar with. "No, I covered everything."

Pierce took a sip of coffee and slowly set the mug on the table. "You didn't mention the AG's attempt to drag the tribe's leaders into the case."

Noah grabbed the back of his neck with his right hand. After a moment he said, "I don't think I need to focus on that too much. If there's no legal basis for the lawsuit, the court will dismiss all the parties."

Pierce looked at Noah and shook his head. "The thrust of your argument to dismiss the lawsuit is one of ripeness. Assuming the Judge grants our motion, the AG can re-file in a few months when the casino opens."

"And we can deal with Ex Parte Young at that time."

Pierce wondered if Noah was seeing the bigger picture. In any conflict, it's better to have allies than to be isolated. It was also just as important to prevent your enemy from acquiring a strong ally. The MCN had come out against the Kialegee Casino. They could prove to be an effective witness for the state. Pierce figured that the battle for a casino in Broken Arrow would only be a passing interest to anyone who did not live in Tulsa County. Whether the Kialegee Tribe was a successor in interest to the Creek Confederacy and entitled to the same treaty rights as the MCN would cast a slightly wider net and interest similarly situated tribes and academics. However, a state's ability to prosecute the individual leaders of Indian tribes could have widespread consequences and impact every state and Indian tribe in the country, including the MCN.

The Attorney General's attempt to expand the U.S. Supreme Court's 1908 ruling could have every tribe, state and federal prosecutor picking a side. It would also put the MCN in a tough position if they helped the state.

"I don't want to wait to expose Oklahoma's attempt to undermine tribal sovereignty. There is a strategic advantage to doing it as soon as possible. By doing it now, we can widen the lens and help the Kialegee gain some allies." Pierce paused and then added, "We can also force the MCN to sit on the sideline."

"You need to go attack the AG's position on Ex Parte Young in our motion to dismiss," Pierce said.

Noah looked instantly uncomfortable. "I wasn't going to completely ignore it. . ."

Pierce gave Noah a look that said he wasn't finished. "Ex Parte Young puts our case on a national stage. Take advantage of the opportunity."

Pierce stood up and slid the complaint back in Noah's direction.

Noah looked deflated. The scale of what Pierce hoped to accomplish settled its weight on him. "I shouldn't have missed that."

"The core of your legal argument is solid. You hit all the major points."

Noah shrugged his shoulders. "Yeah, but I glossed right over Ex Parte Young."

"Stop beating yourself up and tell me what Masters will do next."

Before he could answer, Pierce added, "Don't think like a lawyer. Think like a politician."

Noah racked his brain. "Exploit the media."

Pierce nodded. "He's already staged one press conference at a church close by the site." The numbers in attendance gave Pierce a sense of foreboding. Like a storm was coming. "Masters will keep playing to the masses."

Noah's face twisted into a frown. "We have the stronger legal argument. We'll beat him in court."

"We don't turn a blind eye to what the AG is doing."

Noah hesitated for a moment as he thought of the obvious response. "Are you suggesting we hold our own press conference?"

"No. When we finish our response to the state's complaint, we'll send courtesy copies to the Native American Rights Fund. NARF is an organization dedicated to protecting Indian rights. They'll get the word out that the state of Oklahoma is trying to water down Indian sovereignty."

Noah began pacing across the office. "Fight fire with fire."

Pierce nodded. "Yes, in a manner of speaking. The AG attacked tribal sovereignty, so we'll let NARF make this an Indian rights issue instead of a gaming one."

"Sorry I missed this boss."

Pierce brushed off the apology. "Just do a good job on the motion to dismiss and memorandum of law."

Noah was already halfway out the door.

"I want it by the end of the week," Pierce said.

Over his shoulder he replied, "You'll have it before that."

Chapter Thirteen

Noah handed Pierce twenty-five perfectly typed, plainly worded pages with two days to spare. The next morning, he found Pierce in the conference room up to his elbows in law books. His jacket was off, and the sleeves on the same crisp white shirt he had been wearing the day before were rolled up. Pierce was old school in that he preferred to read legal pleadings on actual paper instead of on his computer. He could focus on the arguments and make notations in the margins and refer back to earlier arguments without losing his place. Noah repeatedly told his mentor that their computer programs would let him view pages simultaneously, but Pierce preferred to spread the pages across the conference room table and use his eyes instead of a mouse to dart back and forth between the pages.

Noah's months of research were painstakingly detailed, and he had worked closely with Payton.

Payton spent countless hours sorting through boxes at the tribal headquarters that contained old records, looking for anything that could be useful. She sent Noah copies of the original tribal rolls and records of allotments of land given to the Kialegee. She scrounged through basements and attics of tribal elders and found journals with handwritten notes of the Kialegee chiefs that attended the treaty negotiations.

Noah focused on several treaties between the Creek Confederacy and the United States from the 1833 Treaty signed by the Kialegee Tribal Town where the Kialegee transferred their lands to the United States in exchange for lands in Eastern Oklahoma to the "Treaty with the Creeks in 1866" which established the boundaries of the Creek reservation in Eastern Oklahoma for all "Creek Indians." He cited to historical sources to detail the organizational structure of the Creek Confederacy. All

Creek tribal towns were autonomous, equal, and owned their lands independent of each other. That was the reason each tribal town that transferred land was a signatory to the 1833 treaty. The documents uncovered by Payton helped Noah work through one hundred and ninety years of treaties, historical documents, court cases and legislation which pertained to or affected the Creeks.

His second argument cited to a recent United States Supreme Court case *Michigan v. Bay Mills Indian Cmty*. In this case the State of Michigan sued the Bay Mills Indian tribe for building a casino on non-Indian lands located over ninety miles away from the tribe's reservation. The Supreme Court ruling dismissed the state's claims against the tribe because the court found that to sue a tribe under IGRA actual gaming must occur on Indian lands. Since the state alleged that the gaming was occurring on non-Indian lands the complaint did not satisfy the criteria under IGRA. Noah adeptly applied the legal holding in Bay Mills to the facts and argued that Oklahoma has failed to state a claim for relief under IGRA since the Kialegee Tribal Town had not yet conducted gaming on Indian lands.

In accordance with Pierce's instructions, Noah cited to every significant case where tribal officials were accused of violating federal law and were sued. He laid out, with wonderful clarity, the *Ex. Parte Young* exception to sovereign immunity. He provided a summary of a long list of Supreme Court cases to illustrate that the *Ex. Parte Young* exception was only to be applied in rare situations and established that despite various attempts by states, no court had allowed tribal officials to be sued under the Indian Gaming Regulatory Act. Noah concluded that argument by citing to the United States Supreme Court ruling in *Seminole Tribe of Fla. v. Florida*, where the Seminole Tribe attempted to sue the Governor of Florida under the *Ex. Parte Young* exception and the Supreme Court determined that it would be inappropriate for the court to undermine the principle of Sovereign Immunity since the Indian Gaming Regulatory Act provides an exclusive remedial scheme.

Despite the skillfully crafted arguments, they were not immune to Pierce's red pen. Pierce filled each page with notations in the margins, edits and redlines that most people, except for his secretary Laura, would find impossible to decipher.

Pierce appeared to be deep in thought when Noah handed him a cup of coffee. He was tired and didn't feel like engaging in morning chit-chat, so he jumped right in as soon as Noah took a seat across from him at the conference room table.

"I think we should cut down some of the historical analysis," Pierce said. "For example, the whole section which discusses the 1893 and 1907 legislation should come out."

Noah considered Pierce's comment and then said, "Those congressional acts terminated the membership rolls of the Five Civilized Tribes . . . that lays the foundation for our successor in interest argument."

Pierce nodded, he understood the argument, but he didn't think they should include it in the motion to dismiss. What he wanted was a crisp motion focused primarily on procedure. He didn't want the court getting weighed down in substantive arguments when the court should focus on the state's lack of authority to bring this case.

However, Pierce looked at this as a teaching moment, so he allowed Noah the opportunity to make a case for keeping it in.

He liked Noah's work ethic and intellect and wanted to bring him along. His zeal needed to be directed and sometimes bridled. Much like a Miami summer thunderstorm: if the storm blew through quickly, it was a rather enjoyable experience. The brief downpour cleaned things up and added vigor to Miami's lush vegetation. But if it hovered or stalled, streets were flooded, trees were toppled, and homes lost power. That was Noah Grayson. With guidance, Noah was surgical and precise. If left to his own devices, he could be a destructive force much like an F-5 tornado cutting a path through a mobile home park.

Noah liked it when he had Pierce's undivided attention. "The Department of Interior used the same rationale when it determined that the Cherokee Nation of Oklahoma is not the historic Cherokee Nation. When their membership rolls were closed, the authority of the Cherokee government ended. That's the reasoning that the Department of Interior used when it decided that the Cherokee Nation and the United Keetoowah Band of Cherokees are both successors to the historic Cherokee Nation and have equal rights to Cherokee lands. Those same facts apply to the Muscogee Nation and the creek tribal towns."

Pierce nodded. "It's a persuasive argument."

"But?"

"But . . . this point goes to the merits of our case," Pierce said. "It doesn't belong in a motion to dismiss. Our legal position is that the state has no legal standing to bring this action under IGRA and the tribe's sovereign immunity prevents the tribal officials from being named in the suit...The court won't consider substantive arguments at this juncture so there's no point in making them."

Noah nodded ever so subtly as he appeared to process Pierce's point. "I understand."

Pierce could see Noah's discomfort and offered him a compliment. "This is excellent work, Noah. You've provided everything we need for the motion."

Noah's brow furrowed while he continued to take notes. It was obvious to Pierce that he was disappointed.

Pierce yawned. "Noah, please stop writing for a minute."

Noah slid his legal pad away. "I'm listening."

"The substantive arguments you drafted are crisp. If the court denies our motion to dismiss, the history of the Creek Confederacy and validation of the Kialegee Tribal Town as a successor in interest will be the lynchpin of our case. You did nice work. But as usual, you got a little ahead of yourself."

Pierce walked around the conference table and gave him a "that-a-boy" pat on the shoulder. Before opening the door to the conference room, he said, "Please get my edits to Laura and tell her I'll be back in a few hours. I'm going home and getting a couple of hours of sleep."

Chapter Fourteen

TULSA, OKLAHOMA

Payton took a swig of whisky and nudged the man sitting on the barstool next to her who had passed out face down. He didn't budge. Even though it was her seventh in the past two hours, she was not drunk. When it came to booze and a few other things she had the constitution of a man twice her size. Tonight, however, her unshakable resolve was a bit wobbly. The problem had to do with a string of confidential emails that had come into her possession. The man on the barstool had been hitting on her and rambled on about being a member of the MCN National Council. Payton didn't give it much importance until a couple of drinks later when he mentioned Merrill Lynch and Bank of America and the pressure they were putting on the MCN to stop the Kialegee casino. After a couple more whiskeys, she coaxed him into letting her read the string of emails.

The first one was from a Managing Director for Bank of America in Merrill Lynch's New York City office to Chief Beaver. Chief Beaver copied the Members of the MCN National Council.

From: Jeff Carson, Managing Director, Bank of America Merrill Lynch

To: Chief Beaver

Chief Beaver,

The loan for the River Spirit has a lock-out provision that requires that the MCN not open any new casino until the River Spirit loan is repaid. Our legal counsel advises that under the applicable covenants of the loan Agreement the MCN must stop the Kialegee project otherwise we may have to provide the MCN with a formal Notice of Default under the Loan Agreement.

Jeff Carson
Managing Director, Bank of America Merrill Lynch

From: Speaker Sam Greene-Speaker National Council
To: Chief Beaver
I don't appreciate the underlying threat of any banker to this Nation. The actions taken by others are beyond our control. I'm in favor of exploring alternative lending solutions concerning our Phase II financing for the River Spirit.

Hvtvm ce heca res.
Sam Greene

From: Mark Barnett, National Council Member
To: Chief Beaver,
I agree with Sam. Our lenders should not interfere with tribal business. We should let them know how we feel and remind them that the MCN has filed a formal objection letter with the NIGC.

Robert Nichols-Chair-Business, Finance & Justice
To: Chief Beaver,
I agree with everyone. Merrill Lynch's attempt to pressure the MCN is inappropriate. Our lock-out provision only applies to future MCN casinos. However, it doesn't matter whether they can hold us in default.   I've confirmed with our Gaming Commissioner and Paul Carson regarding the Kialegee casino's potential impact to our business. If they get their casino

open, we are going to have to lay off people and we are going to have trouble finding financing for Phase II. So it makes sense to assure Merrill Lynch and Bank of America that we are playing ball.

From Paul Craft–CEO Muscogee Creek Nation's Casinos
To: Chief Beaver, Muscogee National Counsel,
*   As you would expect, our banks are calling us daily for up-dates on the Kialegee Casino project, including what the Creek Nation is doing to object to this project. I forwarded the Gaming Commissioner's letter to the NIGC Chair, along with Bank of America/Merrill Lynch threatening emails to the Nation. Please see Jeff's comments below regarding potential default if the Nation does not oppose the project vigorously.*
*   Thanks,*
*   Paul*

From: Jeff Carson
To: Paul Craft
Subject: Letter to BIA NIGC re Kialegee Casino 12-28
SENSITIVITY: Private
Paul-Thank you very much for keeping me informed on the issue. We want to help defend you and the MCN Gaming credit.
*   Keep in mind that under the "joint-jurisdiction" theory, it appears that the MCN can officially object and stop the Kialegee project, which is the intent of the applicable covenants of the Loan Agreement.*
*   Subject to Agent bank counsel interpretation, to do nothing could provoke a Notice of Default and a Reservation of Rights by the Bank group whose rights include among others, the abil-*

ity to interrupt distributions of gaming revenues to the Tribe.
This is not a hammer that anyone throws around loosely, but it
is potential exposure for the Nation that may have to be con-
sidered in their decision making.
   Jeff Carson
   Managing Director, Bank of America Merrill Lynch

Payton waited for him to get up to go to the bathroom, before she asked if she could put her number in his phone. When he stepped away, she forwarded the emails to her account. Her problem was that she didn't know how to use them to generate the maximum damage to the MCN. She wanted to bludgeon the MCN and expose them. But a voice inside her told her that Pierce could put them to better use. Something that could help the Kialegee. While Payton grew up resenting the MCN as they grew fat and rich while her tribe struggled, her feelings didn't intensify into a burning hatred until after Samuel's death. Seeing how hard her father was fighting to make a better life for his tribe and how the MCN painted him to be a lawless villain, something he wasn't, pushed her past the point of no return. Payton felt a tear starting down her cheek and wiped it away, trying to hide the emotions overwhelming her. The only thing at that very moment that Payton wanted was not to feel anything. And what she hoped was after a few more glasses of Jack Daniel's she would be numb and push Samuel and the Kialegee from her thoughts, at least for one night.

*****

Pierce was used to working Saturdays. He was, however, not accustomed to being rousted by the Chief's daughter at three in the morning.

"We've got a problem," she blurted out as soon as she heard Pierce's voice.

Pierce could tell immediately that Payton had been drinking. "Why don't you tell me what's wrong."

He listened patiently as Payton rambled on about having drinks with an MCN council member and explained how she stealthily sent herself copies of confidential emails between Merrill Lynch and the tribe.

"The MCN is getting pressure from its lenders," she snapped into her phone. Pierce sat up in bed and thought for a second. "What exactly did the emails say?"

"Hold on," she said as she pulled them up on her phone and read them to Pierce. In a slightly strangled voice tinged with amusement she said, "Looks like that banker is squeezing good old George's balls good."

Pierce didn't respond right away, processing the information. "You said that we had a problem," Pierce said. "We already know the MCN opposes the casino. This just tells us why." None of it was shocking but there were unquestionably a few revelations.

Payton hesitated. The whiskey was catching up with her. "Yes . . . but this is different. Those fucks are preaching to the BIA and the NIGC that the Kialegee are trampling on their treaty rights, when most of them know we have the same right to be there. The oral history of the Creek Confederacy gets pounded into us from the time we're toddlers . . ." Her voice faded for a moment. "Those assholes know that all the Creek Tribes share jurisdiction over all Creek lands. This isn't about treaty rights. This is about dollars."

Pierce knew there was a good deal of truth in her words.

"One more thing," Payton cut in. "Before the guy passed out, he told me he'd heard that a member from the Oklahoma congressional delegation confided in Chief Beaver that the NIGC is cooperating with the

Attorney General and that they're going to release an opinion that the Broken Arrow land is under the exclusive jurisdiction of the MCN and the Kialegee has no right to the Broken Arrow land."

"The council member shared that with you?" Pierce asked, slightly surprised.

Payton poked fun at his stupid question. "You'd be surprised what a drunk and horny Indian will tell you if he thinks it will get him laid," she said, swilling her drink.

Pierce regarded Payton's news cautiously. He had thought little about the motion of dismiss since they had filed it but if the court ordered a hearing, he suddenly thought Oklahoma's attack on Indian sovereign immunity might not be enough to keep the MCN from staying out of the fray. While most tribal leaders would disapprove of the MCN aligning itself with the state against another Indian tribe, George Beaver could spin it like he had no choice but to cooperate since they were facing the potential loss of treaty rights. His mind turned over all the facts and every angle he could think of. If Chief Beaver or any other member of the MCN testified for the state, he would use the emails like a scalpel to cut the MCN to pieces and expose them to the rest of the tribal leaders. He could also use the emails to create a mess of epic proportions for the NIGC. But that would have to wait until after he exposed the weaknesses in the State of Oklahoma's case. If Payton's news was accurate, and the NIGC issued a written opinion, Pierce suspected that even with the emails in hand, they would not withdraw it before the Kialegee received a favorable court ruling.

He made a mental note to add the NIGC to the growing list of battles he would have to fight for the Kialegee. Dealing with government regulators was maddening, but that's how these standoffs were won. One victory at a time.

Pierce glanced at the clock on his nightstand. "Do me a favor and send me those emails." He wasn't sure how Jeremiah would react to them. Given all the pressure he was under, he could easily come unhinged. "And don't tell anyone about them, not even your dad," Pierce added.

"Okay."

"One more thing, you did really great. As soon as you're done sending the emails you should go get some sleep."

Payton let out a frustrated breath. She could do without the proverbial slap on the back from Pierce. But it was harder for her to ignore his annoying habit of sending her off to bed alone. Her muttered response was barely intelligible.

"I'm sorry, Payton. I didn't catch what you said."

"It was nothing," Payton said in an unconvincing voice. "I'll talk to you in the morning."

Chapter Fifteen

GOVERNOR'S OFFICE
OKLAHOMA CITY

Chief Beaver was informed via intercom that the Governor was holding on line one. Before he could finish his greeting, the Governor asked
him if he could come to the capitol immediately for a meeting. The
Governor wouldn't say what the meeting was about, only that there was
some business that needed to be handled quickly and that she would see
him as soon as he could get there.

Two hours later George Beaver arrived at the state capitol building.
He gazed up at the white dome of the state capitol walking past several
producing oil wells, enormous statues and Centennial Plaza which
contains the flags of each Indian tribe as a tribute to the contributions of
Native Americans to the state of Oklahoma. George started his climb up
the limestone stairs towards the rotunda. A member of the Governor's
staff was waiting for him at the top. When he tried to sign in, he was
politely told by the Governor's assistant that it wasn't necessary. There
was a sense of urgency in his pace as he hurried George through a long
hallway and down several flights of stairs to a door that led to a small
private conference room.

The Governor, Attorney General, Congressman Murphy and Chief
Judge Fennell's law clerk were all present. George assumed when he
hung up the telephone that the meeting had something to do with the
tobacco settlement. When he saw Congressman Murphy, George
instantly knew that the Governor summoned him to discuss the Kialegee
casino project. He could feel the tension in the room spike the moment
he walked through the conference room door. Introductions were ex-

tremely brief. Neither George nor Scott Masters cared much for each other. Scott made little effort to hide his true feelings. He didn't care for Indians. They didn't vote for him. And Indian casinos were a blight on Christian communities.

They both wanted to get the meeting over with and go their separate ways.

The Governor pointed to a chair next to her. "Please Chief, sit over here."

"I assume we're not here to talk about the tobacco settlement," George said, looking around the table.

"The tobacco settlement is contingent on what we've asked you here for," Masters interjected. "The state has generously agreed to forgive 32 million in taxes for your continued opposition to the Broken Arrow casino project."

With a dismissive half smile, George said, "We've held up our end of the bargain. I've publicly opposed the project several times, and the Nation has submitted formal letters of protest to all three federal agencies."

Masters shot the Chief a dissatisfied look.

"We want more from you. We want you to testify at the preliminary injunction hearing in two weeks."

George's gut twisted upon hearing the Attorney General's demand. "Our lawyer has been closely monitoring the case. He didn't mention anything to me about a hearing."

"The hearing will take place two weeks from now as soon as Judge Fennell denies the Kialegee motion to dismiss."

"And you're certain that will happen?"

Masters had a smug look on his face. "The order denying the motion and setting the hearing date will be signed tomorrow."

Judge Fennell's law clerk shifted nervously in his seat.

In George's mind there was no doubt what was happening, but he wanted to hear the Attorney General say that the hearing was fixed. "So, if you know how the judge will rule on the motion to dismiss, I'm guessing you also know how the hearing is going to turn out."

Masters nodded in a skillfully noncommittal way, but other than that he did not respond.

A practiced perplexed expression fell across George's face. "What could I possibly testify about?"

"We'd like you to testify that the Broken Arrow land is under the exclusive control of the MCN and that the Kialegee never received permission from you to open a casino."

The expression on George's face seemed to say, are you kidding me? "I'm a chief, not an anthropologist or ethno-historian. What you need is . . ."

"We have an expert witness," Masters cut him off. Professor Judson from the University of Oklahoma will do the heavy lifting. All you have to do is testify that the MCN provides governmental services and controls the land."

"We don't provide any services. It's eighty acres of woods," George said.

Masters remained unflinching. "Professor Judson will testify that based on his research of the history of the Creeks, the lands in Tulsa County belong exclusively to the MCN. You will simply confirm his conclusion from an Indian perspective."

"Indian perspective," George repeated under his breath, as he gave the impression like he was thinking long and hard on the Attorney General's request. "Is this Professor Judson an expert on Creek history?" George asked in a tone that suggested that he had never heard of him.

"He's a professor of history specializing in Indian cultures of the Southwest. He'll give us what we need," Masters said with absolute confidence.

The last thing George Beaver wanted was to testify against the Kialegee Tribe. He believed that Indians should settle their differences among themselves. They shouldn't rely on non-Indians to do it for them. It reflected poorly on the Indian community. While he wanted the state to stop the casino, he didn't want to play a public role in the courtroom spectacle. George preferred to work through political back channels. He cared about how other tribal leaders viewed him. No matter the reason, if George testified on behalf of the state against an Indian tribe, he knew that his standing among tribal leaders would take a hit.

George smiled and said, "Then, if I were you, I'd stick to your expert and leave it there."

Masters gave him a curious look. "Why would I do that?"

"Because 'Indian perspective' as you put it is a slippery slope. Most of the MCN frown on the Kialegee's attempt to build a casino in Broken Arrow but when it comes to the question of jurisdiction, there are many Creeks, even among the MCN that believe that the tribal towns have the same rights to Creek lands."

"Your point being?"

"It's pretty obvious. If you put me on the stand, you risk the Kialegee's attorney exposing the split among the Creeks concerning the tribal town's rights."

"You don't have to admit to that," Masters spat back.

George looked through his glasses at Masters and said, "I would be under oath."

Masters made a face like he might get sick. "Are you saying you won't help? Maybe we should rethink the tobacco settlement," Masters said in a threatening tone.

The Governor looked at Masters and cleared her throat. It was a signal to him to back off. She then looked at George and said, "This casino is no good for both of us. I hope we can continue to work together."

George nodded. "Governor, I give you my word, we are doing everything we said we'd do to oppose it."

Masters shot George an extremely dissatisfied look.

The Governor studied George's face for a moment. "George, I've known you for a long time. You really don't expect me to believe that you're afraid of being backed into a corner by the Kialegee's attorney. Why don't you tell me exactly what's troubling you?"

George considered the most diplomatic way to put it. Then went the other way. "If the AG had limited his lawsuit to the tribe instead of including the individual tribal leaders, the member tribes of the Oklahoma Indian Gaming Association wouldn't have cared. Now they're teetering on whether they should jump into the fight."

George shook his head, frowning at what he was about to say. "If the MCN testifies for the state that will most likely tip the scales the other way."

Masters rose from his chair. The Governor held up her hand, signaling to the Attorney General that she would like him to remain silent for a minute.

"You're saying that the MCN's involvement in the hearing might do more harm than good."

"That's exactly what I'm saying. I've been telling the other Oklahoma tribes that this is strictly a dispute between the State and the Kialegee and that we should stay out of it."

George glanced over at Masters and back to the Governor. "There's been a lot of blowback over the AG's reckless decision to include the individual leaders of the tribe in the lawsuit. There are several tribal leaders that feel that if the AG can sue the Kialegee tribal leaders, what's stopping him from going after them? If the MCN gets involved in this case, then it's no longer just a dispute between the State and the Kialegee and I suspect several tribes will file motions to intervene. These are gaming tribes with deep pockets. If they jump into this fight, they're bringing some high-powered law firms with them."

George figured the potential for the case turning into a legal free-for-all might concern the Governor. He studied the Governor's face for a moment and thought she looked at ease. Either she was very good at dealing with stress or she was a talented actress.

George had his hands folded in front of him. He turned his gaze on Masters for good measure. "That would make your case a lot more complicated."

Masters shuffled some papers and cleared his throat but did not engage.

The Governor considered George's remarks carefully. She stood and extended her hand. "Thank you, Chief, for meeting with us on such short notice."

"You're welcome," George stood.

The Governor escorted George to the door and handed him off to one of her staff. She closed the door and walked back towards Masters. "Take him off your witness list."

Chapter Sixteen

TULSA, OKLAHOMA

Shortly after Pierce and Noah stepped off the plane, Noah asked him for the rental car reservation. At that precise moment, Pierce realized he had forgotten to turn his cell phone on upon landing. Pierce hit the power button and the color screen came to life. A picture of a spinning globe flashed on the screen, and then the phone beeped as it retrieved messages, voice mails and emails. After a few seconds the beeping stopped and Pierce saw that he had twenty-nine text messages, seven voicemails and nine emails. He was about to scroll down through the text messages, when the phone began ringing.

After swiping the green button with his thumb, he answered the call. "Hello Payton."

"I'm parked outside in 'Arrivals'. I told my dad I'd pick you up."

Pierce continued to walk towards baggage claim with Noah matching him stride for stride. "That really wasn't necessary. We're planning on renting a car."

"There's been a development that my dad would like you to handle this afternoon. He was going to pick you up himself, but I told him I would get you and run you to Wetumka."

"Wetumka? I was hoping to spend this afternoon prepping for to-morrow's hearing."

"Change of plans. Just come on out and I'll explain on the way," Payton said with a trace of urgency in her voice.

After claiming their belongings from baggage claim, the two men made their way outside through the revolving doors.

"There she is," Pierce said. Payton was standing on the curb next to her white jeep. Noah took one look at her and stopped to straighten his tie.

"And who might that be?"

Pierce shook his head. "That's Payton. She's our ride."

"Wow," Noah said, drawing out the word. "You never mentioned that she's an absolute knock-out. Can this day get any better?"

"You've been talking to her for six months. I'm surprised you never looked her up on the internet to see what she looks like or suggested a video call."

Noah shrugged as he took another quick look. "Huge mistake on my part."

Pierce shot him a look that said whatever you're thinking, it's not a good idea. "She's the Chief's daughter."

"Does that make her off limits?"

Pierce looked less than pleased. "You have your first evidentiary hearing tomorrow. Keep your head in the game...Besides, she'd eat you alive."

Noah smirked. "I like the sound of that."

When they got to the car Payton offered her cheek to Pierce and he gave it a quick kiss. She swung open the rear passenger door and gestured to Noah to get in before he could say a word. Noah leaned in and stopped short the moment he came face-to-face with Payton's Husky mix, Kal.

"Stop being a pussy and get in. I already fed him today," she barked at Noah.

Payton looked at her watch. She seemed rushed. "We better get going or we're going to be late."

"Late for what?" Pierce asked.

Payton looked like she wanted to shake him. "I left you three voicemails. If you'd listen to them . . . better yet, if you answered your phone, you'd know."

"Well, I'm here now so why don't you tell me what's going on."

Payton didn't respond immediately, and then glancing sideways at Pierce, she said, "My dad wants you to handle an interview with a Tulsa World reporter . . . The media has been crucifying the tribe and my dad thought it would help to get our side of the story out. He wants you to do it."

Pierce raised a curious eyebrow. He wasn't buying it. Jeremiah's decision to suddenly capitulate to the press sounded suspicious. The media had been attacking the Kialegee Tribe and the project for months.

"Why now?"

Payton shifted uncomfortably. "Don't know."

Payton and Pierce exchanged a quick look. Her expression told him a different story. "Why don't we start over?" He suggested. "And how about this time you tell me the whole story and not just bits and pieces?"

Payton clutched the steering wheel. Her eyes watered. After a few minutes, she said, "A reporter for the Tulsa World told my dad she would run a front-page story about me unless he agreed to give her a story about the Kialegee Tribe and the casino project. She said it was his choice."

For the entire drive, she'd been unable to fight back thoughts of her past and what it would do to the Kialegee and the casino when it was front page on the Tulsa World. Payton had no illusions about who she was, or what she'd done. She just hated herself for putting her dad in such a vulnerable position.

"What kind of story can the reporter write about you?" Noah asked.

Neither Payton nor Pierce bothered to answer the question.

"I'm sorry, Pierce. I know you and my dad have a lot on your plates and you don't need this," she said.

"You have nothing to be sorry for."

Pierce twisted in his seat to look at Noah. "I'll need you to prep the Chief for tomorrow's hearing and go over the list of questions we prepared in case the state calls him as a witness."

"You got it."

Pierce noticed a faraway look in Payton's eyes. "It will be alright," he said to reassure her.

Payton blinked. Her nausea reached its peak when she eased the car through the tribal headquarters' parking lot, passing an overfilled dumpster.

"I'll wait for you here."

*****

Abbey Brody jumped up from her chair the instant Pierce opened the door and walked into the only meeting room in the Kialegee's small headquarters. Wearing a fake smile plastered across her face, she reached out for Pierce's hand. "Abbey Brody, Tulsa World. You must be the Kialegee Tribe's attorney."

Pierce squeezed her hand and then quickly let it go. "Pierce Evangelista, I'll be the one answering your questions." Pierce acted as if he was pressed for time. "Shall we get started?"

Brody nodded. "I'm set up over there," she said, pointing to a table and folding chairs in the corner of a tight room which doubled as the lunchroom. The scent of fried bologna and mac and cheese casserole which still lingered made Pierce's mouth water, reminding him that he'd skipped breakfast in his rush to catch his flight.

Abbey Brody was smart as hell, cunning and very dangerous to be on the wrong side of. If not for her propensity to repel people by her mere presence, she would be writing for the Washington Post or the New York Times. She was a pit bull. From what Pierce had seen from her prior stories about the casino, Abbey Brody had already picked a side and didn't let the facts get in the way of a good story.

Brody wasted no time with pleasantries or softball questions.

"Why would the tribe build a casino over seventy miles away from where they are located and put it next to a school?"

Pierce looked at her for a moment, like a predator that hadn't decided whether he wanted to play with his food or kill it quickly. He took a breath and decided he would give Brody a little rope.

"Ms. Brody, are you familiar with the history of the Creek Confederacy?"

Brody shook her head. "I've done some research and interviewed Professor Judson from the University of Oklahoma on the subject . . . Just to be clear, Mr. Evangelista, it's my job to ask the questions and yours to answer them."

"Of course, I was simply gauging how versed you were in Creek history." The four legs on the folding chair were uneven and wobbled as he talked.

Brody looked over the top of her glasses. "Back to my question."

"Very well, if you'll indulge me," Pierce said, trying to put it all in context. "The Treaty of 1866 created the Creek reservation in Oklahoma. The treaty states that the reservation was created for all Creek Indians. The land was not divided among the tribal towns, nor did it say where each tribal town must settle. In other words, where a tribal town is located has no bearing on anything. The Broken Arrow land is owned by a Kialegee Tribal member. The Kialegee headquarters can be in Broken Arrow just as easily as it is here in Wetumka. In fact, there's nothing that prevents the Kialegee from relocating its headquarters to Broken Arrow . . . In response to the second part of your question, the City of Broken Arrow purchased the land for the school nine months ago, the Kialegee Tribe has owned the land in Broken Arrow for over one hundred and fifty years."

Brody nodded in a way that said she wasn't buying it and said, "But the City started construction of the school before it was aware of the Kialegee plans for a casino."

"That's debatable," Pierce said. "Actually, the city's Master Plan for the area provides that the future zoning for the property where the school is to be located and the area surrounding the casino site is commercial and light industrial. Meaning that if a casino was a lawful use under state law, it would be a permitted use under the city's zoning code."

Brody shook her head, "But casinos are illegal under state law so it couldn't be a permitted use under any zoning category."

"You're missing my point. The future uses for the area are commercial and industrial uses, not residential. My point was only to illustrate that the proposed location for the casino is consistent with the City's plans for the future development of that area. And you know as well as anyone that casinos are legal on Indian land."

Brody's nostrils flared. It was obvious she didn't care for Pierce's answers since he wasn't giving her anything she could use to continue to portray the tribe as trespassers with no regard for the good people of Broken Arrow.

"Why has the tribe been unwilling until now to answer questions about the project?"

Pierce's blue eyes stared right through Brody. He didn't care for the tactics she used to get this interview. "Access isn't a right. It's a privilege. The media and your newspaper, in particular, have painted the tribe as lawless, when no law has been broken . . ."

"The Attorney General obviously doesn't agree with you," she cut Pierce short.

Pierce inched forward in his chair. "I'm aware of Mr. Masters' position. But what law has the tribe broken? The Attorney General sued under the Indian Gaming Regulatory Act. Under the Act, illegal gaming must be occurring for the law to be broken. No gaming has occurred on the property, so how can the tribe be guilty of violating the act?"

Brody listened with a bored expression. "I guess that's for the District Court judge to decide."

Pierce sat back and let out a deep breath. "I'll tell you this much. The only law which has been broken is the city's repeated denial of the tribe's request to connect to the city's water supply. Federal law is very clear on that point. States and local governments cannot deny public utilities such as water to Indians."

Brody looked almost instantly uncomfortable.

"And yet, the city continues to violate federal law and I haven't read a single story about it."

Brody looked down at her notes to avoid Pierce's gaze and regroup.

"But why build a casino that no one in the city wants?"

Pierce smiled cynically. "Are you sure about that?"

Brody nodded.

"That tells me you've only spoken to the handful of folks on the other side of the fence at the construction site and no one else."

Brody played dumb. "I'm sure our people canvassed . . ."

"We've conducted our own polling over the entire city," Pierce interrupted. "We didn't skew it to get a particular result. We wanted to know what the people in the community were thinking so we could use the information to address real concerns and tailor the casino's marketing campaign . . . You'd be interested to know that the majority of the folks were indifferent to the casino but would come if it was open and most others favor it. Very few people outside a small group that live within a one-mile radius had anything negative to say."

"Was the polling by a professional firm?"

Pierce looked at her intently. "Would you like to see it?"

"Please."

Pierce nodded, scribbled something on his legal pad and glanced up at Brody. "Do you mind if I ask you a question?"

"Sure," Brody replied after a slight pause.

"Do you know how Broken Arrow got its name?"

Brody sighed. "I can't say that I do."

Pierce straightened up in his chair. "It's actually an interesting story . . . Broken Arrow was named after a Creek Indian village in Georgia. When the Creeks were forced to leave their homes to make room for white settlements, they renamed the area just east of Tulsa where they settled Broken Arrow."

Pierce looked at Brody with dead serious eyes. "So, going back to your question?"

Brody looked confused. "What question was that?"

"The one where you asked why the Kialegee would want to go to Broken Arrow when they're not wanted there."

Brody's eyes got big. "I don't believe I said that."

"Said it . . . implied it, the message was crystal clear," Pierce insisted. "So, after the Creeks settled in Broken Arrow and white settlers began moving in and squeezing them out, do you think the Creeks wanted them there?"

"No, I suppose not."

"And yet, here we are." Pierce looked at his watch. "That's all the time I have for today. If you'll excuse me, I have a hearing to prepare for." Pierce pushed his chair away from the table and started in the direction of the door.

Brody managed an unconvincing smile. "Would it be possible to get a few minutes with the Chief? I still have a few more questions."

"You're getting ahead of yourself, Ms. Brody. After we read your article, we'll decide whether you've earned that privilege," Pierce said just before opening the door and closing it behind him.

Chapter Seventeen

UNITED STATES DISTRICT COURT FOR
THE NORTHERN DISTRICT OF OKLAHOMA

A hundred people were crowded into the small courtroom, filling the wooden benches that squeaked whenever someone moved. Indians sat together on the defense side of the courtroom whether they supported or opposed the Kialegee and whites filled the opposite side behind the Attorney General. There were a few empty seats on the Kialegee's side, but the white faces chose to stand along the back wall instead.

Nikki took her place at Counsel's table between Pierce and Noah just as the bleary-eyed bailiff yelled "All rise".

Chief Judge Fennell looked down past the end of his nose, over his reading glasses at the packed courtroom. "The court has disposed of the procedural motions. If there are no other motions, the court is prepared to move forward with the evidentiary hearing on the state's motion for a preliminary injunction."

"We have no other motions pending Your Honor," Masters' voice filled the room.

Judge Fennell flipped through the pages of the pretrial briefs and witness lists.

"Mr. Evangelista, how many witnesses will you call?"

Pierce rose from his chair. "Three, Your Honor."

"Mr. Masters, how many will you call?"

"We have twenty-one," Masters said proudly.

Judge Fennell stopped writing and looked up. "Are twenty-one witnesses necessary for the state to prove its case?"

"Your honor, we have seventeen members from the community that will be directly impacted if this casino is allowed to move forward. They would all like an opportunity to be heard."

"Pick one person to testify on behalf of the group."

"Yes, Your Honor."

"Mr. Masters, the state has filed the motion for the preliminary injunction. You may proceed."

Masters walked importantly to the wooden podium.

"May it please the court. The State of Oklahoma has filed this action against the Kialegee Tribal Town and officials of the tribe to stop the construction of an illegal casino in violation of the Indian Gaming Regulatory Act and the Gaming Compact signed by the tribe and the State of Oklahoma."

Masters contended that the property on which the casino was being built was located more than seventy miles away from the tribe's headquarters. He made the same arguments that he made in his complaint and pre-trial brief, only his performance was better in person.

"The land in Broken Arrow does not belong to the Kialegee Tribal Town. There's no lease or anything that gives them rights to the land," Master's voice boomed as he launched into his opening argument with a ministerial zeal that any black preacher would envy. He painted a picture of lawlessness and the criminal element that would prey upon the good citizens of Broken Arrow if the casino was permitted to open. Then he launched himself into a fifteen-minute discourse on Oklahoma's history and how tribes must peacefully coexist with the citizens of Oklahoma.

"This case is much bigger than the Kialegee Tribe trying to build an illegal casino on land that doesn't belong to them. If the Kialegee's illegal actions go unchecked, we will open the floodgates to a much bigger problem and the entire state will be vulnerable to cherry picking as tribes will put casinos anywhere they please."

The indignation registered on Nikki's face before she could prevent it. Noah scribbled notes and slid them across the table to Pierce.

Masters let the judge and everyone in the courtroom ponder casinos popping up everywhere like fast-food franchises.

Masters started again, this time in a confident and businesslike tone of voice. "The State will prove that the subject land is under the exclusive control and jurisdiction of the Muscogee Creek Nation. The Indian Gaming Regulatory Act requires governmental control and jurisdiction for a tribe to lawfully operate a gaming facility." Masters turned and waved his finger at Jeremiah, who was sitting in the front row, for dramatic effect. "The Kialegee have neither and therefore absolutely no right to game in Broken Arrow."

Jeremiah didn't react. Instead, he remained outwardly serene, choosing to let the courtroom drama play out, but his heart rate notched higher.

Judge Fennell's normally calm demeanor turned to one of overt irritation. He removed his reading glasses and glared at Masters from the bench. "Counsel, this is a United States Federal Court, not a State Court where the rules governing courtroom decorum are more relaxed. In my courtroom, I insist that you refrain from any more theatrics. You will have ample opportunity after we adjourn to perform for the media. Do you understand what I'm saying?"

"Yes, sir."

"Are you done with your opening?"

Masters nodded. "Yes, your Honor."

"Good, now take a seat."

Pierce had planned a brief opening, and after Masters' long-drawn-out diatribe he made it even shorter. He did a twelve-minute opening statement citing to the controlling case law and Department of Interior's legal memorandums regarding Indian gaming laws, treaty rights and applied them to the facts surrounding the Kialegee Tribal Town and the Judge appeared to be interested in every word.

Pierce explained that all four Creek tribes are part of the Muscogee people and were all organized under the Oklahoma Indian Welfare Act, which provided for a revival of self-government among the Native American tribes. Pierce asserted that each of the four were successors to the historic Creek Nation, which ceased to exist in 1907 when an Act of Congress permanently closed the Creek membership rolls and terminated the authority of the Creek government. He pointed out that the Kialegee Tribal Town was federally recognized as an independent Indian tribe in 1941, thirty-eight years before the MCN. Before winding up with his strongest argument, Pierce briefly touched on the State's misapplication of the *Ex Parte Young* doctrine and the court's lack of personal jurisdiction over the individual tribal leaders.

Then he turned his attention to the United States Supreme Court decision in *Michigan V. Bay Mills* which clarified that Indian Tribes have Sovereign Immunity and the Indian Gaming Regulatory Act only authorizes a State to sue a tribe to enjoin Class III gaming activity that violates the Tribal-State compact.

"The United States Supreme Court made it clear that Class III gaming means the playing of Class III games. There has been no playing of Class III games on the property, nor has the State alleged in its motion that the Kialegee Tribe has played Class III games on the property. The State's complaint is based on supposition that Class III gaming may occur in the future. And that, Your Honor, cannot abrogate the Tribe's Sovereign Immunity."

Finally, Pierce seized on an opportunity presented by the Attorney General when he sued to enforce the Tribal-State compact. He pointed to a provision in the compact under the "Remedies" section that required the parties to arbitrate disputes.

"Your Honor, the state itself has not complied with the Tribal-State compact. Specifically, Part 12 provides that parties must first refer disputes arising under the Compact to arbitration under the rules of the American Arbitration Association. The findings of the arbitrator would be subject to review and enforcement by a federal district court. The state has failed to comply with this provision and is, therefore, prevented from suing the Kialegee Tribe in Federal Court. Thank you, Your Honor."

"Is that all?" Judge Fennell asked.

Pierce nodded as he sat next to Nikki.

Judge Fennell looked over at the clock. "It's almost lunchtime. We'll recess and reconvene at one o'clock."

*****

Nikki picked a diner about three-blocks from the courthouse famous for home-style southern cooking, a location that she thought would be far away enough for them to talk about the case.

Payton slid into the booth next to Pierce while Jeremiah, Nikki and Noah sat across from them.

"So, what do you think so far?" Payton asked Pierce, searching his face for a reaction.

Pierce just shrugged. He thought Masters sounded more like he was stumping hard to garner votes from folks whose inflated sense of self-worth and uncompromising Christian values made them easy to manipulate than making an opening statement.

"Let's see what his expert witness has to say," Pierce said, speaking on automatic as his mind focused on his cross-examination.

Noah nodded in agreement. "Masters parading around the courtroom like a peacock with his fire and brimstone theatrics won't win this trial."

Nikki imitated Masters' buttery drawl, "The entire state will be vulnerable to cherry picking as tribes will put casinos anywhere they please ...What a turd."

Pierce smiled and dabbed his mouth with a napkin.

Pierce was a formidable trial lawyer. But everyone sitting at the table realized theirs was an uphill battle. Pierce wasn't from Oklahoma. He was an outsider representing an impoverished tribe that the citizens of Tulsa now hated with a burning certainty.

Chapter Eighteen

Judge Fennell rapped the gavel at 1.15 p.m. and the courtroom came to order. The State called its expert as its first witness.

"Please state your name and occupation for the record."

"Professor Alfred Judson. I am a professor of history at the University of Oklahoma in Norman, Oklahoma."

"What classes do you teach at the University of Oklahoma?"

"I teach classes on the history of the Native American tribes of the Southwest."

"And is the Creek Nation's history an area you are an expert in?"

"Objection, Your Honor. Mr. Masters has not laid the foundation to establish the witness as an expert."

"Sustained."

"Professor Judson, can you provide the court with your educational credentials?"

"I received my Bachelor of Science from Mississippi State and earned my doctorate in history from Texas Christian University."

"And what was the subject of your doctoral dissertation?"

"The Comanche Tribe . . . In particular, the warlike culture of the Comanche. I compared aspects of the Comanche culture to other war-driven cultures such as the Celts and Spartans."

Masters handed the witness a thirty-two-page document. "Professor Judson, I've handed you a report entitled Creek Tribal Towns." Are you familiar with this report?"

Judson nodded. "Yes, I wrote it."

"Your Honor, the state would like to offer this report, Exhibit S-1, into evidence."

"No objection," Pierce said.

"Professor, can you tell me whether the Creek Tribal Towns have any rights or claims to the lands reserved for the Creeks under treaties with the U.S.?"

"Objection Your Honor, Mr. Masters is leading the witness."

Judge Fennell nodded affirmatively during the objection. "Sustained."

Masters shrugged off the objection. "Have you read the state's complaint against the Kialegee Tribal Town?"

"Yes, I have."

"What is your expert opinion about the Tribal Town's claims of jurisdiction over Creek lands?"

"They don't have any rights to Creek lands."

"And why don't they have any rights?"

Professor Judson spent the next ninety minutes answering the Attorney General's questions and lecturing on the history of the Creeks. He explained that tribal towns were no different than Indian bands, which were single communities that united with other bands to form a tribal government but have no independent status. The professor acknowledged that while a few tribal towns signed several of the earlier treaties with the United States, that was only ceremonial to account for everyone in attendance.

"The Creek Nation was represented by the Muscogee. That was the only Creek Tribe that the United States recognized and negotiated with. In fact, several treaties even refer to the Creeks as the Muscogee."

Professor Judson detailed a "tier" structure and applied it to the tribal towns. He concluded that despite three tribal towns organizing under the Oklahoma Indian Welfare Act, they were second tier tribes with no treaty rights or claims to the Creek reservation lands. That was his final opinion.

"We have nothing further from this witness," Masters announced.

"Cross-examination?"

Pierce flipped through his notes as he walked slowly to the podium.

"Good afternoon, Professor Judson."

"Good afternoon."

"Professor, have you ever done any research on the historic Creek Nation prior to writing the report the state entered into evidence earlier today?"

"I've done some general research on the Muscogee Creek Nation."

"Anything published?"

"No."

"So, the focus of your research is not the Muscogee Creek Nation or the Creek Tribal Towns. Would you agree with that statement?"

Judson nodded. "I would agree."

"In your research of Creek Indian history, did you read any of Morris E. Oplar's thirteen published papers?"

Professor Judson frowned. "I'm familiar with his work."

"Does that mean yes that you've read them?"

"Not all thirteen."

Pierce was tempted to ask him how many, but instead said, "Doctor Oplar was an acclaimed ethnographer and cultural anthropologist who wrote extensively on the Creek political structure."

Masters pushed back his chair, poised to make an objection.

"In Doctor Oplar's 1937 report entitled "History and Contemporary State of Aspects of Creek Social Organization and Government," Doctor Oplar concluded that Creek Tribal Towns were in fact autonomous, each with its own political organization and leadership." "Do you agree or disagree with Doctor Oplar?"

"I disagree with Oplar. As you said, his report was written in 1937," Judson answered with a haughty attitude.

Pierce was developing a good sense of the man on the witness stand and the buttons he would need to push. "Are you familiar with the seminal case *Harjo. V. Andrus*?"

"No."

"That's a little surprising," Pierce said to himself in a low voice, but loud enough for Judson to hear him. "The United States District court in *Harjo. V. Andrus* discussed at great length the history of the Creek Nation."

"Objection, Your Honor, this is a cross-examination. Mr. Evangelista is supposed to be asking questions, not lecturing to the witness."

Pierce jumped in. "Your Honor, I'm simply laying the foundation for my next question."

"Overruled but get to your question quickly."

"Yes, sir."

"Professor, would it surprise you to learn that the District court in 1978 accepted Oplar's findings and recognized the political autonomy of the Creek Tribal Towns?"

Judson feigned confusion. "Are you asking me whether I'm surprised or whether I knew about the court's ruling?"

"You've already answered that you were not aware of the most important case concerning the Creek Nation's history . . ."

Masters yelled over Pierce. "Objection, Your Honor."

"Sustained."

Pierce said nothing for a moment. "Have you heard of Doctor Robbie Etheridge?"

"Yes."

Pierce raised one of his thick eyebrows in a manner that said he was pleasantly surprised. "Are you familiar with her work?"

"Yes."

"I'm not going to ask you if you've read all her work because she's the most published authority on the historic Creek Nation."

Judson shook his head with contempt.

"Doctor Etheridge has opined that the tribal towns were an alliance of sorts of 44 independent tribes, each with its own chief. She also asserts that the United States was fully aware that the historic Creek Nation also referred to as the Creek Confederacy was made up of autonomous tribal towns."

Judson shifted impatiently.

Pierce held up one finger, indicating that he was almost done with his question.

"Doctor Etheridge cites to memoranda written by the U.S. Solicitor at the time of the treaty negotiations with the Creeks where he describes the difficulties in getting all the Creek leaders together, and the Secretary of Interior's decision to interact with the Muscogee not because they recognized the Muscogee as the leader of the Creek Indians but because they were the most conveniently located."

Judson's face twisted into a frown. "I disagree with Doctor Etheridge."

Pierce could sense the Professor starting to unravel. "With what part?"

"All of it."

"Could you elaborate?"

Pierce's composure and methodical chipping away at the Professor's competency and integrity was sending Judson's blood pressure north.

"I could, but I won't because it's in my report," Judson said dismissively.

"That's fine," Pierce said in a reasonable voice as he prepared to target a new pressure point.

"Professor, did the Muscogee Creek Nation own all the land east of the Mississippi or did the land belong to each of the tribal towns? You didn't address that in your report."

Judson's face appeared to draw a blank. Pierce had drawn first blood.

Masters jumped up, "Objection, Your Honor, this line of questioning is irrelevant."

The question had an ominous feel to it and Masters was trying to buy some time for his expert witness to recover.

Pierce laughed softly. "Of course, it's relevant." He could easily have demonstrated the relevancy of the question, but he didn't want to tip his hand unless the Judge required him to do so.

Judge Fennell looked downward in the direction of the witness. "Please answer the question, Professor Judson."

"Would you like me to repeat my question?" Pierce asked in a tone that suggested to the witness that he knew something that Judson did not.

Judson hesitated. He looked uneasy. "I believe the lands belonged to the Muscogee Creek Nation, but I'm not entirely sure."

"You testified earlier that the tribal town signatures on the treaties were ceremonial. Is that correct?"

"Yes."

"The 1833 Treaty was a treaty of cession. Under that treaty, all land east of the Mississippi was transferred to the United States in exchange for the land in Oklahoma. The tribal towns were signatories to that treaty. Since you don't know with any degree of certainty who owned the land east of the Mississippi how can you say with any degree of certainty that their signatures were ceremonial?"

Judson shifted uncomfortably in his chair.

"Wouldn't you agree that if the tribal towns owned the land where their villages were located, their signatures on the treaties were more than ceremonial?"

"If the tribal towns owned the land, but I never said they did."

"You just said you're not sure who owned the land."

"Objection!"

"Overruled."

"Are you familiar with the language in the 1833 treaty?"

Judson exhaled sharply. "I've reviewed it."

"The language I want to ask you about is the section where the treaty says that the land is taken in exchange for property that belongs to the whole Creek Nation. Isn't the Kialegee Tribal Town part of the whole Creek Nation?"

Judson shook his head. "They are but ownership is communal, and the rights of ownership do not apply to any tribal town independent of the whole."

"The 1852 and 1866 treaties established the boundaries of the Creek lands in Oklahoma. Both treaties say that the lands were set aside for the entire Creek Nation."

Judson's frustration was apparent. "Yes, but again the Kialegee only have communal rights to the land. As long as they were part of the Creek Nation, they have a communal interest in the land same as all the other Creek Indians."

"If the Kialegee Tribal Town exchanged lands they solely owned under the treaty shouldn't they have certain rights and expectations?"

"Under the treaty, the rights flow to the entire tribe."

"Can they be taken away?"

"I don't understand your question."

"What I'm asking is whether the Kialegee Tribal Town lost their rights to the land when they organized under the Oklahoma Indian Welfare Act and became a federally recognized tribe?"

Judson looked across the courtroom towards Masters for help. He appeared to be apprehensive on how he should answer. "The Kialegee rights to occupy the land stem from the treaties that transferred the Oklahoma land to the Creek Nation as a whole. They don't have independent rights."

"So, they lost them?"

"I didn't say that."

"No? Then what are you saying? Do they have rights to occupy the Oklahoma land or don't they?"

"As part of the Muscogee Creek Nation they do."

"Where does it say that in the treaties?"

"Objection Your Honor, asked and answered."

"Sustained. Move along, Mr. Evangelista."

"Professor, are you familiar with Assistant Secretary of the Department of Interior's opinion on the subject of shared jurisdiction?"

"No."

"Really? You should read it sometime. It's the most important position statement on the subject of successors in interest to come out in the last twenty years. If you read it, you might change your mind."

"Objection. Your Honor, Mr. Evangelista is badgering the witness."

"Sustained," Judge Fennell said in a tone that signaled that he wasn't going to tolerate much more.

"What about the Curtis Act of 1898, have you heard of it?"

Masters rattled off another objection. "The witness has already testified that he is unfamiliar with the Department of Interior's position on successors in interest."

"Your honor, I am asking about a historic piece of legislation specific to the Five Civilized Tribes."

Judge Fennell took off his glasses and rubbed his eyes before instructing the witness to answer the question.

"Yes, I am familiar with the Curtis Act."

"Did the Curtis Act terminate the Creek Nation?"

Judson shrugged. "No."

"Did the Act terminate the Nation's membership roles?"

"Yes."

"So, in your opinion closing the roles did not terminate the Creek Nation?"

"That's correct."

"Would you agree that the Muscogee Creek Nation applied for federal recognition under the Oklahoma Indian Welfare Act in 1979?"

"I suppose so."

"Is that a yes?"

Judson nodded. "Yes."

"If they never lost their status as a federally recognized tribe after the Curtis Act closed their roles, why do you think they filed for federal recognition 39 years after the Kialegee Tribal Town?"

"I don't know," he said.

"Did Muscogee Creek Nation file for a different type of recognition than the Kialegee Tribal Town?"

Judson exhaled a tired sigh. "I don't understand the question."

Pierce nodded. "You testified earlier that the Kialegee Tribal Town was a second-tier tribe. Did the Muscogee Creek Nation apply for a different type of Federal recognition?"

Judson took a long time to answer, which in itself was an answer. "No, I don't believe they did."

"Is there any federal law that creates distinctions between federally recognized tribes?"

Judson shrugged his shoulders. "I don't believe there is."

"So how did you arrive at your conclusion that the Kialegee Tribal Town has a lesser status than the Muscogee Creek Nation?"

"I said they were a band. That has nothing to do with their federal status."

Pierce looked at him with his best poker face as he handed him a copy of the Federal Register. "Do you see the Muscogee Creek Nation on the list of federally recognized tribes?"

"Yes."

"Do you see the Kialegee Tribal Town on that list?"

"Yes."

"Is there an asterisk by their name or anything reflecting that the Kialegee Tribal Town is a band or has fewer rights than the other federally recognized tribes?"

"No," Judson offered brusquely.

Pierce took a moment and read his notes. "Professor are you familiar with Federal Rule 25 USC 476(f)."

Judson made a face and stared straight through Pierce. "No."

Pierce walked over slowly and handed him a copy of the regulation.

"The law says that it's illegal to take any action or render any decision that diminishes the rights of an Indian Tribe. Don't you think your testimony here today that the Kialegee Tribal Town is a second-tier tribe with lesser rights than the Muscogee to the lands given to all Creeks by treaty diminishes the Kialegee?"

The expression on Judson's face said it all. He looked like the captain of a ship that had been broadsided by a torpedo.

Masters jumped to his feet and shouted. "Objection!"

Judge Fennell paused and thought for a moment. "Mr. Evangelista you've made your point that there is no such thing as a second-tier tribe under federal law."

Congressman Murphy's jowls flushed red, and he clenched his jaw in anger. He had heard enough and lunged past those seated next to him towards the exit.

Pierce turned and pretended to glance at his notes. He briefly locked eyes with Jeremiah and gave him a quick wink before turning back around.

Jeremiah's subtle shift in his expression, a tight smile barely visible told Pierce what he wanted to know.

"Your Honor, I have no further questions," Pierce said.

Chapter Nineteen

Jeremiah remained surprisingly calm. His eyes narrowed slightly when he read the headline of the lead story in the Tulsa World. "Expert Testifies that Kialegee Tribal Town has No Right to Casino." If Jeremiah had not been there to see Pierce with his own eyes dismantle the state's expert, the Tulsa World's story would have distressed him. Abbey Brody's article was buried on page three of the local section. By the time Jeremiah finished reading both articles, his mood had soured. The stories served as both a reminder and a warning. They gave Jeremiah a sense of foreboding that the fight had only just begun.

It was just after eight in the morning when Jeremiah left the hotel lobby and began the four blocks walk to the courthouse. The strong morning sun had already baked everything dry. Jeremiah could feel the heat coming off the sidewalk. He had walked no more than a block and he could already feel the sweat creeping between the roots of his hair. This summer would be hotter than any in recent memory.

He picked a shady spot across the street from the courthouse and reached into his pocket and fished out a pack of cigarettes. With all the press milling around, sneaking out during a break to catch a smoke was painfully complicated. Jeremiah figured he would get one last fix and it would have to last him until they broke for lunch. He took a deep pull of the cigarette and watched the people filing into the courthouse. He initially thought the Attorney General's decision to sue the tribal leaders was reckless, but with each passing day Jeremiah became more convinced that it was a calculated maneuver aimed at gutting any support the Kialegee might receive from other tribes.

The breadth of the blowback from an unlikely source was not something Jeremiah had ever thought about until now. He knew when he broke ground on the casino that the state would fight him. What he hadn't planned on were the other Oklahoma tribes plotting against him. No tribe publicly attacked the Kialegee, but several of them were busy working back channels trying to convince the Bureau of Indian Affairs to issue a ruling against the Kialegee's claim of shared jurisdiction. Sacrifice one to save many was the easiest way to protect their sovereignty. There was a growing concern among the tribes that the formidable political forces already lined up against the casino could influence the court to rule for the state on all counts. They hoped that a negative decision from the BIA would render the state's case moot and the Attorney General would have no choice but to dismiss his complaint. Jeremiah was keenly aware of the rumblings in tribal circles, blaming the Kialegee for the potential shit storm that was now at every tribe's doorstep.

Jeremiah casually took another drag from his cigarette and watched a television van almost wipe out a pedestrian. He waited for the rest of the Business Committee before entering the courthouse building. The security guard offered him words of encouragement. Jeremiah smiled, nodded politely and felt a flicker of hope.

Abbey Brody pounced the moment Jeremiah stepped off the elevator.

"No comment," he insisted as he moved past her towards the courtroom.

Brody fired off her question, anyway. "What did you think about what the state's expert said?"

Jeremiah hesitated and then glanced at the reporter. "No comment."

A second reporter circled close to Jeremiah. "Ken Frierson Associated Press. What did you think about Mr. Evangelista's cross-examination yesterday?"

"He did a good job."

"If you lose are you going to appeal?" Brody fired.

Jeremiah leveled her with the same expressionless eyes all Indians used when someone had pushed something too far, "No comment," he said, moving away from her and the handful of reporters that began to circle.

Everyone gawked when Jeremiah stepped into the courtroom. The proceedings would not start for another thirty minutes, but dozens of people milled about or looked for seats. The courtroom was already three-quarters full of spectators chatting quietly. The Kialegee Business Committee and members of the tribe filled the first two rows behind the defense table. There wasn't a single unoccupied seat on the Attorney General's side. Payton was a fixture in the farthest corner of the back row. She sat in the same seat the day before, watching the proceedings in her usual quiet but perceptive way, reading between the lines and studying the mannerisms and body language of the judge, the lawyers, the state's expert witness and even some spectators. Juanita sat in the back next to Payton, chewing her nails; too nervous to sit any closer.

Jeremiah walked through the swinging gate. Pierce greeted him warmly, taking special care to shake his hand. Noah unpacked the briefcases and arranged the files while Nikki lounged by the plaintiff's table chatting up the AG's dark suited pack of subordinates.

Pierce put his hand on Jeremiah's shoulder and leaned in. "Nervous?"

Everything about the legal proceeding he'd seen up to now made Jeremiah feel like he'd wandered out onto a very dangerous cliff. One tiny misstep and splat. "A little."

Pierce smiled and said, "Perfectly normal. We're going to have a conversation just like you and Noah practiced."

Jeremiah's concerned look concealed nothing. "How do you think it's going so far?"

Nikki caught the end of Jeremiah's question as she made her way back to the defense table. "The state's expert got humbled and exposed yesterday," she said gamely.

Pierce gave a subtle nod. "We still have a lot of ground to cover."

Jeremiah nodded and glanced over his shoulder at the courtroom, which by that time was standing room only.

*****

At 9:25 am the bailiff stepped forward and yelled, "All rise for the Court!"

Judge Fennell, draped in a black robe, marched to the bench and instructed everyone to have a seat. Turning his attention to Masters, he said, "Call your next witness."

The pastor from the Evergreen Baptist Church took the witness stand.

"Please state your name for the record."

"Doctor Michael Kennedy."

"You are the pastor at the Evergreen Baptist Church?"

"Yes, sir."

"How long have you been the pastor?"

"Five years next September."

"You are familiar with the proposed casino, which is the subject of this hearing, correct?"

"I am."

"How will the casino impact the church, your parishioners and the surrounding community?"

Doctor Kennedy gave Masters a concerned look and said, "Our ministry offers a support group for people suffering from gambling addictions. I would expect that a casino close by will have a negative effect."

"How long has the Church offered a treatment program?"

Doctor Kennedy shook his head. "We don't treat compulsive gambling disorders. We provide a support group to help those with gambling disorders to manage their addiction."

"My mistake," Masters said with an impish grin. "How long have you been providing people a place where they can get help for their gambling problems?"

"Almost two years."

"Is the support group only open to your parishioners?"

"No, it's open to everyone who needs help."

"Does the support group make a difference?"

"Yes. I think it helps quite a bit."

"Why is that?"

The pastor took a deep breath and let it out slowly. "Because gambling like most compulsive disorders isn't really cured, it has to be managed and having a sponsor and people to lean on when you're going through a dark period can make all the difference."

"Tell me, Doctor Kennedy, does this casino pose a greater threat than the others?"

"Well, it's closer."

Masters flashed his toothy grin. "We already have three casinos in Tulsa. I don't think one more can do a lot more harm. Can it?"

Doctor Kennedy fixed Masters with a look and said, "I respectfully disagree. Experts on pathological gambling addiction have shown that the prevalence of this disorder is linked closely to accessibility. The more casinos the more pathological behavior is triggered. There are no casinos in Broken Arrow. Most of the people who attend our support group are going to drive right by the casino to get to our church. The temptation of a casino so close to our church will certainly cause emotional trauma, setbacks and expose new people in our community which may be prone to pathological behavior."

Nikki scribbled in animated fashion, "Hearsay," and slid the note over to Pierce. As far as Pierce was concerned, Doctor Kennedy was a harmless witness. Casinos were legal on Indian land and the effect of legalized gambling on addiction was not at issue.

Judge Fennell glanced over towards the defendant's table, half-expecting to hear an objection. Pierce chose not to make one.

"Nothing further," Masters announced.

"Cross-examination, Mr. Evangelista?"

Pierce didn't think cross-examining this witness would help his case, but he saw it as an opportunity to give Noah some courtroom experience.

"Your Honor, my co-counsel, Mr. Noah Grayson is going to cross-examine the witness."

Pierce turned to Noah. "You're up."

Noah sprang to his feet.

Pierce leaned in and whispered some last-minute instructions. "Keep it short. The witness is a minister. You don't want to go at him with a sledgehammer."

Noah grabbed his legal pad. "Got it."

"Just a few questions," he said as he darted to the podium.

"Evergreen Baptist Church is located at 10301 East 111th Street, is that correct?"

"Yes, that's right."

"How far is the church from the casino site?"

"About two miles."

Noah nodded in agreement. He was scrupulously familiar with the Church's website. "Does your church offer any other support groups in addition to gambling?"

"Excuse me," Doctor Kennedy said with one eyebrow raised.

"I mean gambling addiction," Noah corrected himself.

"Yes, we have AA and EDA meetings?"

"And for the record, what does AA and EDA stand for?"

"AA stands for Alcoholics Anonymous and EDA stands for Eating Disorder Association."

"Is that for overeating or disorders like bulimia?"

"Both really."

"What is the EDA support group at your church about?"

"Over-eating and weight management, mostly."

"Doctor Kennedy, you testified earlier that accessibility which I take to mean ease of access triggers compulsive behavior?"

"Yes."

"Do you know how many fast-food restaurants are within a ten-minute drive of Evergreen Baptist Church?"

Doctor Kennedy shook his head. "No, I know that there are quite a few, but I don't have an exact number."

Noah stood there with a smile plastered across his face. "When I plugged the Church's address into my smartphone, I got Papa John, Kentucky Fried Chicken, Subway, Chili's, Popeyes, Chick-Fil-A, Panda Express, Fuddruckers, Applebee, Raising Cane, Jack in the Box and Sonic, all close by."

Gasps and laughter rattled around the courtroom. Masters twitched visibly.

Judge Fennell rapped his gavel.

"Do you think having such easy access to fast food could trigger compulsive eating disorders?"

Doctor Kennedy shrugged, "I imagine it could."

"Just one more question. Do you know how many places within one mile of Evergreen Baptist Church serve alcohol?"

Doctor Kennedy let out a protracted sigh, followed by, "I don't know, but I have a feeling you're going to tell me."

"Eleven." Noah said, before letting Judge Fennell know that he had no more questions.

*****

The State finished its case at four o'clock in the afternoon. At three the state put on its last witness, the person picked by the homeowner's group to represent them and tell the court how the casino was going to irreparably damage the lives of everyone in their neighborhood. Mrs. Carson struggled to keep her emotions under control.

"It's all right, Mrs. Carson," Masters said a hundred times.

Mrs. Carson would nod, take a sip of water, wipe her eyes and emotionally blather about the threat the casino poses to the children, how the casino is going to bring a criminal element to their community and how the neighborhood property values were going to plummet.

Judge Fennell cleaned and re-cleaned his glasses non-stop for an hour. When Masters finally took a seat, Judge Fennell turned to Pierce. "Any cross-examination," he grunted painfully.

Pierce stood. He glanced over at the witness and back to the judge. He spared Judge Fennell and everyone in the courtroom.

"No, Your Honor. We have no questions."

Masters rose and said, "Your Honor the State rests."

Judge Fennell gave Pierce the option of calling his first witness. Pierce advised the court that he would prefer not to have to interrupt his examination of his expert and added that he would ably put on his case in half-a-day.

"Very well, the court will recess until nine tomorrow."

Chapter Twenty

There was a long line of customers waiting to be seated at the Polo Grill and every table was occupied. Scott Masters asked for the private dining room. On a normal night he sat at his usual corner table with his back to the wall, looking out onto as much of the restaurant as possible. As the Attorney General with higher political aspirations, he needed to see and be seen.

When Congressman Murphy entered the restaurant, the General Manager rushed to the front entrance to greet him. Murphy was just under six feet tall, in his early fifties, with a double chin and an over-inflated ego that carried over into a sense of entitlement. The general manager escorted Murphy to Scott Masters' table. Along the way, the congressman slapped backs and shook hands.

"Scott," Murphy thrust his hand forward.

Masters chose a more formal greeting and said, "Congressman."

Masters started off by ordering a bottle of Belvedere, a bucket of ice, two low ball glasses and plenty of olives. Murphy ordered the New York strip rare and Masters ordered the Seared Golden Trout. Murphy advised the general manager that they would call him if they needed anything. Given the delicate nature of the meeting, he didn't want any interruptions.

"Your expert witness . . ." Murphy shook his head, scoffing, "Could he have been any worse?"

Masters took a sip of vodka and tried to think of the most positive way to respond. "He wasn't as strong as I'd hoped for and the tribe's lawyer was better than expected. But we put enough evidence into the record for the court to issue the injunction."

Murphy frowned and shook his head. "Your expert couldn't answer a single question without looking like a total buffoon who was paid to say whatever the state told him to. And that second-tier tribe bullshit . . . what the fuck was that all about?" Murphy's eyes were bugged in disbelief.

Masters looked at him with a furrowed brow. "Have a drink."

Masters realized that the state's expert witness made what should have been an easy win a lot more complicated. He took a sip of Belvedere. "There's enough to support a finding that the MCN are the exclusive owners of the land and whatever our expert missed the Judge can fill in," Masters replied airily, trying to stress that there was nothing to worry about.

"You're playing it a little too loose for my taste."

Masters rolled his eyes and took a big gulp of Belvedere. "Am I?" he asked sarcastically.

Murphy remained intense. "You're locked away in your office in the state capitol. I'm down in the trenches. I see the fear in the eyes of the people."

Masters suspected that Murphy was more worried about his own re-election than the mental state of the people. The last thing he needed was for this self-centered ass to panic. "Relax Patrick, Judge Fennell will do the heavy lifting. We will get the injunction and you're not going to get any bad press."

Murphy attacked his steak with a knife. "I know the judge will grant the injunction," Murphy said, "but will it hold up if the tribe appeals?"

Murphy's words were less a question than a criticism, and Masters didn't do well with either.

"You haven't given him anything to work with. From where I'm sitting, if the tribe's expert witness makes a compelling case tomorrow, we will get overturned on appeal."

"I can handle their expert," Masters said with confidence.

Murphy was about to take a bite of his steak when his fork stopped inches from his lips.

"Scott, you're a good lawyer, but I just want to make sure you've thought this all the way through."

The seared trout was now in Masters' mouth, so he shook his head and washed it down with a swig of vodka.

"Why don't you say whatever it is you came here to say?"

"Your expert put us in a hole."

"Our expert," Masters cut him off.

"He was your choice. That was your first mistake. Your second was not doing your homework on the Kialegee's lawyer. Had you bothered to, you would have learned that the tribe went out and got themselves a real hitter. Mr. Evangelista is a highly regarded litigator who has won some big cases."

Masters exhaled a tired sigh as if to say that Murphy was wasting his time.

"We can't let him build a record that can be used to bury us."

Masters was suddenly suspicious.

Murphy pointed his fork at Masters. "You can't let them put their expert on the stand tomorrow."

"There's nothing I can do."

"There has to be something! If you can't find it in your law books throw the fucking things away and do whatever is necessary."

Masters set the fork down and wiped his mouth with a white linen napkin. "You obviously have something on your mind . . . so just spit it out."

"Nothing specific, but to put it bluntly, you need to do whatever it takes to keep their expert from testifying, even if it means having your people put something in his food that will incapacitate him for twenty-four hours."

Masters' face twisted into an irritated frown. He tossed his napkin down on the half-eaten trout and said, "That won't accomplish anything. Their lawyer will move to continue the hearing until his expert is well enough to testify and the judge will have to grant it."

"Well, you better think of something," Murphy growled.

Masters didn't know what to say, so he kept his mouth shut and poured himself another drink.

Murphy studied him intensely. What he was proposing did not sit well with Masters. "Scott, ask yourself how badly you want to be the next governor. Then take a step back and look at the bigger picture. Because if you lose this case, you not only can kiss the governor's office goodbye, but you'll be out of a job."

Chapter Twenty-One

Pierce slid out of bed and grabbed the running shorts sitting on the chair in the corner. He walked through the empty hotel lobby and out into the predawn morning. He always had trouble sleeping when he was in the middle of a trial. He would visualize every question he would ask and exhibit he intended to offer into evidence. When he finished playing out the entire trial in his mind, he would hit his mental rewind button and re-play a slightly modified version of it over again. Eventually, he would drift off to sleep with his mind searching for the legal gaps in his opponent's case. But the trial continued to play in his subconscious. Sometimes he slept for minutes, other times for hours before a particular thought or legal issue would wake him. Pierce took a quick inventory of his surroundings, stretching one thigh and then the other. Five minutes into his run, he lengthened his stride and launched into high gear. He always ran hard, pushing himself.

That's how Pierce did everything. Most runners did it to get in better shape or achieve personal bests. He ran with a different purpose. For Pierce, running was a cathartic experience where he cleared his mind and viewed the trial from different lenses as he pounded the asphalt in the dark. The exercise was about sharpening his understanding of human behavior. He replayed the reactions by the plaintiff's attorney and the judge's rulings to pivotal as well as less important issues in the trial to get a better read on them. The state's case was on life support and Masters appeared unfazed. Something about Scott Masters wasn't sitting well with him.

*****

Jeremiah walked to the same spot across the street from the court-house and checked his watch. He had thirty minutes before he needed to be in court. He cupped his left hand around the tip of the cigarette and spun the wheel on his lighter. The flame shot up, and Jeremiah took a long, deep pull. He wasn't too worried about testifying. He thought about what Pierce had told him the day before. All he had to do was tell the truth like he and Noah had practiced. Pierce had been right about how the politicians would react and the sideshow that would unfold the instant the Kialegee swam against the current.

Pierce had counseled the Business Committee to get the hand wring-ing and internal debates out of the way. They all had to be on the same page before they moved bulldozers onto the site. From that point on, there was no turning back. Jeremiah wanted this painfully slow hearing in his rearview mirror so he and Pierce could move on to the next obstacle in the Kialegee's path, the alphabet soup of government agen-cies whose covert mission statement had more to do with protecting the interests of the rich gaming tribes and a whole host of issues that had nothing to do with helping poor tribes achieve sustainable economic independence. Watching his tribal members line up for government rations to feed their families was hard enough but not incongruous given that the tribe had been struggling from about the time they started their long march from Georgia. Watching his eight-year-old grandson die, however, was an entirely different matter. Jeremiah stubbed his ciga-rette out on the bottom of his boot and began moving towards the courthouse.

For the third straight day, the hall outside the courtroom was crowd-ed by eight o'clock. The spectators learned on the first day that all the seats were taken by eight-thirty. The deputy opened the door, and the crowd filed in slowly. Pierce was talking to his expert witness, Nikki and Noah were organizing the exhibits when Jeremiah entered the courtroom. He turned to his right expecting to see Payton sitting in the same spot and she did not disappoint. Like him, she was a creature of habit. A few minutes before nine the bailiff called the courtroom to order, and Judge Fennell took his place on the bench. Judge Fennell glanced at the Attorney General and then turned to Pierce.

"Good morning, are you ready to proceed?"

Pierce stood. "Good morning, Your Honor. Yes, we're ready."

"You may call your witness."

Pierce called Doctor Tomás Romero, a professor at the University of Georgia Institute of Native American Studies. Professor Romero prepared an expert report which concluded that while the historic Creek Nation that executed the treaties with the United States was a predecessor to the present-day Muscogee (Creek) Nation, they were not the same tribe. Professor Romero testified that Congress terminated the historic Creek Nation in 1907 when it closed the tribe's membership rolls.

"The historic Creek Nation was not a single tribe, but a confederacy of politically organized tribal towns known as talwas sharing a common language."

Pierce smiled and nodded politely. "Were you present in the courtroom when Professor Judson testified for the state that the present-day Muscogee (Creek) Nation and the historic Creek Nation were the same tribe?"

"Yes, I was."

Pierce cocked his head to the side. "Is it possible that Professor Judson could be right?"

Professor Romero's mouth twisted into a pensive frown. "No, not even remotely possible."

"Can you tell the court why?"

Professor Romero paused as if deciding where to begin. "The present-day Muscogee (Creek) Nation did not organize until 1979 and their constitution provides for a centralized government. The historic Creek Nation consisted of tribal towns and not a centralized system of government. The lack of the unitary system of government was evident both socially and politically among the tribal towns."

"When did the Muscogee (Creek) Nation become the centralized form of government for all creeks?" Pierce asked.

Professor Romero shook his head vigorously and said, "That never happened."

"If the 1867 Creek Constitution provided for a centralized government, didn't that mean that the tribal towns were no longer independent?" Pierce asked.

Professor Romero straightened up in his chair and answered the second part of Pierce's question first. "No, the 1867 constitution did not eliminate the independent tribal towns, they existed alongside the constitution and maintained a distinct, cultural, political and social identity."

"How so?"

"The centralized government was made up of all the tribal towns. They met about once a year to discuss matters that affected all the tribal towns. However, the tribal towns continued to govern themselves. The Creeks believed that centralizing power ran counter to their cultural beliefs and threatened the very fabric of Creek life . . . in fact the Upper Creeks refused to accept the 1867 constitution."

"And where did the Kialegee Tribal Town fit in–Upper Creeks or Lower Creeks?"

"They were Upper Creeks."

Pierce thought back to a question he had asked the state's expert witness. "Professor did the tribal towns own their lands or did they belong to the historic Creek Nation?"

"The Creek Nation didn't own land. The land belonged to the tribal towns."

"And that also applied to the Kialegee Tribal Town? Meaning they owned the land where their villages were located. Is that correct?"

Professor Romero nodded and said, "Yes, and they also exercised control over all the hunting and fishing rights to the lands surrounding their villages."

Pierce handed Professor Romero a very thick document. "Professor, do you recognize the document I've just handed you?"

The Professor opened the report and leafed through the pages. "Yes, this is my report on the historic Creek Nation."

"Your Honor, I would like to introduce this report as Defendant's Exhibit D-1."

Masters stood. "Your Honor, I would like to reserve my right to object to the admissibility of this report until after I question the witness."

"Professor let me cut to the chase," Pierce said. "Did the historic Creek Nation cease to exist?"

Professor Romero nodded. "Yes, the Creek government was diminished in 1907. The Department of Interior did not permit elections after 1907 and permanently closed the membership roles."

"Who are the successors to the historic Creek Nation?"

"All the Creek tribes organized under Oklahoma Indian Welfare Act are the successors to the historic Creek Nation."

"Does that include the Kialegee Tribal Town?"

"Yes."

Pierce let out a slow, pained breath. "Professor, I know I'm beating a dead horse here but since the state's expert testified that the MCN are the only creeks with treaty rights, I have to ask, if you agree?"

Professor Romero's expression said that that was one of the more irrational assumptions he'd ever heard. "No, if the federal government recognized the MCN as the exclusive creek government, it would not have allowed the creek tribal towns to organize."

"Objection! The witness cannot presume to know what the federal government would do."

"Sustained."

"Do all successors have treaty rights and the same rights to the lands of their predecessor tribe?"

Professor Romero nodded, "Yes."

"Thank you."

"Your Honor, I have no further questions for this witness."

*****

Scott Masters' mind was moving at light speed, trying to plot the correct course that would allow him to discredit or lessen Professor Romero's testimony. He hoped to expose an error in his conclusions, or at the very least he hoped to get the professor to admit that his work was not an exact science but more of an exercise of cobbling together information and speculating on how things might have been. Professor Judson's flawed conclusions exposed the state, and he needed to level the playing field. Masters grabbed his notes and walked to the podium with a determined look on his face.

"You testified that the Creek Nation ceased to exist after 1907. Were they ever terminated?"

"No."

"Did they continue to have a chief even after 1907?"

"Yes, but after 1907 the Secretary of Indian Affairs appointed the chiefs. They were no longer elected by the Creek members."

"But the Creeks still had a Chief. Is that correct?"

"Yes, that's correct."

"Was there ever a time between 1907 and 1979 that they didn't have a chief?"

"No."

"So, is it correct that the creeks were never terminated and always had a political structure?"

Professor Romero considered his answer and then said, "In a manner of speaking, the Creeks had a form of government even if it was a shell of the one formed under the 1867 constitution."

Masters dug in. "But regardless of whether it differed from the one formed under the 1867 constitution; they always had a government."

"I suppose you could say that."

A smile creased Masters' face, and he said, "I just did. The MCN was never terminated and maintained its government," Master repeated.

The professor frowned. "I never said MCN. The Creek tribe from 1907 to 1979 was not the present-day Muscogee (Creek) Nation."

"Semantics," Masters hit back.

"I wouldn't agree."

Masters turned and glanced over at Pierce and back towards Professor Romero. "I wouldn't expect you to. I'm not the one paying you."

"Objection."

Judge Fennell looked at Masters sternly. "Sustained."

"There appears to be a legitimate difference of opinion on whether the Creek ceased to exist since they never stopped functioning as a tribe." Masters looked at the witness with a self-satisfied smile. "This raises questions about your successor-in-interest hypothesis." Then he shook his head and said, "You can't have a successor to something that never ceased to exist. Wouldn't you agree, Professor?" Masters asked rhetorically.

The Professor tried to say something, but Masters didn't allow it. "Let's move on to the treaties." Masters was purposely picking up the pace, trying to keep Professor Romero off balance. "Several sections in the treaties that established the Creek reservation in Oklahoma identify the land as belonging to the Muscogee. Is that correct?"

Professor Romero appeared to know where Masters was heading. "Muscogee was the common language of the Creeks and it was common for outsiders to identify all the Creek Indians, including the tribal towns as Muscogee."

Masters let out a protracted sigh and then spoke in a deep, unwavering voice. "I understand that's what you want to believe. But I'm looking at the actual treaty language and it says Muscogee. Since the United States negotiated with the Muscogee is it possible that they intended for only the Muscogee to own the land?"

"No, not really."

Masters frowned and said, "Are you saying that it's not possible that the U.S. intended for the Muscogee to own the land even though the treaties make no mention of the lands belonging to the tribal towns?"

Professor Romero remained steadfast. "Yes, I'm saying that the reference to the Muscogee was not to the MCN and the treaties specifically reserve the land for all Creek Indians, which includes the tribal towns."

"It appears we have differing opinions on what the drafters of the treaties who are no longer alive may have intended."

Professor Romero shrugged and said, "There are primary sources such as journal entries of the participants present during the negotiations that we relied upon to gain a better understanding."

"I'm sure there are," Masters cut him off, "but those are also subject to interpretation so even though you're making educated guesses they're still guesses."

Masters eyed the witness coolly, and after a long moment of thoughtful calculation, he decided not to ask any more questions.

*****

Pierce waited for Masters to take a seat before standing. "I have a short redirect, Your Honor."

"You may proceed."

"Professor, you testified earlier that the historic Creek Nation ceased to exist because congress closed the membership rolls."

The professor could have given a long-detailed response, but he sensed that Pierce preferred concise answers to his questions. "Yes, that's correct."

"What did that mean exactly?"

"It means that no one could be added to the tribal roles."

"Not even lineal descendants of the Creek Indians on the roles?"

"No one."

"The members of what is today the Muscogee (Creek) Nation are not on the 1907 tribal rolls of the historic Creek Nation. Is that correct?"

"Yes, that's correct."

"So, when the last person on the 1907 tribal rolls dies that would mean the historic Creek Nation would cease to exist since it has no members. Is that correct?"

The Professor nodded. "In theory, yes, but the United States government has not recognized the historic Creek Nation as a tribe with sovereign rights for almost a hundred years. The Muscogee (Creek) Nation, Alabama-Quassarte Tribal Town, Tholpthlocco Tribal Town and the Kialegee Tribal Town are the four federally recognized Creek Tribes which descended from the historic Creek Nation."

"Does that make them all Successors-in-Interest with equal rights?"

"Yes."

"Thank you, Professor Romero."

"Your Honor, I have no further questions."

"You're excused, Professor Romero," Judge Fennell said.

The bailiff waited for the witness to exit the stand before handing the Judge a note. Judge Fennell folded the note when he was finished reading it and slowly took off his reading glasses.

Pierce spotted movement out of the corner of his eye.

"We're adjourned until nine tomorrow morning," the judge announced abruptly.

"All rise," the Bailiff shouted.

Everyone in the courtroom stood up.

Pierce let out a quiet breath, "That's interesting." he said, squinting in the direction of the defense table.

"What's that?" Noah asked.

"Masters' legal team started packing up before the court adjourned," Pierce said in a tone that suggested he didn't think it was a coincidence.

Chapter Twenty-Two

Noah, Jeremiah and Payton sat in the hotel conference room eating a lukewarm pizza and talking about the rumor that spread through the courtroom's hallways like a dry autumn wildfire minutes after Judge Fennell abruptly adjourned the hearing.

Pierce and Nikki were only paying half attention to their conversation as they huddled together discussing whether to call Jeremiah as a witness versus resting. Pierce learned to play Cuban dominoes when he was a young boy. His uncle taught him the game and every summer when he visited Miami, he played dominoes with his uncle and watched the old masters play Double 9 dominoes on Calle Ocho. One of the first things his uncle taught him was to pay close attention to your opponent because he would play to his strength and a skillful domino player takes it away. The second was to use deception to keep your opponent from guessing your strength and from exploiting your weakness. His uncle's lessons not only helped him become an excellent domino player, they made him a much better trial lawyer. He had taken Masters' strength away when he exposed the state's expert as predisposed and ill equipped, and in doing so weakened Masters' argument that the MCN were the only tribe with rights to the Broken Arrow land.

Pierce also baited the state into waiting for him to call Jeremiah as his witness instead of Masters calling him. By waiting to cross-examine Jeremiah, the Attorney General would have a wider berth to ask leading questions and expose the Kialegee chief. Pierce hoped that would factor in the Attorney General's decision and he would choose to cross examine Jeremiah instead of dealing with the constraints of a direct examination. It was a calculated risk but one with very little downside because if the state didn't take the bait and called Jeremiah, Pierce would be the one with the opportunity to ask leading questions.

"Jeremiah's testimony could tie up a few loose ends," Pierce said.

Nikki frowned. "It could also expose a crack or two for Masters to slither into. The burden is on the state to prove a likelihood of success on the merits of the case for the court to issue a preliminary injunction. They've presented nothing to suggest their case has any merit."

Pierce had learned the hard way that some judges manipulated the rules or played by unwritten rules when it suited them. "We need to build as strong a record as possible, just as a precaution in case we have to file an appeal," he cautioned, "with all the notoriety and good ole boy politicians working against us, we can't discount that Judge Fennell will find a way to rule that the state has made a palpable claim."

Nikki swept away Pierce's comment with the wave of a hand. "That would require him to completely disregard the fact that the state presented no evidence. He'd have to give them a complete pass."

"It wouldn't be the first time."

Nikki nodded thoughtfully. "Even if he does, how does the casino cause irreparable harm? He can't grant an injunction without it and there's absolutely no evidence in the record for the judge to hang his hat on. Indian casinos are not only legal, there are two casinos within ten miles of the property."

Noah jumped into the conversation. "Except for the casino's proximity to the gambling addiction support group there's no evidence that a third casino would have any negative impact. Quite the opposite, a third casino would contribute to the one hundred and twenty-two million dollars in compact payments received annually by the State of Oklahoma and create more jobs."

Jeremiah's stomach was churning. "If you need to put me on the stand tomorrow. I'll be ready."

Pierce gave Jeremiah a pat on the shoulder. "I don't think we're going to call you. Nikki has a point," Pierce said. "The state has proven nothing, and we already have a strong record."

Jeremiah took a deep breath and couldn't conceal a smile.

*****

Payton sat back with her arms crossed. Gnawing at the back of her mind was the rumor that Judge Fennell's son worked for Congressman Patrick Murphy as a congressional aide and that Pierce didn't seem to care. Payton exhaled a sigh of frustration. "Don't you think you should at least bring it up tomorrow and let the Judge know that you know . . . I mean Congressman Murphy's face is plastered on every channel fighting the casino and the judge's kid works for him?"

It was obvious by the constipated look on Noah's face that the rumor didn't sit well with him either.

Considering the timing of when the information leaked, Pierce wondered if this was an attempt at misdirection. Despite his well-known opposition to the casino, Congressman Murphy wasn't a party to the lawsuit, so there wasn't much Pierce could do with the information other than move for a recusal.

Pierce looked over at Jeremiah. "You haven't said a word. What do you think?"

Jeremiah shrugged his shoulders, not sure what to say.

Just then, Noah mumbled something under his breath.

Pierce thought he heard him but wasn't sure. "I can't understand you when you mumble, sport."

"I said," Noah spoke with exaggerated clarity, "that this Oklahoma good old boy shit sucks balls."

"Yes! Thank you," Payton fist bumped Noah.

Pierce looked at Noah with a slight grin, "You may be right, but this doesn't come close to the conflict of interest that would require the judge to recuse himself."

Payton was thunderstruck. "Are your apprentice and me the only ones who see what's going on here? That's fucking bullshit Clark and you know it."

Noah was already used to Payton's smart-ass personality, so he ignored her.

Jeremiah gave Payton a look that said I raised you better than that. She hadn't seen that look in a long time.

"Sorry, pops."

"There may not be a technical conflict of interest, but it doesn't make it right." Noah drummed his fingers on the table for a moment and then said, "You know what they say when there's smoke there's fire."

"Maybe." Pierce said. "But maybe they want us to think there's a fire, so we take our eye off the ball."

Nikki shot Pierce a quizzical look. "They could be baiting us into raising the conflict so they can get a shot at another hearing with a different expert witness. Let's face it, they shit the bed on this one."

Pierce nodded. "If you're right, Fennell could be waiting for us to raise the conflict so he can recuse himself."

"Come again?" Noah asked, looking confused. "What's the ball?"

"The case, dickweed. Keep up." Payton snapped. Her eyes darted back to Jeremiah. "Sorry pops."

"This rumor wasn't dropped in our laps by accident," Nikki said suspiciously. "They planted it."

"Nikki's right, the state had the burden of proof, not us. They didn't meet it. I say we rest and call it a day," Noah said, sounding suddenly convinced.

Pierce thought about all the time, money and professional resources the state had poured into this case without moving the needle.

Noah recognized the far-away look in his eyes. "It's starting," he said under his breath.

Payton's eyebrow shot up a notch. "What's starting?"

"He's breaking down the case-brick-by-brick. He does that sometimes when he thinks he's missed something."

Noah studied Pierce for a long moment. He could tell something was eating away at him. "What more is there left for us to do?"

Pierce didn't answer right away while he thought about his own way to exert leverage. "Find every chink in their armor."

Noah made a hopeless gesture with his hands. "What good will that do?"

Pierce's gut told him that even if they won the hearing, it wouldn't be the end. The Attorney General wouldn't give up so easily. He would appeal and keep spending whatever it took to fight them. Pierce built a strong record which he could use to file an appeal or defend one. There would be no request for recusal. He would not give the state a "do over".

"You don't wound a snake and let it slither away. You kill it," he said.

Chapter Twenty-Three

At nine thirty, the Judge took his seat on the bench.

"Mr. Evangelista, call your next witness."

"Yes, one moment, Your Honor."

Noah couldn't help but get the feeling that Pierce was up to something. "I thought we decided that we would rest and not call the Chief as a witness?"

Pierce's blue eyes drifted away from his notes and settled on Noah. "I'm not going to call the Chief."

"What exactly are we doing?"

"I'm going to pull back the curtain," Pierce said. He pushed his chair away from the table and stood. "Your Honor, the defense calls Mr. Scott Masters."

The Attorney General's position as a Board of Director and Deacon in the First Baptist Church in Broken Arrow was no secret, but it wasn't newsworthy. Pierce made a calculated decision to push Masters's buttons by supplying the dots for the media to connect. If he teed up the information from a fresh angle, it might give the press a reason to ask questions and dig for a story. Professor Judson wasn't the only expert hired by Masters. He was the only one willing to offer the unqualified opinion that Masters wanted. The Attorney General, however, had hired every ethno-historian and anthropologist he could find that specialized in the Creek Nation and Five Civilized Tribes and paid them to serve in an advisory capacity at great expense to the Oklahoma taxpayers.

Pierce surprised Masters. His eyes darted from Pierce to the judge, then back to Pierce in a state of semi-disbelief. It took him seconds to process what had just occurred before jumping up as if he'd been shot out of a cannon.

"Objection!" Masters shouted.

Pierce plowed forward, talking over Masters. "The First Baptist Church has organized and led several prayer marches against the Kialegee's project. It has also organized a petition drive against the project. Mr. Masters is not just a member of the congregation. He is a Deacon of the Church and sits on the Church's board. I want the opportunity to question Mr. Masters for the purpose of addressing not only an obvious conflict of interest but what may also be an abuse of his elected office."

Masters's eyes and face were glowing with anger and his neck was a deep purple. "Your Honor, Mr. Evangelista should be admonished."

Judge Fennell ripped off his glasses and glared at Pierce. He paused for a split second before ruling. "Mr. Masters is the attorney of record for the State and is not listed on your witness list. You may not call him as a witness."

Masters was shaking. "Your Honor, Mr. Evangelista has blatantly disregarded the rules of this court and he knows it."

The courtroom burst into a murmur of conversation.

Judge Fennell snatched the wooden gavel and gave it several whacks. "Order! . . . Mr. Evangelista, call your next witness."

Pierce picked up his notepad and said, "Your Honor, we are not going to call any more witnesses."

Noah looked over at Masters. Genuine surprise flashed across Masters' face and he tossed his pen on his legal pad the instant he realized that his opportunity to question Jeremiah had slipped through his fingers.

Judge Fennell thanked the lawyers and stated that he considered it a privilege to have such accomplished practitioners in his courtroom. He limited each side to five minutes to present closing arguments. At the conclusion, the Judge announced that the court would reconvene at three and render a decision.

Noah waited for the Judge to leave the courtroom before asking Pierce if he thought he had any chance of putting Masters on the witness stand.

Pierce smiled. "Absolutely no shot."

Noah gave Pierce a disbelieving frown. "Then why did you do it?"

"Something Professor Etheridge said to me got me thinking," Pierce said. "Masters called her and tried to hire her even after she told him that in her professional opinion the Kialegee Tribal Town could exercise jurisdiction over the Broken Arrow land."

Noah shrugged as if to say, "Interesting, but that still doesn't answer my question."

"When she declined, he persisted on hiring her and only stopped after she told him that she was going out of the country and would not be available. She also mentioned that Masters hired three professors that she knew of that also specialized in Creek Indian History."

"Then why did he go with Judson?"

The expression on Pierce's face said, "I think you can figure that out on your own."

Noah was quick on the uptake. "I assume that the other professors gave him the same answer Professor Etheridge did which was why he didn't use any of them."

Pierce gave Noah a look that said, "Keep going."

Noah digested the information and said, "He didn't hire every expert he could find to use them. He hired them so we couldn't."

"Exactly," Pierce nodded.

"Okay, that's a classic move, so what's the issue?"

Pierce paused and looked over at the Attorney General and his legal team as they headed out of the courtroom. With a dire expression, he said, "They aren't a silk stocking law firm. Regardless of the state's vast resources, the AG does not have the luxury of using his client's deep pockets to win a case by outspending the other side. He has a fiduciary responsibility to the taxpayers of Oklahoma. If he hired all those experts knowing he couldn't use them in court, he not only wasted taxpayer money, he violated his oath as the state's top law enforcement officer sworn to uphold the state's laws. This case isn't about enforcing the law, it's about stopping a casino at any cost."

Noah wasn't trying to punch holes in his colleague's position, but on this point he couldn't resist. "Masters wouldn't be the first government official to overspend. I don't see how his excessive spending is even an issue."

"It is if we can show that he knew that the project was legal and still spent taxpayer dollars to serve his personal agenda."

Noah shook his head with a bit of skepticism. "As long as the AG had at least one expert willing to testify that the Kialegee have no legal rights to the Broken Arrow land, he had sufficient legal grounds to bring this case."

Frowning, Pierce pushed down and locked the gold-plated latches to his black leather briefcase. "I didn't do it to build a record."

Noah squinted. "Then why did you do it?"

"Win or lose, this fight doesn't end here. Masters wants to be the next Governor. I did it to send him a message that if he isn't playing by the rules, we're throwing away the rule book."

Pierce picked up his briefcase and gave Noah a look that said let's go.

Noah nodded as he thought about what Pierce had just said. Exposing Masters's overzealous spending of taxpayer dollars to rig a case in his favor wasn't exactly front-page tabloid news, but no candidate wanted negative press just before launching a campaign. While a news story about the Attorney General's reckless spending wouldn't generate a chorus of disapproval, it would serve to send a message that Pierce would turn Masters' life into an archeological dig uncovering every skeleton, no matter how old or deeply buried and make things ugly for him.

As Pierce and Noah exited the courtroom towards the elevator, Jared Crowley, the self-appointed leader of the citizens' group 'Broken Arrow Citizens Against Neighborhood Gaming spotted them and was on the move. He had a smile and a look that reminded Pierce of the southern televangelist preachers that monopolized the Tulsa television channels on Sundays. His suit was a bit shinier than everyone else's and his teeth were a few shades too white.

"Mr. Evangelista," he said as he walked across the room and extended his hand.

"I just wanted to introduce myself and tell you that even though we're on opposite sides both you and Mr. Grayson did a great job," he said while keeping the fake smile in place.

Pierce nodded appreciatively and shook his hand. "Thank you." Just then Pierce's phone vibrated. "If you'll excuse me, I have to take this."

Crowley nodded, and turned his attention to Noah. "We just wanted you to know that despite appearances we really have no issue with the Kialegee."

Noah snickered at the obvious lie. Not to be outdone he smiled and said, "That's nice to hear, but the protesters just outside the Kialegee's property don't appear to share those sentiments."

Crowley nodded as if to say fair enough. "That really has nothing to do with the Kialegee Tribe and everything to do with keeping our neighborhood safe. A casino right next to an elementary school invites all sorts of potential problems. Say what you will, but you can't argue with statistics and the crime rates go up when you put a casino into the picture."

"Actually, any kind of non-residential development statistically increases crime rates." Noah replied bluntly.

Crowley shook his head. "I suppose from a purely statistical standpoint you're right. But some uses attract more crime than others, and a casino so close to a school is a recipe for disaster."

Noah almost laughed but managed to keep a straight face. "Really? Would you like to know what I think?"

Crowley nodded politely.

"I think eighty wooded acres close to an elementary school might be exactly where a pedophile might creep around as opposed to a casino with security guards patrolling the perimeter and cameras that monitor and record all activity around the property."

The elevator doors opened. Crowley looked Noah over from head to toe and put a fake smile on. "Are you coming?" He asked as he stepped in the elevator.

Noah turned and looked back for Pierce. "No, go ahead; we'll catch the next one."

Chapter Twenty-Four

It took ten minutes to bring the courtroom to order. Pierce caught a quick glimpse of the faces of the Attorney General and his team of lawyers as they shook hands and engaged in small talk with a few well-wishers. They appeared to be relaxed and confident as they waited for the ruling. Pierce was more than a little surprised. Lawyers typically relied on several indicators to predict on how a judge might rule. None of those would suggest that they had any reason to expect a favorable outcome. The state had a heavy burden of proof and they hadn't come close to meeting it. The Attorney General backed away from his expert witness's opinion during his closing argument and offered little to rebut the evidence presented by the tribe's expert witness. From where Pierce was sitting, they had completely eviscerated the state's case against the Kialegee Tribal Town, which made their manner that much more curious. It gave him an uneasy feeling that they knew something that he didn't.

When it was quiet, the bailiff directed everyone to rise and Judge Fennell walked into the courtroom. Judge Fennell cleared his throat. "In Oklahoma versus the Kialegee Tribal Town, I find that the State of Oklahoma has satisfied the four elements for the court to grant a preliminary injunction. Plaintiff has demonstrated that it would suffer an irreparable harm if the casino is allowed to open. I find that the harm that the Kialegee Tribal Town will suffer is negligible when balanced against the harm suffered by the citizens of Oklahoma. The State of Oklahoma showed a likelihood of success on the merits of proving that the land belongs to the Muscogee Creek Nation and that the Kialegee Tribal Town has no legal right to assert jurisdiction over the land. Finally, I find that the public interest would be furthered by the granting of the preliminary injunction. I will issue my written order within ten days."

The gasps and shocked faces turned into applause and soft whistles. Jeremiah's face twisted with anger as he processed what he'd heard. Payton blinked her eyes against a sting of tears. Juanita tried valiantly not to throw up. Noah wrote everything down, and Nikki glared at the judge with vile thoughts. She stole a look at the plaintiffs' table and caught a quick glimpse of the jubilant congressman and a grinning Attorney General. Masters' grin was tight, conspiratorial and filled with gleeful satisfaction. There were hugs and smiles and self-congratulation. The judge's ruling dumbfounded most of the reporters covering the trial as the prevailing sentiment among them was that the state had been thoroughly beaten.

Pierce showed no reaction. He sat back in his chair mildly surprised at the audaciousness of the judge. It was an outrageous ruling. One that he was determined to overturn.

Judge Fennell tolerated the excitement for another minute, then directed the bailiff to restore order. His Honor looked at the attorneys. "If there's nothing further this court is adjourned," he said and rapped his gavel.

*****

The news arrived in Wetumpka before Jeremiah did. A small crowd had gathered outside of his home by the time his pickup truck rolled into his driveway. They talked about the ruling and speculated about the casino. More tribal members arrived by the minute. Some by car, others walked the short distance from their homes as soon as they spotted Jeremiah's truck. For a long-suffering people that dared to hope that their lives might finally get better, the judge's ruling felt more like a death blow than a setback. Jeremiah eased past his friends, neighbors, and family. Their eyes filled with unbridled concern and bewilderment. When he got to his front porch, he turned to face the small crowd that now spilled out of his front yard onto the street.

"I'm proud of all of you and the way we've stuck together," Jeremiah started. "This is not over!" Jeremiah raised his voice to make a point. A few in the crowd smiled and others nodded their heads.

"This was a miscarriage of justice. Sadly, this is the same old story we Indians are all too familiar with. But I want you all to know that we are not going to give up. We will continue to fight and appeal the judge's decision."

"What makes you think things will be different the next time?" A voice from the crowd beckoned.

Jeremiah nodded. *A fair question*, he thought to himself. "Because I haven't lost faith, and neither should you. Our appeal will be heard by a court in Denver. They won't care about local politics. They'll focus on the law and what's right," Jeremiah said. His eyes scanned the crowd briefly, stopping on a few nervous faces. "I don't intend to lose this fight."

On the surface, Jeremiah was the epitome of a confident leader. His promise to call a meeting for the next evening at the headquarters lightened the mood when he sent everyone home. On the inside, however, Jeremiah needed one night to clear his mind and lick his wounds.

Chapter Twenty-Five

WETUMKA, OKLAHOMA

Jeremiah and Payton sat on the front porch for hours, saying little, watching as the darkness surrounded the town. Payton offered to cook. Jeremiah declined and reached for the whiskey bottle. He had no appetite for food, and a few belts of Tennessee whiskey in his system would satisfy the hunger pangs stirring within. He drew a breath before lifting the bottle to his lips. Whiskey is meant to be sipped and rolled around the mouth. But Jeremiah didn't care to savor the flavors. What he was interested in was settling his nerves and large gulps was what he needed. What troubled him was knowing that the Tribe was fighting an uphill battle in a process controlled by insiders and politicians. In wrestling with the process, Jeremiah only succeeded in burning bridges, alienating the Bureau of Indian Affairs and upsetting the Oklahoma gaming tribes for bringing the spotlight onto them.

He had blown the trumpet for his people to the point of exhaustion, but few heard him or seemed to care. The trial had pushed him over the edge. When the court granted the state's motion to stop the construction of the casino, a defeated look fell across his face and his head began to spin. He heard Pierce's voice as the press crowded around for a statement, but Jeremiah didn't comprehend what he was saying.

Payton shifted uneasily like she wanted to say something to Jeremiah about his drinking, but instead she looked at her watch.

"It's time," Payton said, "the tribal members are waiting. I'll meet you there."

Jeremiah felt his chest tighten. The sign of an anxiety attack. He had gone through his entire life without suffering one, but with the loss of his grandson, they began. Jeremiah closed his eyes and forced himself to breathe deeply and evenly. Finally, the heaviness in his chest subsided.

Grim-faced and hollow-eyed, Jeremiah heaved a sigh and muttered profanity as he walked towards his pickup truck.

Jeremiah felt his pulse quicken just before opening the door to the tribal headquarters and fished around his shirt pocket for his pack of cigarettes. He decided to have a smoke and gather his thoughts before facing what was waiting for him inside. Twelve minutes later, he finally went in. The table that was usually in the center of the room had been moved out to make room for more chairs. Jeremiah knew all the faces sitting in the sad collection of metal and wooden folding chairs. He looked around the room and identified fear in some of their eyes and anger in others. The one sentiment they all shared was their need for the Chief to lead them. The atmosphere was tense, with a fight just one comment away.

Jeremiah held up his hand, signaling to everyone to stop talking.

Nikki, the Tribe's attorney stood next to the Chief as he explained in as much detail as he could remember the steps that need to be taken to overturn the judge's decision. Words were chosen carefully to avoid a heated discussion about the tribe's future and the shortcomings of the Business Committee. An outcome the Chief wanted to avoid.

Everyone listened attentively, sipping the same bad coffee that they'd grown accustomed to while Nikki gave her recap of the trial. At meetings all members were stakeholders, and anyone could speak whenever he or she felt like it.

"Mr. Evangelista, our lawyer, who most of you have met will work on filing the appeal." Nikki said.

"How long will the appeal take?"

"About a year."

"Why so long?"

"There's not much we can do to speed it up. It's a process." Nikki answered.

"What happens to the building while we're going through this process?"

"We shut down construction and do our best to make sure that the winter months don't cause the building to deteriorate," Jeremiah answered.

Nora heard enough. She jumped to her feet and faced the members, purposely turning her back to Jeremiah as she tried to hijack the meeting. "There is another way. A better one that our Chief hasn't mentioned. We have to face facts," she started. "There is no guarantee that we will win an appeal. In fact, there's a good chance that we'll lose. Nothing has gone right, so there's no reason to believe that suddenly our tribe's luck is going to change."

In what clearly looked and sounded rehearsed Lucinda Wiley, Nora's close friend asked, "What's the other option?"

"We ask the MCN to take over the project. They can take out the investor, so we don't owe them anything and finish building the casino," Nora said.

"How does that help the Kialegee?" One of the members asked.

"The land is owned by a Kialegee member," Nora answered. "In exchange the MCN will agree to pay a monthly lease payment to the owner and also pay the tribe."

Juanita looked skeptical. "Why would they agree to do that? And what about the opposition to the casino?"

"When the casino is finished, it will attract customers not just from the River Spirit but also from the Cherokee casinos so it would make business sense for the MCN because it will be profitable for them. They can pay the investor back from casino revenues once it opens so the only money the MCN will be out of pocket is the cost to finish construction."

Nora gave a confident nod. "That's why they'll do it. To answer your second question, the judge already ruled that the MCN have jurisdiction, so there's nothing the city can do to stop it."

One of the older members, Agnes Randolph, who was known for being blunt asked "How much money are we talking about?"

The question seemed to arouse the crowd. Jeremiah could see he was losing the room.

Satisfied with her audience, Nora took a deep breath and pressed on. "To make sure that during our negotiations we come away with the most money from the MCN, I suggest we retain a consultant to help us."

Nora's proposal made Jeremiah instantly suspicious. But when she mentioned hiring a consultant, he knew. "Sounds to me like you've already cut a deal with the MCN's chief behind the tribe's back," Jeremiah said as if he wanted to spit.

Nora knew Jeremiah wouldn't hurl an accusation unless he knew something. That rattled her. She turned and glared at Jeremiah, her nostrils flaring. She didn't deny Jeremiah's accusation. When Nora spoke again, her voice lost some of its bravado. "I'm trying to save our tribe while you're chasing dreams and turning all the Oklahoma tribes against us."

Jeremiah seized on Nora's mistake. "We are a tribe of 200, not one. The decisions we make, we make as a tribe through the committee after consulting with the elders and our members. Like we're doing here now. You had no right to try to cut a deal with the MCN."

It was unanimous around the room that Nora should not have approached the MCN.

Nora tried to defend her actions, but Jeremiah spoke over her. "We survive because we stick together. Our decisions, good or bad, are made as a tribe." Jeremiah pointed his finger at Nora in a menacing manner. "You had no right to put your personal interest ahead of the tribe's!"

The whispers around the room grew louder. No one dared to speak on Nora's behalf or in favor of the proposed deal with the MCN. It was obvious to everyone that they could not consider Nora's proposal without condoning her actions.

Jeremiah's eyes narrowed and the expression on his face hardened. He had a tribe to protect.

"The days of putting the MCN's interests ahead of our own are behind us. We're the only ones willing to fight for our future. So, let's fight."

Chapter Twenty-Six

MIAMI

The sun was just starting to rise and light up the bay. Noah had already been in the conference room for two hours, slugging coffee and working on the outline for the brief that would accompany the notice of appeal to the United States District Court of Appeals in the Tenth Circuit. The district court filed the order granting the preliminary injunction one week after Judge Fennell announced his ruling. Not a day had gone by since Judge Fennell stopped construction of the casino, that the Kialegee Tribe was not in the news.

Noah listed several points regarding the Kialegee history, which Pierce found to be persuasive. However, Pierce believed that to reverse the District Court's order the better strategy was to argue that the District Court did not have jurisdiction to hear the case. It was a simple black-and-white argument that did not require any heavy lifting by the appellate court. They would not need to dissect the history of the Creek Confederacy to vacate Judge Fennell's order. Pierce raised the court's lack of jurisdiction in his motion to dismiss. The District Court rejected it for political reasons, Pierce suspected. The United States District Court of Appeals, however, was in Colorado and not as vulnerable to the whims and pressure of Oklahoma politicians.

"We lead with the jurisdictional argument. Those facts are not in dispute," Pierce reasoned. "The property is located on Indian land. Under the Indian Gaming Regulatory Act, the State has no right to bring this action. It boils down to the application of a federal law to facts not in dispute."

Noah nodded, "I agree that the jurisdictional argument should be included but the district court wouldn't even consider it. It's not our strongest argument. So, why lead with it?"

Pierce took a small sip of coffee. "The court couldn't consider it. Not without having to dismiss the state's case. There's precedent that supports our position. The other arguments require the appellate court to weigh the testimony of both experts and conclude that Judge Fennell got it wrong. We need to give the court an easy way to dispose of the case."

Noah didn't share his mentor's opinion. "Our research is better than theirs, and you eviscerated their expert on cross. We built a sound record. We need to throw everything we have into our appeal and get the question regarding the Kialegee's rights finally resolved."

Pierce guided Noah through important factors that needed to be considered when appealing a federal court's ruling. One of the most important being that only one in every ten cases appealed, gets reversed. Pierce didn't think that the appellate court would reverse the district court and grant the Kialegee shared jurisdiction over all Creek Confederacy reservation lands based on one expert's testimony. Shared jurisdiction is a complicated issue. Neither the Bureau of Indian Affairs nor the National Indian Gaming Commission offered any opinion through the Department of Justice. Without the benefit of the government's position, the appellate court was likely to remand the case back to the district court. Something Pierce wanted to avoid. He had experienced Oklahoma justice firsthand. The facts not in dispute were enough for the appellate court to reverse the lower court and dismiss the case. The battle over the Kialegee's history and their legal rights would still need to be fought, but not in Judge Fennell's courtroom. The judge had deep roots in the city. Pierce frowned at the thought of Judge Fennell and his hometown brand of justice.

"We have to be tactical," Pierce said, the voice of experience. "We will not restore the Kialegee's treaty rights on appeal. That's a fight for another day. What we have is a reasonable chance of obtaining a ruling that the State exceeded its authority by suing to stop construction of a casino on Indian land."

Noah lowered his eyes towards his outline that contained the details and structure for the appellate brief as he listened without taking notes.

"The myriad of historical facts makes this case complicated. We also have the 'indispensable parties' issue to deal with. The Muscogee Creek Nation and the two other federally recognized Creek Tribal Towns were not parties to the lawsuit. A ruling awarding the Kialegee shared jurisdiction would affect their rights. Meaning, the ruling could be immediately subject to challenge since they were not parties."

Pierce reached for a bagel and said, "We need to make this a simple no-brainer for the court."

"Are you suggesting that we minimize the shared jurisdiction argument in our brief and dedicate more pages to the procedural deficiencies?" Noah asked, with his left eyebrow slightly arched.

"Not at all. I'm just saying plant the seed by leading with the jurisdictional argument. Then do a full court press on the merits. The state's expert didn't present any credible evidence. The burden of proof was on the state, and they failed to demonstrate a likelihood of success on the merits of the case. Without credible testimony from their expert, the state failed to satisfy the first element necessary to get an injunction. We'll argue that the judge erred as a matter of law since there is no evidence in the record to support the order granting the injunction. It's a strong argument and we need to make the state think that's where they're most vulnerable and our primary point of attack."

Noah took up the narrative, "They will have no choice but to concentrate their efforts on this issue to show that the judge's ruling wasn't arbitrary and capricious."

"Precisely." Pierce smiled.

*****

Thirty-three days later, the State of Oklahoma filed its reply brief. Noah read the reply brief carefully. Overall, it was little more than a convoluted recitation of the conclusions in the State expert's report. Their rebuttal to the argument that the state lacked the jurisdiction to sue the tribe was a one-page benign response that appeared to be included as an afterthought. Exactly what they were hoping for.

Chapter Twenty-Seven

TENTH CIRCUIT COURT OF APPEALS
DENVER

A paneled door opened near the dais and the courtroom deputy called "All persons having business with the United States Court of Appeals for the Tenth Circuit are admonished to draw near and give their attention, for the court is now in session. God save the United States and this honorable court. All rise."

Jeremiah, Payton and the members of the tribe's Business Committee who drove through the night to attend the oral argument all stood. The judges paraded out in their black robes. Federal courts decide appeals in three-judge panels. The Tenth Circuit had a long history of being a conservative court. Nicknamed the little Supreme Court because the United States Supreme Court rarely overturned its decisions. The panel consisted of Chief Judge Baron, appointed by President Clinton, Senior Judge Mathews, a President Bush appointee and Judge Holloway, the most recently appointed judge to the court. President Obama appointed him.

"State of Oklahoma versus Jeremiah Tiger, Town King of the Kialegee Tribal Town. Case number 16-5154," announced the courtroom deputy.

Pierce stood at the podium and waited for the Chief Judge to signal to him that he could present his argument.

"Good morning," Pierce said into the microphone. "If it pleases the court, Pierce Evangelista representing the Kialegee Tribal Town."

"Indian gaming under federal law is regulated by the Indian Gaming Regulatory Act and may be lawfully conducted by a federally recognized tribe on Indian land. In the case before you, the Kialegee Tribal Town, a federally recognized tribe was in the middle of construction of a building on Indian land intending to operate a Class II casino."

Judge Baron leaned forward in response to Pierce's statement that the casino would only operate Class II gaming.

Pierce continued, "The United States Supreme Court's recent decision in Bay Mills versus the State of Michigan, specifically ruled that a claim for injunctive relief against the tribe and its officials was not authorized under federal law. Accordingly, the State of Oklahoma has failed to state a claim upon which relief could be granted and, consequently, the district court erred in granting a preliminary injunction in favor of the state."

With only thirty minutes to present his argument, Pierce focused almost entirely on the jurisdictional issues. The legal history of the Muscogee Creek Confederacy and the Kialegee Tribal Town as the successor-in-interest arguments were exhaustively briefed in the record.

Pierce set the stage by briefly outlining the key provisions of the Indian Gaming Regulatory Act relating to Class III gaming. "Section 2710(d) of the Act provides that Class III gaming activities shall be lawful on Indian lands if conducted in conformance with the Tribal-State compact. The Kialegee Tribe and the State of Oklahoma have a signed compact approved by the National Indian Gaming Commission."

Pierce paused for a moment and looked down at his notes even though he didn't need them. "No gaming Class II or Class III has occurred. The Tribe was merely in the middle of constructing a building on Indian land. There are no laws that allow a state to stop legal construction."

Judge Holloway glared at Pierce. "Counselor," he interrupted. "Your client declared that it would use the building for a casino."

"Only Class II gaming, your honor," Pierce replied. "Under the Act, the State has no statutory right to enjoin or regulate in any manner the construction or operation of a Class II casino. That is specifically reserved to the federal government. The state, therefore, exceeded its authority."

The light blinked from yellow to red.

Judge Baron looked over at her colleagues on the panel. "Questions?"

Senior Judge Mathews picked up some notes and adjusted his reading glasses. "I have a question."

"Go right ahead," the Chief Judge nodded.

"Counselor, the Supreme Court in the Bay Mills case did not address whether a state could sue individual tribal officials for violating the Act. This suit names Jeremiah Tiger."

Pierce nodded. "Your honor, Mr. Tiger was only acting in his official capacity and under the precedent established under *Ex Parte Young*, he is immune from suit since Mr. Tiger has not acted contrary to any federal law or the constitution. The compact signed by both the tribe and the state has a dispute resolution provision. The state was required to exhaust the legal remedies in the compact. Which it failed to do. Under Part 12 of the compact, all disputes must be arbitrated. The state never requested arbitration. Finally, Part 9 provides that the Compact shall not alter tribal, federal or state civil adjudicatory or criminal jurisdiction."

Judge Mathews leaned back in his chair and scratched his chin. "In other words, the state is prevented by supreme court precedent, the Act and the compact that it voluntarily signed from suing the tribe or its tribal officials."

Pierce resisted the urge to smile. "That's correct, your honor."

"Thank you," The Chief Judge said, indicating that Pierce's time was up.

On gut level, Pierce thought the argument went as well as he could hope for. Payton fixed her eyes on him. The mix of relief and joy was clear in them. The surge of adrenaline that Jeremiah felt when Pierce started speaking was now a profound sense of satisfaction.

Chapter Twenty-Eight

Scott Masters, the Attorney General, walked with his notes to the podium and stood proudly waiting for the court to signal him that he could begin. For six years, he represented the people of Oklahoma with his eyes on the gubernatorial seat or the United States senate. Masters relished every opportunity to gain publicity, and a courtroom packed with news reporters was exactly what he had hoped would happen.

"Good morning, your honors, Scott Masters, Attorney General representing the great state of Oklahoma," he started, his voice rich, his grin wide and toothy. All that was missing was a Miss Oklahoma beauty pageant sash draped across his chest and a half-wave to complete the picture, Pierce thought.

Masters droned on for twenty minutes, painting the Kialegee Tribe as interlopers, sounding more like a televangelist preacher on a pulpit than a lawyer. Switching gears, he dwelled on the righteous people of Broken Arrow. The proximity of the casino site to churches and schools and the increased crime rate associated with casino operations. He detailed the extensive research conducted by the state's expert, an eminent scholar proving that the only beneficiary of the treaty that established the Creek reservation was the Muscogee Creek Nation.

The mood suddenly got tense when Scott Masters suggested that the court had no choice but to affirm the district court's order.

"Who wants the first question?" The Chief Judge asked, looking over at the panel.

Judge Holloway leaned in. "Counsel, your client sued a federally recognized tribe for threatening to game on Indian land. A right specifically reserved to tribes. I wonder if you understand the statute at issue."

"Sir," Masters looked puzzled. "Is that a question?"

"The land where the construction was stopped by the district court is Indian land. Is it not?"

Masters cleared his throat. "The Indian land in question is exclusively under the jurisdiction of the Muscogee Creek Nation. A requirement under the Act to game on Indian land is the ability to exert jurisdiction and governmental authority over the land. The Kialegee has no right to assert jurisdiction over the land."

Chief Judge Baron rubbed her temples, giving the impression that she was having a problem processing Masters' argument.

"There's nothing in the record that states that the Bureau of Indian Affairs officially concluded that the Muscogee Creek Nation has exclusive jurisdiction. Isn't that correct, Counsel?" The Chief Judge asked.

Masters tried valiantly to suggest that the federal government agreed with the state. "Your honor, the Chairman of the National Indian Gaming Commission sent my office a letter stating that the Kialegee has no jurisdiction . . ."

"I've seen the letter," Holloway interrupted. "But you realize that is advisory, nothing more. It is not appealable by the Kialegee and therefore not a final agency action."

Before Masters could think of a response, Judge Mathews hunched over his microphone. "It's my understanding that the Chairman of the National Indian Gaming Commission is a member of the Muscogee Creek Nation. Doesn't that sound like a conflict of interest?"

Chief Judge Baron arched an eyebrow as she glanced over at Judge Mathews. "We're getting off topic here."

Mathews forced a well-bred smile and turned his attention back to Masters. "Counselor, you argued that the state can sue the tribe because the Kialegee can't exercise jurisdiction over the land. Is the land Indian land?"

Masters gritted his teeth and nodded. "Yes."

"Then can you point out where in the Act it provides that a state can sue a tribe over gaming activity on Indian land where the state or the Indian Gaming Commission contend the tribe lacks jurisdiction over the land?"

Masters shot a look at the attorneys from his office as if to say, "you failed to anticipate and prepare me for this line of questioning."

Masters pondered the question for a minute, then finally said, "Your honor, the Act needs to be read in concert with the district court case *Miami Tribe of Oklahoma v. United States* which determined that only lands within the Tribe's jurisdiction qualify as Indian lands under the Act. Since the Kialegee Tribal Town does not have jurisdiction over the land its actions violate federal law. Therefore, this lawsuit by the state against Mr. Tiger is allowed under *Ex. Parte Young*."

Judge Mathews sighed and almost smiled. "Back to the jurisdiction question. I feel like we've come full circle, Mr. Masters."

"With all due respect your honor, this issue has been carefully vetted by the National Indian Gaming Commission. It is their responsibility to make determinations concerning jurisdiction . . ."

Judge Mathews interrupted him, making no effort to hide his dissatisfaction. "In effect, I assume you're arguing that it's the State's position that advisory opinions issued by the National Indian Gaming Commission expand the jurisdictional reach of the state to allow it to bring claims not authorized by the law enacted by Congress?"

Masters was still composed, but clearly agitated. "Your honor, I believe that you are mis-characterizing the state's position."

The lawyers in the courtroom began to look at each other. Nobody tells a judge on the Tenth Circuit Court, the last stop before the Supreme Court, that he doesn't grasp the nuances of the argument made to the court.

"Counsel, are you familiar with the rule of statutory construction expressio unius est exclusio alterius?" Judge Mathews asked. "It means that if the Legislature has not expressly given you authority under the law you cannot presume to have it." His question sounded more like a stern lecture.

Masters frowned, a quick sharp grimace as if his hemorrhoids had suddenly flared up. "Yes, your honor."

"Nowhere in the Indian Gaming Act does it allow a state to sue a tribe gaming on Indian land. Correct?"

Masters started to respond but was abruptly cut off.

"At this juncture a yes or no answer will suffice since I've been asking the same question for the last ten minutes."

"The Kialegee Tribe under the compact with the state consented to suit under the limited waiver of sovereign immunity . . ."

"As part of the Dispute Resolution provision," Judge Mathews cut him off.

Master nodded.

"Under that provision, the state is required to demand arbitration before filing suit. Did the state ever request arbitration?"

"The extenuating circumstances required that the state pursue a preliminary injunction to prevent irreparable harm to the community. The tribe would have continued to move forward with construction during the arbitration process." The hole that Masters was digging himself into was starting to look like a grave.

The panel peppered Masters with questions for an additional twenty minutes. However, at the appellate level it didn't necessarily mean that the court was leaning in a particular direction. In some cases, it was nothing more than good theater.

Chapter Twenty-Nine

OKMULGEE OKLAHOMA

Randall Yahola was elected Principal Chief of the Muscogee Creek Nation in a special election after charges of embezzlement and racketeering were filed by the U.S. attorney against George Beaver and the Tribe demanded his resignation. Randall had been in office eighty-nine days when a copy of the Tenth Circuit Court's decision concerning the Kialegee Tribal Town's appeal came across his desk.

Unlike his predecessor, Randall was not one to engage in political maneuvering or agree to a deal just because everyone walked away with something. He spent his early years living with his maternal grandmother in Okemah, Oklahoma with a population of roughly three thousand scattered throughout the county. Okemah a predominantly poor Creek Indian community's only claim to fame, was that it was the birthplace of folk music legend Woody Guthrie. From there he was sent to live at an Indian school. When he was eighteen years old, Randall went to work for the Oklahoma Department of Corrections. He spent the next thirty-five years as a correctional officer guarding prisoners that the justice system considered too dangerous to be anywhere but in a maximum-security prison.

Randall lived in an isolated bubble, having little contact with people that weren't Indians, correctional officers or convicted criminals. He trusted few people and was suspicious of everyone not in his inner circle. He didn't care much for white people, but he tolerated them. His feelings towards the three Creek tribal towns that left the Creek Nation were mixed and complicated. When the three Creek tribal towns broke away from the Creek Nation to become independent and federally recognized tribes, they turned their backs on the tribe. While they were Creek Indians, and some were even kin to Randall, when they left the Creek Nation, they abandoned all the rights given to the Muscogee Creek Nation under the treaties. In Randall's eyes the Kialegee, Alabama-Quassarte and Thlopthlocco tribal towns were all squatting on Muscogee Creek land.

He was pugnacious and promised to rid the Muscogee Nation of those who had been easy to corrupt and fell hopelessly addicted to lining their pockets at the tribe's expense. Randall had a small group of loyal followers. They were almost cult-like in their devotion and commitment to him. His followers did not number nearly enough to get him elected. Most of the tribal members that elected him were not voting for him inasmuch as they were voting against the corruption and the constant embarrassment of federal agency investigations into missing grant monies and reputed kickbacks. Randall ran for chief at the perfect time and his "us against the world" and "damn everyone and everything that isn't Creek" ideologies seemed more palatable on election day than did the status quo. Almost everyone working in the tribe's administration was fired in his first week as Chief. Those that survived the carnage walked softly around him.

With a displeased look on his face, Randall Yahola studied the court's order. He didn't bother to read the whole thing. He was only interested in the last sentence that read:

'We REVERSE and REMAND to the district court with instructions to vacate its preliminary injunction and to dismiss the State's complaint with prejudice.'

What that meant to him was that Jeremiah would soon start up construction again. Randall first met Jeremiah at the Indian school. Jeremiah was three years behind him, but he was such a gifted athlete that he competed against the older boys. What stood out about Jeremiah even at a young age was how hard he trained and played. He was not like the other boys who made up excuses to avoid practice. Jeremiah kept a mental scorecard and battled in every basketball and lacrosse practice as if it was the last minute of the state championship.

By Jeremiah's senior year Randall along with carloads of tribal members from the nearby towns attended the games just to see him play. There was even gossip that Jeremiah would go to a big-time white college on a lacrosse scholarship. Like many gifted Indian athletes before him, however, Jeremiah never left the reservation. Over the years, Randall and Jeremiah occasionally crossed paths at the annual Green Corn Ceremony. From what Randall remembered of those grueling practices in the steamy summer heat, Jeremiah would never quit. Now his motivation to succeed was much deeper. Far more personal.

The site where the Kialegee was constructing the casino abutted the Creek Turnpike. Most of the River Spirit's customers drove past the location every day to and from work or on their way to gamble. There was little doubt that the accessibility of the Kialegee casino location would take business away from the River Spirit. If Randall believed what the tribe's head of casino operations was telling him, the Kialegee casino once open would siphon off twenty-four percent of his tribe's casino revenues. The River Spirit Casino had just finished construction of a new hotel and expanded gaming floor.

Randall tossed the piece of paper and tried to think the situation through. There weren't many things that scared him, but this was one of them. With the MCN hundreds of millions in debt, it didn't matter that the state couldn't stop the Kialegee casino, he would have to do it. Randall knew that he would need to do whatever was necessary to stop Jeremiah and protect the River Spirit Casino's revenues.

*****

Jeremiah read the court's order several times. He didn't comprehend all the legal arguments, but he understood that the appellate court overturned the injunction. He sat on the front porch listening to the rain with the order rolled up in his hand, afraid to let it go, afraid if misplaced the tribe's victory would disappear. When the day began, it was a typical February day; the Kialegee Tribe was invisible. A casino promised a senior center, health care, a youth center with a swimming pool and better schools. Now the day held promise, and the sun was shining on the Kialegee.

Jeremiah wrote the names of the people he needed to call. First on the list was Pierce. He had questions and wanted to fully understand the court's decision so he could explain it to the tribal members.

Pierce explained to Jeremiah that the court's decision stopped short of ruling on the shared jurisdiction issue. "The court found that the state had no authority to stop construction of the casino . . . What it means," Pierce continued, "is that the Bureau of Indian Affairs and the National Indian Commission could still find that the Kialegee Tribal Town doesn't have jurisdiction over the Broken Arrow land."

Jeremiah swallowed hard and digested Pierce's explanation. "So what's our next step?"

"You finish construction and open the casino."

Jeremiah carefully considered his next question as Pierce's answer would factor heavily into the tribe's plans. "And what about the Bureau and NIGC?" He asked.

Pierce reminded him of the original plan. "They can't do anything until the casino is open. If they issue a Notice of Violation, we'll fight it. If they follow that up with a closure order, we'll fight that. Meanwhile, your casino is making millions. The tribe will have the resources to fight them for years until we wear them down. Indian casinos once they get open don't get shut down. So, get open," Pierce said.

In a perfect world the court would have resolved the lingering juris-dictional question and there would be nothing for the Kialegee to fight about. But nothing perfect or easy ever came the Kialegee's way. Jeremiah hated loose ends, but if the tribe still had a fight ahead of them, he liked the idea of amassing a war chest.

After speaking with his lawyers, Jeremiah contacted David Johnson, to get all the subcontractors back to work.

*****

When Scott Masters got to the top of the Capitol steps, he was be-sieged by reporters shouting questions. The press that he cajoled into broadcasting his every move as he prepared to make his run for the Governor's office was the last thing he wanted to see. Reporters shouted questions at him.

"The Court of Appeals unanimously overturned the District Court's decision. Is the State going to appeal the decision to the Supreme Court?"

"Of course," he said, looking worn out and uncertain. "This wouldn't be the first time a court got it wrong."

"Do you know if the Kialegee will resume construction of the casi-no?" A look of annoyance flashed across Masters' face. "You'll have to ask them."

His confident demeanor was gone. His answers sounded like politi-cal spin.

"Now if you'll excuse me," he broke away trying to avoid more questions.

Chapter Thirty

NATIONAL INDIAN GAMING COMMISSION
WASHINGTON D. C.

Lyman Rampersad saw the new Attorney General for the Muscogee Creek Nation sitting in the waiting room to his office. The harried look on his face made him suspect that Muscogee Nation was about to lean on him for something big. The Chief called Lyman the night before and insisted that he clear his morning. Other than to say that Travis Alexander would be in his office first thing in the morning, the Chief had been vague about its purpose. Lyman, a Muscogee Creek Indian on his mother's side, was fifty-six years old. His hair was long, thick, and black, swept back into a ponytail. He had been Chairman of the National Indian Gaming Commission for three years. Prior to being sworn in as Chairman, Lyman served as Chief Justice of the Muscogee (Creek) Nation Supreme Court, the highest court of the tribe.

"Can we get you some coffee?" Lyman asked.

Travis lifted the Starbucks cup, "I'm good."

The two men exchanged a few pleasantries and Travis caught Lyman up on tribal gossip before getting to the reason for his visit.

"You know construction on the casino started back up again about a month ago," Travis said.

Lyman took a sip of coffee and nodded, "Yes, I know. I've been keeping tabs on the activity on the Broken Arrow Site."

There was a pause and Travis said, "The Chief sent me here to find out what you're going to do about it?"

"There's not much I can do at the moment," Lyman frowned.

"Why not?"

"Because they're not gaming right now."

"But they are going to . . . the freakin sign on the top of the building says Red Creek Casino in bright neon lights."

Lyman had a look that suggested that Travis being a lawyer himself should know better. "I can't bring an enforcement action until actual gaming is occurring on site. C'mon Travis, you know better than to press me. A cop can't give you a speeding ticket because you announce you're going to speed at some point in the future. He has to catch you speeding."

Travis frowned, "It's not me doing the pressing. I'm just the Chief's messenger. He wants you to issue the closure order now."

Lyman studied Travis and wondered if he was giving the Chief legal advice or saying yes to whatever the Chief wanted. "It doesn't work that way, Travis. I already issued an Indian Lands Opinion finding against the Kialegee Tribal Town. I'll issue a Notice of Violation the same day they open. But I can't do it before."

Travis's eyes narrowed; his jaw clenched and in a slightly elevated voice said. "I don't think you understand, the Chief isn't asking here."

Lyman held his tongue and didn't snap back. He could see that the Chief had unrealistic expectations, and they were weighing heavily on Travis. There was a pause in the conversation in which Travis appeared to settle down and organize his thoughts.

He rambled for a bit about the construction. Then Travis explained that the Creek was doing everything they could behind the scene to sabotage the Kialegee. He explained that they contacted everyone doing business with the Kialegee and threatened to close their accounts. The Creek operated nine casinos, so for most vendors keeping the Creek business was more important than doing business with the Kialegee.

"At first, it was working," Travis explained. "Their food and liquor suppliers walked off the job and no slot machine distributor in Oklahoma would sell them slot machines."

Lyman listened with his feet up on his desk and hands clasped behind his head quietly wondering whether any of this could blowback on him since the Creek were openly threatening slot machine distributors and his office regulated slot machines.

"Do the Kialegee know that the Creek are threatening their vendors?" Lyman asked.

Travis shrugged, "You know how the Moccasin Telegraph in Indian Country works, nothing stays a secret for long."

Lyman rolled his eyes as if to say that he unfortunately knew it all too well.

"We knew that they would figure out the food and liquor because there are too many vendors and we don't do business with all of them," Travis said before taking a sip of coffee. "But we didn't expect them to find slot machines. Those little pricks found slot machine distributors in Canada and Europe willing to do business with them."

"I didn't realize that Jeremiah was so resourceful," Lyman mused.

Travis scoffed, "I don't think he had anything to do with it."

"Who then?"

"I'm sure his lawyer from Miami is responsible."

"Well, folks from Oklahoma are fickle. When they don't see games they recognize they'll move on," Lyman said trying to sound reassuring.

"Maybe," Travis nodded, "but it comes down to pay-outs. We have a lot of debt to repay, so we have no choice but to keep the pay-outs on our machines lower. If they have looser slots, it won't much matter whether people recognize the games. Folks like to win and if the slots at the Kialegee casino pay out more than we do, that's where people will go."

Travis frowned as if this was grievous news for everyone and then he said, "We can't let them get open."

Lyman shrugged his shoulders. "Nothing we can do. They have excellent lawyers. If we cut corners and don't follow the law, they'll expose it and we'll all be worse off."

"So, how long before you can shut them down?"

"We'll issue the closure order the day the casino opens. They'll have thirty days to file their response. Once the order is final, they'll appeal it. I'll hand pick the administrative law judge and make sure he expedites the hearing."

Travis didn't seem to care about the process. "How much time are you going to allow them to remain open?"

"Six months, give or take."

Travis flinched. He wasn't sure the River Spirit could survive for six months with the Kialegee taking away their business. "What do you want me to tell the Chief?" He asked, sounding worried.

Lyman offered a phony smile. "The truth," he said.

Chapter Thirty-One

BROKEN ARROW

Payton was spending twenty hours a day at the casino. What started as two days a week at the satellite office as part of her deal to be reinstated morphed into a full-time commitment. Overnight, Payton became the unofficial eyes and ears of the tribal elders. The casino development team grew to rely on Payton because she had a genuine talent for managing people, which included the Business Committee. The Business Committee and elders trusted Payton because she was one of them and always told them what they needed to hear and not what they wanted to hear. Jeremiah was happy to see his daughter embrace her new role with such gusto. For the first time since Payton's mother died, he didn't worry about the path she'd chosen.

With only three weeks before the grand opening, the "To Do" list grew longer with each passing hour. Everyone was working at a frenzied pace. There was an army of computer engineers in red pull over shirts bearing their company logo scampering around the server rooms and casino floor checking the security systems and back of the house servers, synchronizing the internal computer codes and protocols of all eight hundred slot machines to allow the casino floor to function as one system.

Chef Demetri tested recipes and complained hourly that the menu for the restaurant was not finalized. With such little time left, Chef Demetri worried that his staff would not have enough time to master all the menu items. He demanded a ritualized and organized way of preparing the dishes. Only through repetition could they achieve consistency and excellence. The recipes had to become second nature. Otherwise staff could not perform under high stress.

Jeremiah hired a nationally known bar expert and celebrity, Nick Roberts to design the bar and create a unique drink menu. He watched the television show about failing establishments "rescued" by Nick and his team of experts regularly and was star struck when he flew to Las Vegas and met him personally. When Nick invited Jeremiah to appear in one episode, he was completely sold, and Roberts was hired. The personnel assigned to work with the tribe to create signature cocktails for the casino were mixologists that routinely appeared on the television show.

Nick arranged for Iggy Oremonesi, a Michelin Star chef, to fly in from Chicago to create the menu for the casino. Iggy was small in stature, big on ego. When he landed in Tulsa, he held up five fingers and told Jeremiah that's how many minutes he had to wait in Oklahoma's oppressive summer heat. At sixty-three, Iggy had not cooked profession-ally for fifteen years. However, he carried on as if they had awarded him his Michelin rating yesterday. For him there was no middle ground or collaboration. Nick hired Iggy to bring his menu to Tulsa and heaven help anyone who didn't consider it to be culinary genius. His bellicose and irascible temperament was the reason that the restaurant after two months' time still had no menu.

Payton looked over the latest menu items on the whiteboard. The starters included Giant Pretzel & Beer Cheese Fondue; Street Taco Sampler, Deconstructed Nachos and Lollipop Chicken Wings Tossed in a Jack Daniel's infused BBQ sauce, and blue cheese dressing.

"What the fuck," she mumbled to herself as she moved on to the main dishes that included Pork Porterhouse finished with a rich maple glaze, Rack of New Zealand Lamb and Akaushi Butler Steak Frites in a red wine glaze.

The door to the kitchen swung open. "Iggy!" Payton didn't mean to shout, but his name exploded out of her. Iggy sat at a table looking over the food inventory list, pretending not to hear Payton. Chef Demetri chuckled. Finally, Iggy said, "Oh, hello Payton. How can I help you?"

"Iggy, we talked about the menu a hundred times," Payton started. "There's nothing on that whiteboard that says down home comfort food."

Iggy hesitated, took a deep breath, then shot Payton a look of sheer bewilderment.

"I talked to Nick last night. These are the menu items he wants to go with."

Tension was rising by the minute. Their impromptu meeting showed all the signs of not ending well. As their voices grew louder, Chef Demetri and the kitchen staff looked for excuses to be elsewhere.

Payton thought briefly about firing Iggy on the spot but caught herself before the situation spiraled out of control. She realized that trying to bulldoze Iggy was getting her nowhere and took a different approach. She walked over and gently rubbed Iggy's shoulders. Iggy instantly stiffened and then sank a few inches in his chair.

Leaning over, she whispered in his ear. "Food that uses smoke in the presentation and desserts that look like artwork will not appeal to Okies. The food is beautiful, but it says little about Oklahoma and the Kialegee culture."

Iggy rolled his eyes and grimaced. He had this conversation with Payton on several occasions, and each time it ended in a stalemate. "Indians aren't going to be our customers. People are coming here to eat and gamble, not to get a history lesson," he said sarcastically.

Payton spun Iggy around in his chair and as easy as flipping on a light switch, she licked her lips seductively. It was the same look she had perfected during her photo shoots to make men fantasize about her.

It was obvious what Payton was doing. But it didn't matter, any desire or willingness Iggy had been feeling to continue to argue with her had vanished.

"How many restaurants have you visited since you've been here?" she asked.

Iggy rattled off a few names.

"None of those are local spots," she interrupted. "You have no clue what Okies like to eat,'" she said.

Iggy resented the implication but kept his cool.

Very diplomatically, Payton encouraged Iggy to have dinner with her. "I'm taking you out tonight. Nothing fancy, just good Okie food."

He shook his head slightly on reflex, unsure. "I don't know."

"How else am I going to convince you?" Payton insisted.

Iggy hung his head and said, "What time?" He realized that she wasn't going to leave until he agreed, and he had a lot of work to do.

*****

Payton stopped at a few of her favorite local restaurants and collected menus before swinging by the DoubleTree Hotel. She was determined to give Iggy a crash course in Oklahoma comfort food.

Iggy was already outside when Payton rolled under the covered driveway. She was fifteen minutes late, but Iggy knew better than to mention it.

They drove to the Tally Good Food Café on historic Route 66.

Payton flashed Iggy a warm smile and said, "You're in good hands. I promise."

Payton ordered Iggy Chicken Fried Steak with Mac & Cheese and beans and cornbread for sides.

She ordered grilled catfish for herself and let Iggy have a few bites.

Iggy enjoyed the Mac & Cheese in particular. "This takes me back to my childhood," he said, smiling at the memory. "I can't remember the last time I had Mac & Cheese."

Payton patted his hand and said, "I know you're targeting the millennial demographic, but they're not the ones that feed the slot machines. The biggest slot players are people over forty."

Iggy was busy cleaning his plate with a piece of cornbread and taking a bite of it. He swallowed the cornbread and took a sip of sweet tea before asking a question. "And how do you know this?"

Payton rolled her eyes. "All you have to do is walk the casino floors and look at who's sitting in the chairs. The Red Creek Casino will be a local's casino. If those folks want a fancy steak, they're going to Prime or Mahogany's steakhouse, not our place."

"The River Spirit has Ruth's Chris Steakhouse," Iggy countered.

"And the Hard Rock casino also has a steakhouse. We're just offering more of the same. We need to offer value. Good food at good prices," she smiled. "I like that write that down," she chuckled.

Iggy seemed skeptical. "I understand your point, but to compete with the River Spirit and Hard Rock we need to offer a high-quality and unique menu that you can't find anywhere else in the city. Especially since we don't have the amenities those casinos have."

Payton disagreed. "That's not our target demographic. Our players in the afternoons are retirees and, in the evenings, the hundred thousand people that live in Broken Arrow looking to spend their money gambling not on expensive food."

"Did you know that buffet revenues are directly tied to slot revenues? When the buffet has a good month revenue wise slot revenue is also up," Payton continued.

Iggy gave her a quizzical look. "And where did you pull that from?"

"I've been doing a lot of research. And I followed it up with a call to the General Manager over at the San Manuel casino in California. He confirmed that slot players, same as bingo players don't usually eat in their restaurants other than the buffet because they want to spend their money gambling, not eating."

"I guess we can put a few items like the chicken-fried steak and fried chicken on the menu," Iggy said sounding like he was coming around to Payton's way of thinking.

"More than a few," Payton said, sensing she was getting close to convincing him. "We also need to take the New Zealand Rack of lamb off the menu. That's an expensive item for us to carry, and no one is going to order it."

Iggy sighed. It wasn't as simple as swapping out a few appetizers and entrees. "So, who's going to break the news to Nick?"

Payton ignored the question. The Tribal elders gave Payton a second chance, and she would not blow it worrying about what Nick had to say. He had never visited Tulsa. She thought he should focus on rescuing bars instead of barking orders from one thousand miles away.

After dinner, Payton and Iggy stepped out into the Tulsa night. Payton placed a doggy bag in the back while Iggy slipped into the passenger seat.

Payton didn't want the jeep to smell like leftover food, so she rolled the windows down before pulling into traffic. Iggy felt increasingly uncomfortable as the chilly night air whipped around the jeep.

"Do you mind rolling the windows up?" Iggy asked.

A smug smile played at her lips. "Aren't you from Chicago? You should be used to a little cold."

"Ironic, isn't it, but I can't stand the cold. If I had a choice I'd live in New Orleans or Miami."

"Then why do you live in Chicago?"

Iggy shrugged. "I married a girl from Lake View. So, you could say I'm stuck there."

"Enough said," Payton smirked, sounding satisfied.

When she pulled up to the hotel, Payton reached into the back seat and handed Iggy a bunch of paper.

"What's this?" Iggy grinned.

"Your homework," Payton replied. "Look through those menus. I expect you to pick six entrees by tomorrow."

A look of concern washed over Iggy's face as there was still an important loose end to deal with. "And what about Nick? He's not going to be happy about the changes to the menu."

Payton resisted the urge to say, "Fuck him." She couldn't help but smirk at the thought of telling Nick and his gigantic ego to go fuck himself and revved the throttle to let the engine roar with power. "Don't worry Iggy," she said calmly, like there wasn't a thing in the world to worry about. Payton let the jeep creep forward, "You can't make an omelet without breaking a few eggs," she said.

Iggy gripped the menus and watched Payton navigate out of the hotel property and turn onto Yale Ave.

Chapter Thirty-Two

OKMULGEE, OKLAHOMA

The instant that Travis Alexander's jet touched the tarmac in Tulsa, the phone in his jacket pocket vibrated.

The text message read: "*Chief wants to see you as soon as you get back.*"

Travis headed straight for the tribal headquarters. When he walked through the reception area just outside the Chief's office, Mary, the Chief's executive assistant shot him a look that told him all he needed to know.

"They're waiting for you," she said.

"How long have they been waiting?"

"About thirty minutes," she said. "You better get in there. You know the Chief doesn't like to be kept waiting."

Sitting around the conference room table was a tall, thin and sharply dressed man, Pat Craft, the Chief Executive Officer of the Muscogee Gaming Enterprises and the River Spirit Casino. To Pat's immediate left was Jason Hawkins, the Police Chief. Jason was a big intimidating figure who looked like he was itching for a fight and seldom lost. Next to Jason was his deputy, L.J. Wind, whose primary purpose was to drive the Police Chief around, shake hands and interact with people so that the Police Chief wouldn't have to. At the head of the long table was Chief Yahola.

There weren't any smiles.

"Have a seat Travis," The Chief said pointing to a seat directly across from where the other three were sitting. The instant that Travis sat down, his chair felt like a hot seat.

Travis reported on the meeting with the Chairman of the NIGC. He did a quick review of his notes to make sure that he didn't leave out any important detail.

When he was finishing up, Travis took a deep breath and shook his head in frustration. "I pushed the Chairman as hard as I could, but he wouldn't budge. He won't start enforcement action right now."

The Chief remained composed, but he was clearly agitated. "How long before they shut them down?" He asked.

Travis's voice was quick and nervous. "We talked about the NIGC's timetable for closing the Kialegee casino. Best-case scenario, six months."

"And what's the worst-case scenario?" Pat Craft asked.

"Well worst-case scenario is that they don't get shut down. But that's unlikely, so a more realistic scenario is that the lawyers for the Kialegee drag out the closure for six months to a year longer," Travis said.

Everyone sitting around the table stiffened.

A morbid silence fell over the meeting. Finally, the Chief asked a question on everyone's mind. "Can we afford to wait on the NIGC?"

Pat Craft was careful to couch his response in a manner to suggest he could weather a brief storm. He thought the River Spirit could survive the six months and longer if necessary. He slid copies of a report across the table.

"We've run numbers. If the Kialegee takes ten percent of the River Spirit's business, we could survive until they get shut down," Pat said.

"Survive," the Chief repeated grimly as he methodically flipped the pages of the report. The Chief recognized Pat's answer for what it was, a slick non-answer. His gut told him that ten percent wasn't a realistic scenario. The Chief peeled off his reading glasses with an air of exasperation and tossed the report to the side. "Ten percent sounds optimistic.

What if they take more than ten percent of our revenue?" The Chief asked.

Craft didn't want to upset the Chief. He had met with outside law-yers to discuss a contingency plan. The Chapter 11 bankruptcy laws designed to protect struggling businesses did not apply to Indian tribes. "We can loosen our slot hold to make sure our customers don't flock to the Kialegee casino. Our lender, like it or not, is in the boat with us. They can't foreclose on Indian land, so they'll have to renegotiate a lower payment. They can't afford to let us go under. We can also lower our operating expenses by laying off some of our staff."

The Chief felt his heartbeat increase ten beats per minute. He didn't like Craft's answer. Particularly, the part about cutting jobs, that meant firing tribal members.

"Travis."

"Yes, Chief."

"The Kialegee are trespassing on Creek land. What's keeping us from shutting them down?"

"Nothing." Travis jotted a quick note and continued saying, "The FBI and the U.S. Marshals won't stick their noses in a tribal conflict. The Broken Arrow Police have no jurisdiction on the land, and the Federal District Court already tried to shut them down. So, we shouldn't have any obstacles."

His mind ticking along, the Chief turned his attention to the Police Chief.

"Jason, what do you think?"

The Police Chief, a man of few words and limited social skills, grunted, "The NIGC's excuses are horseshit. Lyman is a bureaucrat. He won't risk his neck to help his tribe. When it comes to Lyman and the NIGC, I think we're drilling a dry hole."

The Chief nodded gravely and looked at Pat Craft. He didn't care for Pat Craft. He was the highest paid tribal employee, making almost twice as much money as the Chief, and that bothered him. Every time Pat pulled up to the tribal headquarters in his Mercedes-Maybach GLS with a price tag of two hundred thousand dollars wearing two thousand-dollar suits, his mood soured. To make matters worse, Pat Craft was a white man in charge of the tribe's most important asset. The money generated by the tribe's casino enterprises paid for the tribe's operations. But until the Chief could find an Indian capable of running the casino, Pat Craft had job security.

"How much of our business will the Kialegee casino really take from us if they remain open for six months? And this time don't sugarcoat it." The Chief snapped at Pat.

The wrinkles growing on Pat's forehead as he thought about the question told the Chief all he needed to know. Pat re-shifted, cleared his throat, and said, "Worst-case scenario, they could take fifty million in revenue from the River Spirit. More if they're allowed to stay open longer than six months."

The Chief didn't flinch, but he was clearly troubled. He and Jason had been hatching a backup plan. If the NIGC agreed to step in and immediately shut down the illegal casino, it wouldn't be necessary. Otherwise he was prepared to do it himself. Before Travis left for Washington, he brought him into his inner circle to make sure that any legal obstacles were dealt with.

"Jason, how much time do you need to get the Lighthorse ready?"

The plan was to roll into the casino with the MCN's version of its Special Weapons and Tactics team. They would take control of the site and immobilize all activity, shutting down any possibility of the casino opening.

"Two days, three tops," Jason replied.

L.J nodded in agreement.

"We'll need to secure a search warrant from the MCN tribal court," Travis offered. "Otherwise, we could give the feds a reason to interfere."

The Chief nodded. He appeared to be weighing his options or lack of them. After a long pause he said, "Get the warrant and shut them down now."

Chapter Thirty-Three

RED CREEK CASINO
BROKEN ARROW

Jason Hawkins kept his eyes on the parking lot in front of the casino. He set up a command post at the technical college across the Creek turnpike and surveyed the casino from there. With the scheduled opening only two weeks away, employees and contractors were working seven days. By 6.30 PM on Sunday evening, the parking lot had emptied with just a few cars left.

The police chief ordered the two teams of Lighthorse to move in. Minutes later, eight black SUVs blitzed into sight, turning off the Creek Turnpike and onto the casino road. The lead vehicle stopped twenty feet from the main casino entrance. Five SUVs came to screeching halts in line with the lead vehicle while the other two circled around to the back of the building. For the raid the Lighthorse officers were armed with M4 Rifles with optics, 12-gauge shotguns and tactical vests. Ten men wearing black masks carrying assault weapons stood behind open SUV doors waiting for orders.

Jason Hawkins looked through binoculars. "Is everyone in position?" He asked.

The deputy was monitoring the mission on a closed circuit. "Yes, sir."

"Go," Hawkins ordered.

*****

After the court of appeals reversed the district court's ruling Congressman Murphy and the community opposition to the casino faded. To cut costs, David reduced security to one guard per shift. Larry Miller worked the evening shift. He was unarmed and the only security he provided was signing in food deliveries and checking everyone's I.D. badges. When Larry saw the flashing lights, he cracked the door open and saw men dressed in tactical masks with assault rifles moving in his direction. All he could think of doing was to scream for Payton as loud as his vocal cords would allow.

The first team charged through the entrance, weapons hot. The IT workers busy on the floor systematizing the slot machines scattered like cockroaches in all directions. The laser scopes mounted on the weapons painted the casino walls with red dots.

The second team used a battering ram to breach the rear door. Moving reflexively, they entered the casino with tightened grips on their weapons and eyes gleaming.

Payton heard the screams and looking out of the restaurant window she saw lights on top of SUV's flashing frantically. She knew she only had seconds. Instinctively, she reached for her cellphone and sent Nikki a text message. *"Lighthorse raiding casino. Tell dad to stay away."*

Adrenaline slammed through the veins of the Lighthorse officers as they moved through the casino, rounding up the workers at gunpoint. Chef Demetri stumbled out of the kitchen and was thrown down to the ground. He laid on the floor with the point of an assault rifle aimed at the back of his head.

"Officer, when you search me you will find a knife in my pocket. I'm telling you so we don't have a problem," Demetri said.

"Why the fuck do you have a knife?"

Demetri had a terrified look. "I'm a cook. I use it to cut food."

The Lighthorse officer pressed the tip of the rifle against the back of Demetri's skull. "Pull it out slowly and lay it next to you. Any sudden movement and I'll put a bullet in your head," he warned.

Officers Billie and Larney led the second team through the offices, gathering all the laptops, cell phones and thumb drives they could find.

The grim-faced employees had been rounded up like prisoners of war. A few of them huddled together, shell-shocked and holding hands. Others tried shrinking into the background. What terrified them most was not knowing what would happen next. Scared to make eye contact, they sat on the floor, whimpering each time the armed guards barked at them.

Officer Lucian Huft gawked at Payton.

"You," he yelled.

Larry sitting directly across from Payton gave her an apologetic glance. The officer pointed his weapon at her, expecting to see fear in her eyes, but instead he was confronted with a defiant expression. There was no fear, only a burning rage in Payton's eyes. Officer Lucian Huft grabbed her by the hair and gave it a savage yank.

"You're coming with me," he growled.

Lucian threw Payton into the count room. The most isolated and secure room at the end of the long hallway. When he patted her down, his hands lingered on her breasts and between her thighs.

Lucian sucked his teeth as he eyed her.

Payton stayed quiet, trying to read the situation. With all the Lighthorse milling around, she hoped that Lucian was only trying to scare her. Payton turned and tried to reason with him. But when she looked into his eyes, they were vacant and dark. She instantly felt that things were going from bad to worse.

Lucian slapped Payton across the face. She staggered for a moment.

He kept his predatory gaze locked on her. "Turn around cunt."

197

Payton turned and faced the wall, but from the corner of her eye, she caught a glimpse of him loosening his belt with one hand. She could feel his gun pressed against the small of her back.

"Take your pants off," he snarled.

"Fuck you, Lucian," She snapped. "That's right motherfucker, I recognize you through that bull shit mask."

Lucian jabbed his weapon so hard into Payton's back that on reflex she turned around and faced him. He put his hand around her windpipe and squeezed.

"Lucian, you don't want to do this," she said in a muffled voice, barely audible as he choked off her air supply.

Payton reached for his hand, trying to pull free. Lucian released his grip and stepped back. At the very moment that Payton's head tilted forward, gasping for air, he pistol-whipped her face with the butt of his gun. Payton crashed face first to the floor with a crack, like a melon landing on concrete.

Lucian was standing over her when Officer Larney rushed into the room, gun drawn. Payton lay on the floor, twitching, weeping quietly. Blood ran from her mouth.

Larney glared at Lucian. "What's going on?"

Lucian shrugged, gave a dumb look and said, "She resisted, so I had to put her down."

A look of annoyance passed across Larney's face when he noticed Lucian's loosened belt. "Fix your pants and get the fuck out of here," he said in an angry growl.

Lucian's shoulder sagged, and he avoided eye contact with his fellow officers who had rushed in the room after Larney.

Larney barked at the other officers. "Clean her up and put her into one of the SUVs. She's under arrest."

Hawkins watched on the monitor as the two teams secured the site with no trouble. He smiled with satisfaction and called out for a quick "sit rep" from both teams. One by one, each man checked in.

Hawkins entered the building with a smile on his face and a jovial bounce to his step. He continued around the casino, sidestepping slot machines that had been knocked over during the raid. He stopped at the employees sitting on the floor. There were fifteen in total. Twelve of them were white and the other three were Indian. Hawkins knew he couldn't arrest white people. So, he ordered the twelve released but confiscated their tools and equipment as evidence. They transported the other three to the Okmulgee county jail.

"Sir," a young officer approached the Police Chief. "I tracked down Jeremiah. He's on the line," he said, handing him the phone.

"Jeremiah, this is Chief Hawkins. We need you to come down to the casino. It's urgent." He said.

News of the raid travelled quickly. Nikki made sure of it, calling as many Kialegee tribal members as she could.

"Jason," Jeremiah said. "I'm in our tribal headquarters in Wetumka with about one hundred of my tribal members. If you got something to say to me, you can come here. But I'd bring more than twenty men if you want to make it back to Okmulgee in one piece," Jeremiah said.

When Hawkins hung up the phone, he was no longer smiling.

Chapter Thirty-Four

The call with the news of the raid came in the middle of the night. Pierce was still half asleep and bewildered when Nikki said in a voice bereft with tension, "The MCN took the casino at gunpoint."

Pierce blinked his eyes open. "What did you just say?" He asked, trying to make sure that he heard Nikki correctly. The news didn't immediately sink in. Pierce played Nikki's words over in his mind. Sitting up in disbelief he said, "Tell me what happened."

Nikki told Pierce everything she could piece together from the string of telephone calls she made to anyone she could think of that might have been at the casino at the time of the raid.

"The Lighthorse raided the casino. They confiscated all the laptops," Nikki said. Her voice was tight and full of emotion. "Chef Demetri checked himself into St. Joe's hospital complaining of chest pains."

A premonition hijacked Pierce's thought. "Was anyone hurt?" He asked.

Nikki thought about it for a moment. Everything happened so fast that the casino staff was just starting to compare notes and piecing together what happened.

"Most of the staff and the contractors were let go. Only Payton and three employees were arrested and taken to county jail."

Almost as if he could read Nikki's mind, Pierce asked, "Is Payton okay?"

Nikki wondered herself. The rumor mill was churning out different stories. The only common thread was that a few of the employees saw her carried out and put in the back of an SUV.

"The plea hearing is scheduled for tomorrow morning in tribal court. I'll know more then," Nikki said.

"I'll catch the first flight out and meet you there."

"Not a good idea," Nikki cautioned. "Your presence might actually complicate matters. You're a bit of a lightning rod. Since the MCN can't do anything to you, they may take it out on Payton and the others if you're there."

Nikki was already thinking of a battle plan. The plea hearing in tribal court would be straightforward. She would enter pleas of "not guilty" and bond out all four defendants. What she needed was for Pierce to do the heavy lifting and come up with a plan to get the casino back.

"I'll call you tomorrow morning after the arraignment," she said.

When the conversation ended, Pierce sat in the room in stunned silence. His mind processing what he heard, torn between looking for a solution and personal revulsion over the fact that certain groups in Oklahoma broke the law without consequences. There was no accountability, and the government turned a blind eye. He spent the rest of the night on his computer researching case law and running the gamut of legal theories. The MCN raid of the Kialegee casino was unprecedented. Reminiscent of a time when larger, more powerful tribes sent war parties in the middle of the night to raid small defenseless villages. Ironically, this type of aggression was the reason for the creek tribal towns banding together to form the Creek Confederacy.

Pierce was a great lawyer, but he wasn't a magician. He knew that challenging the MCN's actions in an Oklahoma court would be a waste of time. The court for the Western District of Oklahoma already sent the Kialegee a clear message. He needed a plan that didn't involve rushing into federal court in Oklahoma. That's what the Oklahoma politicians, and the MCN were not only expecting, they were counting on it.

To regain control of the casino site, he would have to devise a plan that was brilliant as it was unpredictable. To do that, Pierce required the help of unquestionably the best lawyer he'd ever worked with.

*****

Moses Black sat at his usual table at Starbucks sipping coffee, watching and listening to people's conversations as they waited in line. He was from an older generation and found people to be infinitely more interesting than being hypnotized by his smartphone. Dressed in a golf shirt, khaki pants and Italian loafers, he looked the part of a wealthy retiree living the good life in the sun instead of one of Florida's most accomplished trial attorneys. To his friends he was just "Mo the mush." He had been Pierce's mentor when Pierce graduated from law school. Now, they were just good friends. There wasn't a lawyer Pierce trusted and respected more than Mo. As soon as Mo heard about the raid, he offered to help.

The sixty-eight-year-old graduate of Columbia Law School was a seasoned and battle tested litigator. His string of courtroom wins included a range of cases that garnered national exposure from environmental contamination, bank fraud, and a class action against the big tobacco companies. Mo could handle any case. He was a lawyer's lawyer, a seasoned expert in the courtroom, and exuded a confidence that was contagious. Mo had an analytical mind and worked a problem from every angle, focusing on the most minute and seemingly insignificant detail. By the time he was ready to cross-examine the expert witness for the other side; he knew the expert's report better than they did. And his ability to manipulate the details helped him cast a shadow of doubt with juries. Moses had a saying that he used when the other lawyers on his team grew impatient with his deliberate style, *"Measure twenty times and cut once."*

Pierce ordered two premium dark roasts. He knew better than to ask Mo if he wanted another cup of coffee. Mo did his best thinking when sipping coffee. If his cup ran empty, he would stop in mid-sentence and fill it before continuing his thought. Pierce never counted, but he guessed that Mo drank at least twenty cups a day.

Pierce placed a cup directly in front of Mo, pulled a chair out and said, "Thanks for doing this." Mo shrugged it off and reached for the cup of coffee.

Out of habit, Mo sized up his former protégé, and made an instant assessment. "Let me tell you what I think," he started.

Pierce nodded.

"I think you've been up half the night reading cases on Indian law trying to figure out a way around the Creek Nation's sovereign immunity so that you can get them into court."

Pierce sighed and rubbed the stubble on his chin tiredly. "All night."

Mo heaved a theatrical sigh, shrugged and said, "You can't get around it. I can't figure out why you would want to sue the Creeks?"

Mo brought the cup to his lips and took a big gulp. "When did you become so predictable?"

"What's your point?" Pierce asked.

"My point, Pierce, is simple. You're dealing with a place where people break the law, and it goes ignored." Mo set his coffee cup on the table and leaned forward. "Assuming you can sue the MCN, you're back in federal court in Oklahoma where you got your ass handed to you."

"We won on appeal."

"And how long did that take?"

Pierce was shaking his head, agreeing with him. In tandem, they sipped their coffee and went over every detail.

"You have to throw out the Indian rule book," Mo said. He waved at the girl behind the counter to warm up his coffee.

Pierce laughed. "She's a barista, not a server."

Mo scoffed at the remark. "I come here all the time. She knows me."

"We need to sue in Washington D.C." Mo said.

Pierce knew Mo was right. Trying a case in Oklahoma was a fool's errand. "And how do we do that?"

"First, forget about suing the Creeks. That's a lost cause. Before we can get to Washington, we need a different legal argument and a different defendant," Mo said.

Pierce listened, sipped his coffee and reminded himself that Mo had never handled an Indian case. Though it could be more of an advantage than an obstacle. "Let's hear it," he said.

"What's a treaty? Mo asked. "I'll tell you. It's an agreement between two sovereign governments."

Pierce nodded, eyebrows arched.

Mo plunged ahead. "The key word being agreement. The Kialegee Tribe signed the Treaty that set aside the land in Oklahoma."

"I know," Pierce said.

"I know you know." Mo smiled. "But you need to look at this from a fresh perspective."

Mo took a sip of his coffee and made a face. "Jesus, I hate lukewarm coffee. That girl never came."

Pierce raised an eyebrow as if to say I told you so.

"Give me a minute," Mo said and cut in front of everyone online and asked for the young lady to refill his coffee.

"Okay, where was I . . . Oh yes, looking at this issue through a different lens. The Kialegee gave up their land for the land in Oklahoma. The land belonged to them and not the Creek Confederacy."

Pierce sat quietly, listening to Mo.

"This is nothing more than a breach of contract case. And that's how we should write the complaint. The United States breached the contract with the Kialegee by refusing to allow them to exert jurisdiction over the land in Broken Arrow."

"This has never been argued before," Pierce said. "At least not as a simple breach of contract."

"Right," Mo nodded. "But it is a breach of contract and there's ample case law."

Pierce closed his eyes for a few seconds and tried to put Mo's reasoning into perspective. "We just need to convince a court that this is nothing more than a contract case."

Mo took a sip of his hot coffee and seemed satisfied. "We downplay the Indian Law angle and stress that this case is not about gambling. This case is about the United States breaching a contract with the Kialegee by not allowing them to assert their sovereign rights over their land. Land that they received in exchange for the land that only they owned in Georgia."

"And that means . . ."

"We sue the United States government in Washington D.C.," Pierce said, finishing Mo's sentence.

Mo flashed a toothy grin. "Yes, and when the court rules for the Kialegee, we kick the MCN out of the casino for trespassing on Kialegee land."

Chapter Thirty-Five

OKMULGEE COUNTY JAIL

Payton sat with her back wedged, and her shoulders touching both walls. Her eyes closed, hardly registering the chatter outside her jail cell or the rancid odor which smelled like a mixture of urine and cabbage. She didn't know if her jaw was broken. She could feel swelling and tenderness along her jaw and below her ear. She could hardly move her mouth and when she tried, it felt like torture.

A Department of Corrections officer at the far end of the corridor yelled her name.

"Payton Tiger."

Payton's eyes fluttered and then opened. She could hear footsteps and voices approaching.

Just then the officer along with two Lighthorse police officers appeared by the cell door ready to escort her to the Muscogee Creek tribal court.

"Time to go," the correction officer's voice boomed as the cell door opened.

Payton tried to get up and was rewarded with a wave of nausea.

Dozens of Kialegee Tribal members filled the benches behind the defense table in the courtroom to support Payton and the three employees that had been arrested. By ten in the morning, it was standing room only, and the courtroom was packed with chatter from all directions. With such a large crowd, the Lighthorse kept additional officers stationed inside and just outside the courtroom. The Lighthorse kept a nervous watch on the group of Kialegee Tribal members.

A few minutes before eleven, Payton was escorted from a small holding room. The handcuffs were removed, and Payton took her place next to Nikki. The left side of Payton's face was swollen to a point of being unrecognizable. Nikki froze as she stared at the red and purple bruises.

"Jesus," Nikki mumbled.

Payton took a deep breath, one that made her grimace. Through clenched teeth, she said, "Nice suit. Did you buy it in the Men's section?"

Judge Harjo assumed the bench, and the courtroom was silenced.

"Payton Tiger," a bailiff announced. Payton rose to her feet.

Judge Harjo noted the interest from the media and scanned the indictment in the file.

"Are you Payton Tiger?"

"She is your Honor." Nikki said.

The judge raised his eyes from the file. "I'd like to hear from Ms. Tiger."

"Judge, the Lighthorse broke Ms. Tiger's jaw last night during the raid. She can't talk above a whisper without pain."

Judge Harjo looked over at Payton. "I'm going to ask you a question. You can answer it by nodding your head."

"Is Ms. Slayer your attorney?"

Payton nodded.

"Let the record reflect that Ms. Tiger has confirmed that Ms. Slayer is the attorney of record."

"Ms. Slayer, I am holding here an indictment. Have you been provided with a copy of it?"

Nikki nodded. "Yes, Your Honor, I received it ten minutes ago."

Judge Harjo glared at the prosecutor. "I am required to read it in open court. Ms. Tiger, you are being charged with possessing unlicensed gaming devices in violation of Muscogee Creek Nation Gaming Law NCA-12-184. You are also being charged with operating an unlicensed gambling enterprise in violation of Chapter 21, Section11-104(B) of Muscogee Creek Nation Code."

Harjo caught his breath. "Do you understand the charges against you?"

Payton nodded.

"Do you understand that if you are convicted you could be sentenced to serve five years in the state penitentiary?"

Nikki stood next to Payton with her fake smile plastered across her face.

"Your Honor, Ms. Tiger is not an employee of the Red Creek Casino or an owner. The two charges require ownership or at the very least a formal relationship with the enterprise . . ."

The judge cut Nikki off in mid-argument. "Save it for the trial counselor. I just want a plea. Guilty or not guilty."

Nikki nodded and kept the fake smile in place. "Not guilty."

Judge Harjo scanned his calendar. The trial is set for Monday, December 12. All pretrial motions must be filed by November 20.

"Your Honor, I'd like to request bail for Ms. Tiger." Nikki said.

Judge Harjo turned towards the prosecutor.

Trevor Joseph argued that bail should be set at five hundred thousand dollars.

Trevor began a windy narrative, recounting the events that led to the raid. He was careful to paint the MCN as innocent bystanders and pointed out that the illegal casino if allowed to open would hurt the tribe and Creek families. He argued that the raid was necessary to protect the future well-being of Creek children. After several minutes of standing on a soapbox, Trevor Joseph closed by saying, "Judge, this is an ongoing and dangerous criminal enterprise extending down to the Cuban Mafia in

Miami. In fact, we have information that there is another shipment of illegal gambling devices en route."

Nikki's first impulse was to laugh, and loudly but she quickly realized Trevor was dead serious. She jumped to her feet. "Dangerous criminal enterprise, Cuban Mafia. Sounds like we have the making of a John Grisham novel," Nikki repeated, mocking Trevor.

A few observers in the courtroom chuckled.

Nikki dropped her smile and said, "Your Honor, Payton Tiger is indigent. A Five Hundred Thousand Dollar bond is the same as sentencing her to serve months in jail until her trial. Payton was raised here in Oklahoma. She lives with her dad in Wetumka and is not a flight risk."

The judge listened to Nikki's argument, giving no clue about his thoughts, so she kept grinding. "Payton did not resist arrest and did not deserve the beating she received at the hands of the Lighthorse. Your Honor, the Lighthorse assaulted Payton, and she needs medical attention."

"I'm not blind," the judge said in an irritated tone. Judge Harjo was displeased with the theatrics displayed by both sides and glared at both lawyers. Though it was ideal fodder for the reporters in the back of the courtroom. He looked closely at Payton, her bruised face and decided. "Ms. Tiger, can you afford five hundred dollars?" The judge asked.

Payton nodded.

"Bail is set at five hundred dollars," Harjo rapped his gavel. "Next case."

They brought the other three defendants into the courtroom one at a time. Each one entered a plea of not guilty and all three bonded out for fifteen hundred dollars.

When the hearings were over, Payton turned to Nikki and said, "Get me out of here." Her voice was a whisper, but it had a forceful, almost desperate quality to it.

Chapter Thirty-Six

MIAMI, FLORIDA

In the war room of Mo Black's law firm, there had been considerable and sometimes belligerent debate over the details and legal arguments to be included in the Kialegee Tribe's complaint against the United States. Ira Katz, Mo's ever-cautious junior partner, was displeased with having to share the spotlight with Noah Grayson, a young inexperienced associate from a rival firm.

To make matter's worse he was Pierce Evangelista's protégé. Pierce and Ira went way back, but not always to good places. They had a long history of conflict. Pierce was the rising star at the firm and Ira who had more seniority was passed over and stuck behind him. When Mo left the firm for a better offer, Ira jumped at the opportunity to work as Mo's second chair and get out from under Pierce's considerable shadow.

At forty-one years old, Ira was below average height and not handsome in the classical sense. His large curved nose jutting out between his black brows made him appear to be disagreeable. His arrestingly deep voice made him hard to forget. The office staff were divided when it came to Ira. Some of them thought him to be aloof, and others thought him to be unbearably rude. The one thing they could all agree on was that Ira Katz was a hard-working lawyer dedicated to his craft.

It was well past midnight, and the progress was slower than either Ira, or Noah liked.

Stretching the muscles of his neck, Noah mused over the wording of a sentence much like a painter putting the finishing touches on his masterpiece.

"The complaint is over one hundred pages we need to cut it in half," Ira said.

"There's so much history, and I've only included the most important facts," Noah argued defensively.

Ira carried the coffee to the table and poured two cups. "The goal here is to set out enough detail to support the claims that the United States violated its treaty with the Kialegee. We need to trim the complaint down and put everything in the exhibits."

Noah swiveled his head a few degrees and stared at Ira's fleshy face. "It's not that simple. There's a historical progression that needs to be laid out. The treaty uses the word Muscogee in several places that can lead one to jump to the conclusion that the treaty was with the MCN. But if you're privy to the events that led to the treaty, you would know that isn't the case."

Ira had neither the patience nor desire to listen to Noah's long narrative. "The Department of Justice won't dispute that the treaty existed. They'll argue that the MCN are the only tribe with treaty rights. But that's a fact question which gets us past a motion to dismiss. The complaint only needs to put the judge and the U.S. government on notice of the Kialegee's claims. Save the historical proof for later in the case," Ira insisted.

Noah disagreed. He was armed to the teeth, and he wanted the Department of Justice to know it. "The only way to convince the court that the Kialegee Tribe are also beneficiaries is to eviscerate the government's argument." Noah scooped sugar into his coffee, gave it a violent stir and then said, "And this complaint which meticulously lays out the Kialegee history does just that."

Ira preferred thoughtful and tactical complaints that set out enough detail in the allegations to state a claim for relief and nothing more. It was a strategy that he believed kept defense counsel off balance. The complete history would come later. "Cut fifty pages."

Noah threw up his hands. "Impossible."

Ira fixed Noah with a withering stare, all the while wondering how he could have been talked into working with such a neophyte. "The complaint is too long. There is too much detail," he said in a combative tone.

Noah's eyes were bugged in disbelief. "You can't be serious? Understanding what led to the treaty is as important as the treaty itself." He wondered how Jeremiah would feel if he glossed over the tribe's history to appease Ira's demand to cut fifty pages. Noah droned on about the numerous battles and thousands of Creeks who died in them.

Ira looked on with a furrowed brow.

"The Treaty of Fort Jackson, by and between the United States and the Creek Indians, includes the signatures of both the Kialegee Chief and the Kialegee First Warrior," Noah continued.

Ira thought about ways to silence him. "Are you done?"

"Almost." Noah pressed on. "The United States' push for removal produced the Treaty in which the Creeks ceded their eastern homelands for lands in Oklahoma. Georgia and Alabama militias forcibly rounded up Creeks and sent them to Oklahoma. One hundred and sixty-six Kialegee families were relocated to Oklahoma."

Ira shrugged. "Sad story but this is all parol evidence and inadmissible in a breach of contract case."

Noah yawned into the back of his hand. The yawn wasn't from boredom, but from fatigue. "The parol evidence rule prevents the introduction of evidence if the language of a contract is clear and unambiguous, that's not the case here. The Creek Treaty of February 14, 1833, secures a country and permanent home to 'the whole Creek nation of Indians'. These words made it clear that the Creek Reservation in Oklahoma was to be the permanent home to all Creek Indians not just the MCN. If the United States maintains that the MCN alone exercises jurisdiction over the entirety of those lands, there is an ambiguity and we have an exception to the parol evidence rule."

Ira frowned and said, "But nowhere in the complaint do you assert that there is any ambiguity in the treaty language."

"I don't believe that an ambiguity exists," Noah said. "The plain language of the treaty indicates that the Creek Reservation is the property of all Creek Indians. My point is that any interpretation that attempts to vest jurisdiction solely in the MCN creates an ambiguity and opens the door to parol evidence."

Ira shook his head in a slow, disapproving way. "You need to rework this argument to lay a better foundation for the parol evidence exception. It needs to be clearly laid out in the complaint."

Noah agreed to take another look. "What about the successor in interest argument?" he asked.

Ira inhaled sharply and thought about it. "That argument is solid. If the Muscogee Tribal roles were closed the Muscogee Tribe identified in the treaties ceased to exist when the last enrolled member died. Making the MCN and the three tribal towns all equal beneficiaries of the treaties."

Ira walked around the table and headed for the door. "You can leave that argument in."

"I will be in my office taking a power nap. Come get me when you cut the complaint down to fifty pages."

Chapter Thirty-Seven

SAINT FRANCIS HOSPITAL
TULSA

They climbed out of the car and headed into the emergency room of Saint Francis Hospital. Neither Nikki nor Payton had visited Saint Francis since Sam died there. Sam's death tore at Payton. His absence was a jagged wound that would never heal. When she walked through the emergency room door, her memory of Sam manifested as real physical pain and Payton thought about turning around. But her alternative was the free Indian clinic, a frightening, antiquated facility where a patient's chances of developing a hospital-acquired infection were greater than being cured. Payton filled out the required forms and passed it to the nurse on duty. She then invited Payton to wait for the attending physician in exam room six. Nikki sat in the far corner of the room while Payton sat with her legs dangling off the examining table. As she wrestled with her thoughts, Payton's sinuous frame seemed to shrink away, and her chin dropped. Payton looked lost and helpless.

Doctor Connie Childress entered the exam room in a crisp white lab coat and stethoscope dangling around her neck.

Grabbing the chart off the back of the door she asked, "You must be Payton Tiger?"

Payton nodded.

The doctor examined the bruising and swelling. "This might hurt a bit," she said as she manipulated Payton's jawbone.

Payton pulled back in obvious pain.

"I'm sorry," the doctor said in a sympathetic tone. Taking a tongue depressor and handing it to Payton, she said, "I want you to bite down and hold it in place with your teeth."

Payton couldn't do it without grimacing in pain.

Doctor Childress scribbled notes and looked up at Payton.

"So, how did this happen?"

"She was hurt during the raid on the casino," Nikki said.

A hint of recognition flashed across the doctor's eyes. The raid was all anyone could talk about. "So, the Lighthorse did this to you?" The doctor asked, her tone more accusatorial than inquisitive.

Payton's eyes watered.

Doctor Childress shook her head in disgust and wrote "panoramic x-ray mandible," on a form. "It looks like you have a fracture of your mandible. I'm ordering an x-ray so that we can determine the best way to treat it," she said.

Doctor Childress smiled as she stood. "Okay Payton, someone will be by shortly to take you to get x-rayed. I'll be back right after."

*****

The x-ray confirmed that Payton had a fractured jaw. The doctor displayed the images on a computer screen. Pointing to one image doctor Childress said, "You see here, this is a pretty clean break. There are no displaced breaks in the bone. So, I think the proper course of treatment would be a maxillomandibular fixation which in plain English means I'm going to wire your upper and lower teeth together to hold the jaw in place so that the bone can heal properly."

Payton wanted to ask how long her mouth would have to be wired shut but all she could manage to murmur through clenched teeth was, "How long?"

215

"About six weeks. We're going to move you to another room and give you some local anesthesia. Then we'll start the procedure. I'm going to keep you overnight. You should be good to go in the morning," the doctor said reassuringly.

*****

Noah concentrated on shortening the complaint, making slow and steady progress. He had his sleeves rolled up and his tie loosened, as if he'd been performing manual labor. After six hours of plodding, he was done. A fair compromise, he decided: seventy-two pages in length and one hundred and seventeen footnotes.

When Ira finished reading it, he looked up sharply, paused, holding the complaint in his outstretched hand for a moment, giving the impression that he was considering tossing it back in Noah's direction. He could see that Noah was a young man with considerable potential, but there were holes yet to be filled by training and experience. At that moment, Pierce and Mo walked into the war room. Ira reached into the breast pocket of his jacket and withdrew a red pen. While Mo and Pierce read through Noah's draft, Ira furiously crossed through sentences and scribbled notations in the margins.

As Noah watched Ira, his tired eyes flashed with anger, but he bit his tongue.

"The section in the complaint about the Kialegee's being marginalized should come out. The tribe's lack of economic prosperity pulls at the heartstrings but it's not relevant to a breach of contract case," Ira said, touching off a tense conversation.

Noah snapped. "The lack of economic prosperity goes to damages. The actions by Interior violate federal policy of ensuring that Indians do not suffer interference with their efforts at having a strong self-government which requires an economic base to fund it."

"It's not necessary, and it takes the judge's eyes off the ball. These arguments can be raised in summary judgement." Ira hammered away, leaving both Mo and Pierce with the impression that that these two had been bickering for the last few days.

Ira offered a windy critique that ended with, "The complaint should be limited to the argument that the Kialegee has treaty-protected rights of shared jurisdiction within the Creek Reservation and ownership of the Creek Reservation in common with all other Creek tribes tracing to the Creek Confederacy within the State of Oklahoma. Everything else is superfluous."

"You're making a mistake," Noah mumbled almost under his breath.

With his right hand, Mo began scratching the back of his neck, something he always did when wrestling with a difficult decision. He understood that judicial reasoning should exclude all emotion. But it rarely did. Judges were human who did not always detach themselves from the real people behind the cases they considered. The MCN's seizure of the casino at gunpoint and the attempted rape of the daughter of the Kialegee's chief by a Lighthorse officer were deplorable acts. He knew they would not be mentioned in any order issued by the court, but Mo also suspected that like most reality television shows that hook viewers into tuning in every week, including a blurb about what occurred in Oklahoma might entice the judge to dig deeper.

Up to this point, Pierce hadn't said anything, while he assessed the situation. What was obvious became more so. This was no longer about filing the complaint; this was personal to Ira.

It was clear, at least to Pierce, that Ira's baggage had not been left behind. Pierce didn't have to wonder whether Mo would make compromises to assuage Ira's ego. When it came to writing a complaint, Mo only cared about the facts, precedent and a well-organized and persuasive legal argument.

Pierce explained that the Department of Justice and the NIGC had no historical research on the Kialegee, relying primarily on the case *Indian Country, U.S.A., Inc. v. State of Oklahoma Tax Commission* to establish that the MCN had exclusive jurisdiction over the Creek reservation.

As Pierce spoke Ira adjusted his body, raising one leg over another, then deciding against it. Pierce was the last person Ira wanted advice from which made it difficult for him to sit still.

"The court in the *Indian Country* case did not consider whether Kialegee is part of the Historic Creek Nation, nor was the Kialegee ever part of that case and the Court never decided what tribes comprise the Creek Nation. It only dealt with the MCN. The United States government has erroneously relied on this case to deny the Kialegee their rights. Up to now, the Kialegee never challenged the rulings so there was never a need for the government to actually engage an ethno-historian to research the role the tribal towns played in the Creek Confederacy."

"The court could independently take judicial notice of historical sources," Ira said smugly, straining at the leash to get his way. "In fact, we can include them as exhibits to the complaint. Otherwise the complaint becomes cumbersome."

Pierce was struck by Ira's tactics. He'd never known him to substitute his own agenda in favor of what was best for the client. In fact, he always considered Ira to be principled and pragmatic. It wasn't like him to leave anything to chance that could help the client. "The court could dismiss our case for failure to state a cause of action if its persuaded by the *Indian Country* opinion."

Laying out the history of the tribe in the complaint served an important purpose. It educated the court and safeguarded against the court relying on the *Indian Country* case as dispositive of any issue concerning the Kialegee.   There was no guarantee that the court would review extraneous documents. Pierce did not want to rely on the judge to fill in gaps. The complaint needed to walk the judge down a path that led to an inescapable conclusion.

Mo knew Ira would think he was picking a side. He shifted to the "we," mode now, something he invariably did when a potentially unpopular decision was at hand. "This is a concerted and coordinated scheme to deprive the Kialegee of basic rights. Had it not been for corrupt politicians and bureaucrats, the Kialegee Tribe would have equal rights to the Creek reservation land. This isn't a run-of-the-mill breach of contract case. This is systemic, reprehensible behavior. We cannot expose this without providing details."

Mo's comments triggered memories and feelings of earlier days when he was a young lawyer competing against Pierce.

Ira's left eye twitched. "I appreciate your input, Mo," he said, attempting to smile.

Chapter Thirty-Eight

The months of inactivity that followed the first stoppage of the casino project taxed the Kialegee's resources as the tribe used funds from the line of credit earmarked for construction to repay the interest payments. With the contingency monies almost depleted, Pierce negotiated with vendors to extend credit to the tribe with the promise that they would be paid once the casino opened.

The raid of the casino, however, threatened the viability of the project. With the casino property under the control of the MCN, credit sources dried up. Fear and humiliation became Jeremiah's daily companions. His only reprieve was his daily call from Pierce that came like clockwork every morning at 8:30.

"Good morning Chief. How's it going?" Pierce started with the typical morning pleasantries.

"Had a little ruckus last night. A group of subcontractors got some liquid courage and drove out here. Started banging on my door at three in the morning."

"Did you call the police?"

"Payton is still a little rattled, she wants no part of the police. Besides, these folks are good people under financial stress, same as us. They were just blowing off some steam. No need to complicate their lives further with arrests," Jeremiah said.

"What happened?

"I invited them in, made a pot of coffee and we sat around my kitchen table and talked while they sobered up. A couple of them may lose their businesses if they don't get paid soon," Jeremiah said sympathetically.

"You weren't a little concerned?"

"Not really. These boys weren't drunk enough to wander into an area where a bunch of Indians live looking for trouble. One time that happened was General Custer and we all know how that turned out."

"Indeed. How is Payton doing?" Pierce asked. "I've called her a few times, but it's hard to understand her. She sends me texts. But her texts have so many emojis, I wonder if she's texting in code."

Jeremiah laughed. "She's doing better. That contraption which is keeping her jaw shut is coming off in a couple of days."

Pierce worried about Jeremiah. With the line of credit gone, and the tribe buried under a mountain of debt, Jeremiah was beginning to show signs of strain and frustration. "How much longer can you last?" Pierce asked, referring to the state of the tribe's finances.

Jeremiah couldn't help but grimace. "If we use what we have left to service the credit line, I figure two months before we're out of money."

"Have you given some thought to what I mentioned the other day?"

Jeremiah shrugged. "You mean bringing in another investor?"

"It's the only way. The group here in Miami are not gaming guys. They're just businessmen who like big returns on their investments. They're willing to take some risk, but they have their limits which is why they pulled the line of credit."

"I get it," Jeremiah said.

"We need someone with deep pockets who understands the risks and the potential upside. Someone that can fund the tribe the rest of the way."

Jeremiah nodded unsure why anyone would be willing to throw money at a project that was now under the MCN's control.

"Dave tells me he hasn't had any luck getting a crew on site to seal up the building," Pierce said.

"He won't. It's being guarded 24-7 by Lighthorse officers. They run off anybody that steps foot on the property." Jeremiah took a deep

221

breath and let it out slowly. He couldn't suppress another vile thought about the MCN. "I'm afraid there won't be much of a building left when we can finally get back on the property." Jeremiah's words trailed off but were bitter, nonetheless.

Pierce listened to Jeremiah with growing concern. He rarely thought of his job in terms of love or hate. It was a profession, not something that easily affected his moods, good or bad. However, he was not just committed to the Kialegee cause in which he truly believed; he was emotionally invested in them.

With the casino held hostage, Pierce suspected it would be tough to sell an investor on the project. The individual that Pierce thought of that might be enough of a cowboy and gambler to take a flier on the Kialegee was none other than Michael Lanigan.

The Lanigan family was one of the original gambling pioneers. During the early years, Michael's father built and operated six of the first casinos on the famed Las Vegas strip. Today, the Lanigan family has diversified into oil, cattle, formula racing and aviation but still owns the largest and most profitable casino in Las Vegas.

Pierce didn't know Michael Lanigan personally, but thought he could gauge his interest through his legal counsel, Audrey Ross.

*****

Audrey was six months old when her family moved to Las Vegas. Her father was a pit boss in Michael Lanigan's casino. She attended UNLV and earned her degree in hospitality. During the summers she worked at Lanigan's casino. Audrey was smart and motivated, and she got things done. It didn't take long before Michael took a personal interest and mentored her. She was a rising star, and Michael grew to rely on her insightful opinions. After graduating from UNLV, Audrey attended Harvard Law School with Michael's blessing and with one condition, that she work for him after she got her law degree. Pierce and Audrey never crossed paths at Harvard or at alumni events, but they knew of each other mostly by reputation.

She wasn't beautiful, but some men found her appealing. There was an equal number that found her harsh and intimidating. She dressed conservatively but fashionably and always wore her hair pulled back. Audrey was a quick study, and apart from Michael she never worried about having a filter. She cut through bullshit and red tape with equal dexterity. She was smart as hell, cunning and a ball buster of the first order.

Audrey reviewed Pierce's proposal and was intrigued by the structure of the deal more than the gaming opportunity. While the casino in Broken Arrow represented an interesting but risky deal, she never came across an Indian gaming deal where the developer could own the casino. As she understood the federal law, non-Indians could only manage a casino for seven years. Pierce's proposal allowed a third party to own the casino. Under Pierce's structure after twenty-five years, the third party would turn over the casino ownership to the tribe. If it wasn't because someone with Pierce's stature in the legal community submitted the proposal, Audrey would have immediately thrown it in the garbage.

When she mentioned the deal to Michael, in a forceful voice fueled by his Irish temper he said, "Jesus Christ, Audrey! I'm in Aspen skiing with my family and you're interrupting me with this nonsense. We get pitched a hundred deals a week."

Audrey didn't wait long to fill the silent void that followed his admonishment. "Michael, have you ever seen an Indian casino deal for twenty-five years?"

"Impossible."

"I'm not so sure."

"If there was a way to manage an Indian casino for longer than seven years, why hasn't it been done by now?"

Audrey couldn't answer Michael's question. However, she told him that the law firm that submitted the proposal is an elite firm recognized for defending some of the world's largest financial institutions and companies. "They wouldn't risk their reputation by sending a proposal that didn't have merit. I also did a deep dive on Mr. Evangelista. Everyone I spoke to said he's a brilliant lawyer. One lawyer actually referred to him as a legal assassin."

Michael chuckled. "I like that."

Michael sensed something in Audrey's voice. "There's something else on your mind. What is it?"

A gut feeling preoccupied Audrey. Her first hunch was that Pierce did not randomly take a shot in the dark. She assumed that Pierce specifically identified Michael as a potential investor he believed would have an interest. Her second hunch was that Michael wasn't the only one to receive a proposal. It was only a matter of time before others would see the actual value in the proposal.

Audrey shrugged. "We're probably not the only ones that received this proposal."

Michael's voice was suddenly less agitated. "Call him and ask him to provide you with the legal support for a twenty-five-year deal. If you get it, send it over to our Indian law expert in Sacramento."

The next morning Audrey had an email.

> *Ms. Ross,*
> *Individually owned gaming operations on Indian Land is authorized in the code of federal regulations under 25 C.F.R. § 522.110(c). Part 522 allows tribes to license individually*

owned gaming operations provided that "not less than 60 per-cent of the net revenues of the income is paid to the Tribe."

I have also included two Indian Lands opinions issued by the NIGC which authorizes Non-Indian owned class II and Class III gaming operations.

These regulations allow gaming by non-tribal entities that are conducted on Indian lands. 25 U.S.C. 5 2710(b)(4)(A) ("A tribal ordinance or resolution may provide for the licensing or regulation of class II gaming activities owned by any person or entity other than the Indian tribe and conducted on Indian lands, only if the tribal licensing requirements include the re-quirements described below) . . . and are at least as restrictive as those established by State law . . . ").

Under these laws, the Tribe can enter a lease agreement with a renewable license for twenty-five years. As for proof of concept, you need look no further than your own backyard.

I have attached a copy of the order from the United States District Court, District of Nevada in CROSBY LODGE, INC. v. NATIONAL INDIAN GAMING TRIBAL GAMING COM'N 803 F.Supp.2d 1198 (2011). The Court specifically recognized that a non-Indian may own a gaming enterprise on Indian land.

Sincerely

Pierce Evangelista

When Audrey telephoned the senior partner at the Sacramento firm and requested his opinion, his first reaction was to laugh and tell her to save her money.

John Earl exhaled loudly, as if the request was so repugnant, he wanted to tactfully tell her she was wasting his valuable time. "Ms. Ross, I served on the committee responsible for drafting the Indian Gaming

Regulatory Act in 1988. I assure you there's no way for anyone to own the casino but the tribe. I could go on for hours explaining why it's illegal but, in a nutshell, they legislated the Act with the specific intent of keeping organized crime and gaming interests out."

Audrey read Pierce's email twice and was working her way through the documents. From what she read, she was starting to think that Pierce's structure was not only viable but could be a game changer.

"So, no matter how carefully nuanced the argument is in favor of a non-tribally owned casino, I can assure you it's a scam," Earl insisted.

Fifteen minutes into the call, Audrey massaged her temple as if suffering from a migraine. "Mr. Lanigan would like you to review the information," she ended the call, clearly exasperated.

Three days later Audrey Ross received a short email from the Sacramento firm.

> *Ms. Ross,*
> *Our firm reviewed the material forwarded by your office.*
> *We were surprised to learn that there indeed is legal authority*
> *for non-tribally owned gaming on Indian land.*
> *Cordially,*
> *Jeff Nelson*

Audrey noted that John Earl did not call or email. He seemed incapable of admitting he was wrong. Wasting no time, she forwarded the firm's email to Michael and followed it up with a text message. Ten minutes later Michael was calling.

"I'm cutting my trip short and flying back on Friday. See if you can schedule a meeting with the lawyer on Saturday in Las Vegas," his voice took on an excited tone.

Audrey knew Michael could be laser focused, impatient and unwavering when he wanted something.

Audrey started to speak but Michael cut her off. "Send me his number, I want to talk to him."

"Michael it's almost ten on the east coast. I'll call him in the morning and schedule the meeting."

"Text me the number," Michael ordered in a booming voice that was almost a full-blown yell.

Chapter Thirty-Nine

Mickey Lanigan started the Lanigan family gambling empire with money borrowed from his mother which he used to buy a stake in the Flamingo Hotel and Casino, becoming partners with mob accountant Meyer Lansky and his organized crime associates. Worried that associating with known criminals would hurt his future business prospects, two years later, Mickey sold his interest in the Flamingo and bought the El Cortez.

Over the years, Mickey engaged in land speculation and continued to buy stakes in Las Vegas casinos. His son Michael added to the family legacy by changing the blueprint for the casino industry and building the Barbary Coast Hotel and Casino on only 4.3 acres. Gone were the days of casinos needing large footprints of land. Casinos like the famed Flamingo which sat on a forty-acre parcel were relics. Michael understood the value of land in Downtown Las Vegas and accumulated over twenty-five percent of the available real estate. He doubled the Lanigan fortune by selling land to casino developers Steve Wynn and Sheldon Adelson. What soon followed was a concentration of fifty-one resorts and casinos on a small stretch of South Las Vegas Boulevard known as the Las Vegas strip. When the dust cleared, the Lanigans had an interest in eight of those casinos.

*****

At precisely 10:15 PM, Pierce's cell phone rang.

"Pierce, this is Michael Lanigan. I hope I'm not catching you at a bad time," he said.

Pierce glanced at his watch. "No, Mr. Lanigan. You're fine."

"Michael. If we're going to be in business together, please call me Michael," he said, making no effort to hide his enthusiasm. "I'm flying back to Las Vegas tomorrow and I'd like to meet with you on Saturday."

Pierce didn't answer right away. "After a brief pause, he said, "Michael, I'm in Miami. I'll check the flights and . . ."

"I know where you are," Michael interrupted. "I can have my plane at Miami International Airport waiting for you on Saturday morning."

Pierce didn't understand Michael's sense of urgency. It would be months before the court ruled on the Kialegee's lawsuit against the United States. It was impossible to know the reason after talking to him for only a few minutes. From personal experience, Pierce knew that men like Michael liked to be in control. Setting the time and place for the meeting gave him a degree of it. Time was not a luxury the Kialegee possessed. The money was about to run out and an unfinished casino without financial resources wasn't worth much. The tribe desperately needed a financial partner with deep pockets.

"I'll be there," Pierce said trying to read between the lines, still unsure of Michael's agenda.

*****

The Bombardier Global 6000 touched down in Miami just before sunrise. Michael insisted that Audrey meet with Pierce and size him up on the flight to Las Vegas. She sat at the bathroom vanity staring at her face in the mirror. She applied a bit of makeup to hide the circles beneath her eyes and arranged her hair with more care than usual. Then she dressed quickly—a woven cold shoulder blouse, plaid pencil skirt, black velvet Louboutins—and headed for the passenger lobby.

Audrey's eyes visually canvassed the lobby before settling on the man sitting in the tan leather chair sipping coffee. Even sitting, she could tell he had broad shoulders beneath the dark suit. She introduced herself as the senior vice president and chief counsel for Lanigan Holdings LLC. However, Audrey's position transcended any title the company could bestow on her. She was Michael's right hand. A trusted confidant, a bulldog when he needed her to be and surrogate daughter.

Pierce smiled as he stood up, extending his hand. "It's a pleasure to meet you Ms. Ross." Audrey grabbed it. "If you're ready, let's get going. We can talk on the jet," she said.

The flight attendant placed two expressos on the table between them and handed Pierce a menu.

Audrey poured sugar into her cup. "I ordered you a double espresso but if you prefer American coffee Nicole can brew a fresh pot."

"This is fine. Thank you," Pierce said.

Audrey slid the sugar towards him and stirred her coffee with a spoon. "I know in Miami the espresso already has sugar in it, but this is Italian not Cuban coffee so it's unsweetened," she cautioned.

Pierce nodded, took a sip and held on to his cup as the jet climbed to fifty-two thousand feet.

After breakfast, Audrey wasted little time pulling out her laptop and discussing Pierce's proposal. Instinctively, she liked the simplicity of the structure. Over the years, she had seen her fair share of partnership agreements that were so cumbersome that the projects never got off the ground. Despite the layers of complex regulations governing Indian casino projects, Pierce constructed a unique approach that elegantly worked around the regulatory limitations.

She was eager to dive into the agreements. Pierce studied Audrey as she addressed his proposal point by point. He could see that she was smart and much like Michael she liked to take control of every situation, no matter how small, from when they boarded the jet to the coffee they drank. He also guessed that she rarely failed to close a deal on terms that Michael Lanigan wanted. What he hadn't figured out was the reason behind the full court press Michael Lanigan and his team were giving him for a small casino in the middle of Tulsa.

Audrey took a deep breath; she clearly wanted an answer to a particular question. Finally, she asked. "How many are you pitching the Kialegee deal to?"

There was a short gap in the conversation as the flight attendant brought them two waters and disappeared.

Audrey took a calculated sip. "Well, we're not interested in getting into a bidding war. Just curious if you have been shopping this deal or whether you came to us first," she said, her smile coaxing him along.

"You're the first I've met with," he said. "I've only sent out five proposals."

Audrey did not bother to hide her displeasure. "I assume you're not going to tell me who else received a proposal."

Pierce managed both a frown and a smile at the same time, as if the idea was preposterous. "What I will tell you is that you're the only one to ask me for the law that allows for the structure. No one else has received an email from me that cites to the regulation. And that regulation is a virtual needle in a haystack."

Audrey obliged with a smile of her own as if she felt some relief, even if it was a brief reprieve.

"We have an Indian casino project that we've been looking at. Much bigger than yours, but the numbers don't work if we're limited to seven years. The tribe defaulted on a loan a few years back so no lender will touch them. If we can restructure that deal where we can control the property for 25 years, Michael will sign on the loan and develop the casino."

"*And there it is*," Pierce thought to himself. The reason for the high-pressure tactics.

Audrey followed up with an extended overview of the project and ended with the desire to retain Pierce to represent Michael as lead outside counsel.

He appeared to consider the offer for a moment. He stared at her with hard unblinking eyes as if the trip to Las Vegas to meet with Michael was a complete waste of his time. Pierce spoke softly, but firmly. "If all you wanted was my firm's help why go through all this trouble of flying me out? We could have handled this on a conference call."

"Michael doesn't hire anyone he hasn't met. As for the Kialegee project, we have a level of interest, if we can make some changes."

"Changes?" Pierce raised a curious eyebrow.

Audrey nodded. "We have some ideas for that project. Michael thought that by seeing our operation it would be easier for you to understand his vision.

"And what might that be?"

"I'll let Michael tell you. After we land, I'll give you a tour of our properties and then we'll meet Michael for dinner."

Chapter Forty

Michael stood five feet ten inches tall and easily tipped the scales at two hundred and sixty pounds. His rugby-playing physique at Creighton University was a thing of the past, thanks to countless beers and an insatiable sweet tooth. He blamed his drinking on his Irish Catholic upbringing and his addiction to desserts on his pastry chef.

Dinner at Michael's Gourmet room began with stone crabs. "We get the stone crabs flown in every morning from the same seafood supplier that supplies Joe's Stone Crabs in Miami," Michael bragged. "It's really a good story. About sixty years ago, give or take, Jessie Weiss, the owner of Joe's was losing big and out of money. He had already placed his watch and wedding ring in the pot. He had nothing left to bet, and my old man refused to extend him any more credit. All that crazy Hungarian had left was his exclusive deal for stone crabs. Joe's was already the largest buyer of stone crabs and controlled the market. My dad took the bet and Jessie lost that hand. He's been supplying us exclusively ever since."

Audrey put on her game face. She heard the same story more times than she could count. With each passing year, the stakes grew larger and the events surrounding the infamous bet more desperate. She figured that she would never know what really happened, but Micky and Jessie probably negotiated a deal for stone crabs with Michael paying handsomely. Michael's version was much more entertaining dinner conversation.

When the main course was finished so were Michael's stories. He instructed the wait staff to bring over the pastry cart and place several desserts on the table so that Pierce could sample all of them. Then for Audrey's benefit, who was shooting him a disapproving look, Michael said, "our pastry chef has won the James Beard award two years in a row. It would be a shame if you didn't taste them."

Audrey frowned. She'd heard that before.

"Do you drink scotch?" Michael asked Pierce.

Pierce smiled politely. "I'm afraid good scotch is wasted on me. I wouldn't be able to tell the difference between average and the really good stuff."

Michael held up three fingers signaling to the staff to bring three glasses of Balvenie 1961. "Smooth scotch is a lot like sex with a good woman. Deep and slick, warm and satisfying and she doesn't linger when you're finished."

Pierce lifted the glass of scotch to his face and ran it back and forth under his nose.

Michael raised his glass, his eyes moving from Pierce to Audrey. "To Mickey. Who used to say that the rest of the world saw things and asked why but he would rather dream and ask why not?"

Michael spoke generally about the Kialegee Casino project. He explained that the casinos in Tulsa were vulnerable because they were copying the Las Vegas casino model. Las Vegas catered to tourists. "Las Vegas has almost forty-five million visitors a year," he said. "Tulsa gets a minuscule fraction of that. The better business model is to go after the locals and let the others fight over the visitors."

Michael believed that like his casino the Kialegee casino should focus on people within a one-hour drive of the property. "That's why we have bowling alleys, a twenty-five-screen movie theater, eleven restaurants and 4,600 seat equestrian arena with a show floor all on our casino property."

Pierce began to understand Michael's approach.

"Our equestrian arena is booked fifty weeks out of the year with rodeos, horse shows and even BMX events," Michael boasted. "The bowling alleys have leagues almost every night."

Michael tapped on the rim of his glass letting the waiter know he wanted another scotch. "What I'm getting at is that my casino is full every day and night by more than just by folks that come here to gamble. But the people that come for the movies or to bowl or the folks that are in town for a horse show also gamble and they gamble in my casino."

Michael took a sip, his eyes never left Pierce. "All casinos are busy on the weekends. The war is waged and won on the other days. Choices, variety, options, I don't care what you call it but a casino with a steak house, a buffet and a showroom does not keep the locals coming back if there's a better alternative which doesn't exist in Tulsa."

Michael exhaled loudly, as he finally arrived at the climax of his long-winded pitch. "I'm willing to do the Kialegee casino project on two conditions. First, the Kialegee turns over the development rights and control for all seventy acres not just the nine acres that the casino is sitting on. I also need a thirty-five-year term not twenty-five years."

Pierce knew that the Tribe did not have any plans or resources to develop additional acreage. "What exactly are your plans for the property?"

There was a gap in the conversation, both Audrey and Pierce took a sip of scotch as Michael reached down next to his chair and grabbed a rolled-up site plan for all seventy acres.

"My team only had a day to pull this together so it's still pretty rough," he cautioned.

"A family-oriented lifestyle center with plenty of green space, entertainment and eating venues anchored by a casino," Michael announced as he unrolled the rendering and smoothed it out on the table.

The centerpiece was a large green rectangle with a long pool in the middle. Around the large green field was lush landscaping and a tree-lined pedestrian perimeter. The central green and pedestrian walkway was surrounded by buildings, each architecturally unique. Michael pointed to the tall building at one end of the rectangle. "That's a twelve-story luxury apartment tower. Next to it is a boutique hotel with a rooftop pool." A pause, a sip, and Michael continued to walk Pierce through the plan. "This would be the beer garden and microbrewery featuring local brews, and dining. Next to it is a country western bar. And on the far end is the new casino and the cineplex movie theater."

Pierce noticed that the new casino building was about three times the size of the current Kialegee casino. "What about the existing casino building?" Pierce asked.

"It's still there," Michael said pointing to it. "We're going to keep it for customers that prefer a more intimate casino setting and also have a casino with all the bells and whistles that we have here in Vegas," Michael said before turning his attention back to the green space in the center. "The water feature will be constructed with piping underneath so we can freeze the water and children can ice skate on it during the winter months."

Residential apartments, townhomes and other amenities such as gyms, coffee houses and other local shops filled in the remainder of the property.

"Phase 2 will have twenty-five hundred residences all within walking distance of the casinos. I've been playing with this concept for a long time. I had my people size it and place it on the Kialegee land." Michael said with eager precision.

"Why thirty-five years instead of twenty-five years?" Pierce asked.

"It will take anywhere between five-to-ten years before both phases are completed,"

Audrey interjected. "We need to capture a full twenty-five years of operation."

Pierce's face revealed nothing but deep concentration. Michael's plans for the property exceeded his expectations. It was a first-class project and the additional entertainment venues and activities would make the Kialegee property a premiere destination. With Michael Lanigan in charge of operations, the Kialegee's casino would have a huge advantage over the other casinos in Oklahoma. Persuading the tribe of the merit of Michael's development plan would hinge on the additional ten years. Tribes were reluctant to give up control of their land. Based on his brief experience with the Kialegee, Pierce wasn't sure how the Business Committee would respond to Michael's demands to add another ten years and include the entire site in the deal.

Pierce turned his attention from the rendering back to Michael. "You said you had two conditions."

Michael and Audrey shared a look. "Audrey believes that you're smarter than the lawyers I have working for me and I agree with her."

Pierce quickly realized where the conversation was heading. He ticked off several reasons why he couldn't work for Michael. His logic was sound with the most compelling reason being that he had unfinished business with the Kialegee. He needed to see the lawsuit against the United States through to the end.

Michael shrugged, breathed deeply and took a mouthful of scotch. "Fine, don't come work for me. You can represent me in my other deals as outside counsel."

Audrey leaned forward in her chair. "Once the deal with the Kialegee is finalized, we'd like you to get a conflict waiver signed by the Tribe. That way you would be free to represent Michael," she interjected in a tone that left little doubt that the condition was not negotiable. The faintest of smiles creased Michael's mouth. "We're going to do great things together. Starting with the Kialegee project."

Pierce knew his law firm would see landing a client like Michael Lanigan as a huge win. He did, however, have some reservations about switching sides. Up to this point, he had always represented Indian tribes. He would need to make it clear that while he would represent Mr. Lanigan, he could not be bought. But that was a conversation for another day.

Chapter Forty-One

WASHINGTON D.C.

Kathleen McDonough spent the last three hours analyzing the Kialegee Tribe's lawsuit. She had read it at least a half a dozen times. She was the best of the small cadre of high ranking United States Department of Justice lawyers. Thin and delicate in appearance, Kathleen was poised, tough, absorbed everything, noticed everything and remembered every detail. When she was thirty-four years old she was lead trial counsel for the prestigious Commercial Litigation Branch of the Department of Justice. Over the next five years, Kathleen won every major case she tried for the United States.

By the time she turned thirty-nine the rush she felt from the high-profile cases was gone.

Winning no longer filled the void created by the string of late nights of eating take-out and poring over legal briefs. She was beginning to feel an emptiness. A hole she realized could no longer be filled by professional accomplishments and accolades. What she wanted most she could never have if she continued to work in the Washington office. No matter how many lies she told herself Kathleen knew that success meant 100-hour weeks, interrupted dinners, cancelled vacations and no time for a family. She also realized with each promotion it would only get worse.

On October 3rd, Kathleen requested a transfer to the Idaho office. It was a lateral move which coming from the Washington office made the transfer seem like a demotion. It was like asking to be traded from the New York Yankees to the Portland Sea Dogs. Her request came as a shock to Ben P. Moran, the United States Attorney, since he had been considering Kathleen for a promotion to Deputy Assistant Attorney General in charge of the Commercial Litigation Branch.

On November 14th, the United States Secretary of the Interior's office was served with the Kialegee Tribe's lawsuit. Kathleen was in the middle of writing closing memos and transferring her case files when the call from the Attorney General came.

"Kathleen, I just received a copy of a lawsuit filed against Interior."

Her insides jumped. She didn't like the sound of that.

The Attorney General didn't waste any time. "I'd like you to handle it."

She wanted to return to her close out memos. "Sir, I'm flattered but I'm only here until the end of December."

"Idaho will have to wait."

Kathleen reluctantly agreed as if she had any real choice in the matter. She swallowed hard and said, "Yes, sir."

Before she could say another word, the line was dead. She was filled with disbelief and cursed herself for not having the courage to say "no". But she knew it wouldn't have changed anything. The fact that she worked twelve-hour days, six and sometimes seven days a week for the past sixteen years didn't count for much when the Attorney General set his mind on something.

Kathleen grimaced and looked out of her window. "Shit," she said under her breath with dread at what might lay ahead.

*****

Moses Black's request for a preliminary meeting with the Justice Department was not common practice. However, Moses always made it a point to request a meeting with opposing counsel immediately after filing a lawsuit. He liked to use it to intimidate the other side and give them a glimpse of what they were up against. Moses made it a point to always take charge of the meeting much the same way he took over the courtroom. He liked to compare it to a historical meeting of two generals in the middle of the battlefield to discuss concessions and terms for surrender. If there was no capitulation, then the battle began, and the terms of any future surrender would be more egregious than those originally proposed.

*****

At first Kathleen wondered how to handle the request. It was not customary for justice lawyers to meet with opposing counsel until after the judge issued a scheduling order. If Kathleen had her way, the case would be dismissed on a procedural technicality and there would be no need for that order. Like a grandmaster in chess, Kathleen had one move that could have the ripple effect that she hoped for. She could move to dismiss the lawsuit because the tribe failed to exhaust administrative remedies, a requirement that had to be satisfied when suing the government. By the time the tribe refiled the lawsuit, she would be in Idaho with her husband, hopefully pregnant and the case would belong to another justice lawyer.

But after doing her research on Moses Black and Pierce Evangelista, something clicked and she was suddenly torn between her desire to start her new life and the challenge of battling Pierce and Moses in the courtroom.

Like most successful trial lawyers, Kathleen was wired differently. They are driven, direct, aggressive and focused on winning. They are modern day gladiators and the courtroom is their arena. The better ones believe they can control or influence what happens in the courtroom and jump at the opportunity to test themselves against the best competition.

241

Kathleen was not immune to the competitive fire that burns in trial lawyers, so she decided to agree to Moses' request for a meeting.

*****

At twenty minutes after ten Moses Black cleared the security checkpoint at the Department of Justice building. Moses entered the conference room with a spring in his step and a trial briefcase in tow. Kathleen stood up to meet Moses. "Welcome. I'm Kathleen McDonough with the Department of Justice," she said pleasantly.

Moses grabbed her hand and with a beaming smile said, "Nice to put a face to a name. Please call me Mo." He turned his attention to the two gentlemen standing behind Kathleen.

"Lyman Ramparsad, Chairman of the National Indian Gaming Commission and this is John Harrington, my General Counsel."

"A pleasure to meet you both," Mo replied, shaking their hands.

After the pleasantries and small talk were concluded, Kathleen said, "You asked for the meeting Mo, so the floor is all yours."

Mo started with a methodical description of the treaties with the United States signed by the Kialegee Tribal Town and the promises contained in them. He stressed that the tribe despite being federally recognized and owning land presently has no rights to govern. There were several points during the meeting when Mo belabored a topic beginning with heartfelt ramblings about a tribe beset by deepening poverty, alcoholism, and drug addiction.

Kathleen and the others politely listened. After about an hour, Lyman Ramparsad began to shift uncomfortably. He listened for a few minutes glancing at his watch several times before finally saying, "Everything you've said this morning is in your complaint. Do you mind telling me the purpose of this meeting?"

Mo said nothing for a moment. He just stared at the Chairman then forced a smile. "I was wondering if I'm missing something. Because after reading the treaties, it's clear that the Kialegee has treaty rights and they're being ignored by the United States. So, do you mind telling me why?"

John Harrington looked annoyed. "The Chairman is not going to take part in your fishing expedition. If you have nothing else, this meeting is over."

Mo sat back in his chair, smiled and winked at Harrington. "But I do. I'm just getting started."

Kathleen could see that the meeting was beginning to unravel. To ease the tension and bring the meeting to a productive end she said, "As a professional courtesy, I want to tell you that the United States will be filing a motion to dismiss your lawsuit for failure to exhaust administrative remedies."

"I see," Mo said. "But just humor me for a moment. Forget about procedure and focus on what's right. The Kialegee are a federally recognized tribe and are being denied the right to govern on their land and pursue economic development to improve the lives of their members. I'm sure you've read the treaties by now. Think about the merits of the tribe's case."

Harrington scoffed at the comment. Kathleen kept a neutral expression. "We don't get to the merits," she said.

Mo shrugged, fixed Kathleen with a look, and said, "I'm not so sure."

Kathleen slid a copy of the government's motion to dismiss across the table towards Mo.

"There's no final agency action denying the Kialegee's sovereign rights. Until that occurs the tribe cannot sue. It's all laid out in the motion."

Mo had maneuvered Kathleen to the exact spot he wanted her. The legal profession is many things, but stripped down to its basic elements, it's about research and being better prepared than the other side and adjusting to the curveball when it comes and since there's no case with a perfect set of facts it almost always does.

Mo waved his hand at the document as if he was shooing a fly away. Then he reached into his briefcase, fished out a red folder and handed it to Kathleen. "The Kialegee Tribe exhausted administrative remedies over thirty years ago when they were denied a tribal court. That counts as a denial of sovereign rights and a final agency action. It's all in the folder."

Mo had just hit Kathleen's curveball out of the park and for a split second the expression on her face looked like a pitcher that had just given up the tying home run in the ninth inning. Then back to a poker face. "First I've heard of this," she sounded skeptical. Thinking on her feet, she countered, "You have a statute of limitations problem. The tribe should have sued at the time when they were denied."

Mo had anticipated that response. He had the gift of all great tacticians. He could focus on the smallest detail and never lose sight of the overall picture. "The statute of limitations doesn't apply. The Tribe isn't appealing the government's decision. It is being proffered to establish a foundation that the tribe has already been administratively denied sovereign rights. The NIGC's advisory opinion issued last year while not a final agency action reinforces the government's actions thirty years ago."

Kathleen nodded slightly; it was a novel argument, but she pretended to be still unconvinced. After a long moment of thoughtful calculation, she said, "Thank you, Mo. We will review the information and let you know if we still intend to file a motion to dismiss. Is there anything else?"

Mo nodded. "Actually, there is." He wanted them angry, foaming at the mouth. Ready for a no-holds-barred brawl. The only way to get it was by throwing hand grenades. He reached back into his trial bag for a blue folder. Staring at the Chairman with a look that would be impossible to mistake for anything but disdain, Mo handed the folder to Harrington. "This is a public records request for all the Chairman's records. We want all communications with the MCN for the last twenty-four months. All meeting logs, phone calls, texts and emails from all phones and email addresses, including personal ones. To be clear, all communications with the MCN, any representative of the MCN including but not limited to their employees, lawyers and lobbyists."

The Chairman looked like he wanted to reach across the table and strangle Mo. He mumbled something under his breath and then asked, "What does this have to do with the Kialegee's lawsuit?"

Mo calmly looked at the Chairman. "I don't have to answer that. Under public records law, I'm entitled to it." It was a shot in the dark, but the Chairman's reaction was enough to convince Mo that he might be on to something.

The Chairman spun out of his chair abruptly. "We're done here. Let's go John," he snapped and headed for the door.

Harrington eased from his chair and with a nod, slid out of the conference room.

Kathleen's face didn't reveal much, her voice was flat and steady as if measuring every word.

"Is there anything else?"

Mo looked at Kathleen and felt a sense of accomplishment. The gloves were off, and Mo was relishing the fight. A smile creased his face. "No, that's all for today."

Chapter Forty-Two

KIALEGEE TRIBAL HEADQUARTERS
WETUMKA, OKLAHOMA

"The Business Committee is ready for you. Please follow me," the young woman, Jennie said in an energetic and reverent voice. Her exact title was secretary to the Chief, but her responsibilities were rather vague. She was loyal to Jeremiah and a formidable gatekeeper respected for her ability to shoot down unwanted visitors.

Pierce had only visited the tribal headquarters once. But something so unprecedented as beating the State of Oklahoma and suing the United States for the Kialegee's treaty rights made him something of a local celebrity to most tribal members.

Seated around a long table was the Kialegee Business Committee. At the head was Jeremiah. To his immediate left was Juanita. Next to her was Cora Jimboy, a retired teacher who had taught almost everyone seated at the table. Then Roley Buck, a rugged old cuss who rarely put off fishing to attend a meeting, but this one warranted it. He looked much older than sixty-five, with no front teeth and thick wrinkles. Nora Johnson sat on the opposite end of the table.

Even after being censured by the Business Committee for meeting with the MCN without the tribe's approval, Jeremiah still suspected her of secretly feeding information to the MCN. He was careful and only discussed the casino with Nikki and the three other committee members. When Nora was present, Jeremiah deferred all discussion concerning the casino. But a tall white man built like a linebacker and wearing a suit was impossible to hide in Wetumka and news that Pierce was in town with an opportunity to help the tribe save the casino had made it to Nora and there was no keeping her away.

All the folding chairs were taken by tribal members. Folks stood two rows deep, shoulder to shoulder.

Jeremiah started the meeting by introducing Pierce to the tribal members in case there was anyone that didn't know him, at least by reputation. When Pierce talked, every eye in the room was focused on him. He began by telling the tribe about Michael Lanigan and his offer to partner with the tribe. There were a few whispers in the crowd. Pierce handed out to each Business Committee member a smaller version of Michael's site plan for all seventy acres. He took his time walking them through the entire proposed development. When he finished, he laid out Michael's terms.

Nora gave an indignant snort. "Thirty-five years! Another white man trying to take advantage of us."

A look of annoyance passed across Jeremiah's face. "I don't see how someone spending a half a billion dollars to develop our site and giving the tribe half of everything is taking advantage of us."

"Of course, you don't," Nora glowered.

Juanita exhaled and shook her head in disbelief. "It takes years to repay a half a billion dollars."

"Then maybe we shouldn't do it. That's our land. We shouldn't turn it over to some white man, we don't even know. If you ask me, dealing with white folks has never turned out good for us." Nora's tone was acidic as always. A few heads in the crowd nodded.

Cora cleared her throat, twirling the rolled-up site plan between her nervous fingers. "Chief, I have a question for the lawyer."

"Go ahead."

Cora peeked out over her glasses. "Mr. Evangel . . . what happens to the tribe if you lose the case?" She started somewhat sheepishly. "The tribe is in no condition to pay back a half a million, let alone a half a billion dollars."

Pierce watched the proceedings in his usual perceptive way, reading between the lines and looking for the motive behind the questions and comments. There was little doubt in his mind that Michael Lanigan's proposal was more than a lifeline for the Kialegee Tribe. It was an opportunity for sustained economic development that would change their lives for the better. He was also sensitive to their concerns and fear that it could all be taken away. The Kialegee's history was littered with broken promises and a stolen birthright. His eyes moved across the faces in the crowd before setting back on Cora.

"There are several factors to consider. First, the tribe is using the money it borrowed to build the casino to make payments on the line of credit your investors arranged for the project. Before long, you will run out of money. Until the court rules on the Kialegee's lawsuit, borrowing more money to pay back the money the tribe already owes is next to impossible. Mr. Lanigan has agreed to pay off the tribe's debt for the development rights for all seventy acres. Win or lose the case the tribe would have no debt."

Nora frowned and dismissed the proposal as absurd. "There's got to be a catch."

Jeremiah tensed, but not in a way that would be visible to the others. He bit his tongue and sat with arms folded across his chest; knowing Nora would challenge everything that Pierce said.

"There's no catch," Pierce corrected her.

Pierce looked at the silent faces staring at him and turned Nora's indictment into a question. "If the tribe didn't have to pay back their existing loan under any circumstance would you support it?" Pierce asked Nora.

Pierce's audacity caught her by surprise.

Nora glared at Pierce. "I won't support thirty-five years."

Roley seemed to soak the words in for a second, then cleared his throat. When he spoke, he spoke with a deep voice and seemed to weigh every syllable. His measured demeanor contrasted with his grizzled exterior. "I trust our lawyers," he said standing up so everyone in the room could see him. "What some of us up here seem to be missing is that this is an insurance policy. Win or lose in court we don't have to pay back the money we owe. Win or lose we're better off than we are right now."

Roley picked up a cup, spat in it, wiped his mouth on his sleeve, and said, "Now, I think we're gonna win this case in Washington." He relied on idioms that the members related to. "But as a tribe, if it weren't for bad luck, we wouldn't have any luck at all. So, we need to hope for the best, but plan for the worst. When I saw this plan for our land, I thought I was dreaming. If we have to give up control of our land for thirty-five years and we get to own all of this," he said, holding up the site plan. "I'm for it."

Juanita nodded her head in agreement. Cora wore a worried frown and asked the Chief if she could ask the lawyer another question. Jeremiah nodded.

"Mr. Attorney," she started. "Let's say we agree to the proposal and Mr. Lanigan pays our loan off but sits on our property without developing it. What happens then?"

"The tribe will have a development agreement with Mr. Lanigan that will establish timetables for developing the property. The tribe can cancel the agreement if the project isn't developed."

Nora's face twitched as if Pierce's response had caused her physical pain. Her gaze jumping from Pierce to Nikki and back again. "I'd like to hear from the tribe's real lawyer," she said brazenly trying to create a sense of doubt among the tribal members. Some tribal members had grown tired of the risks taken by Jeremiah with nothing to show for them but debt and an unfinished building. Cracks were forming. Some members were questioning the wisdom of standing up to the MCN. Jeremiah needed one last push. Once the tribe defaulted on the credit line, that's all Nora would need to recruit the younger tribal members to her side.

Nora didn't bother to hide her skepticism. "Isn't it true that even if we have a provision in the agreement that lets us cancel, Mr. Lanigan has the money and influence to keep our property tied up for years? So, there is a lot of risk to the tribe." Her words were an overstatement, but not without a kernel of truth.

Nikki's lips pursed into a perceptible frown. Nora glared at Nikki, but she refused to look away.

"That depends."

"On what?"

"Well, there's a big risk that the tribe won't be able to pay the investors and lose almost everything if they don't partner with someone that's willing to help. That's more than a risk actually that's reality." She let everyone consider that for a moment. "Then there's the unlikely scenario where Mr. Lanigan pays off the Tribe's investors and chooses not to develop, keeping the tribe and the property tied up in court for years." Nikki paused again. "The only way Mr. Lanigan makes money after spending millions paying off the tribe's obligations is by developing the property. There'd be no reason for him to sit on the property," she let out a long wavering breath. "So, I don't consider that risk to be real. I agree with Pierce.

We can draft the agreement to protect the tribe by giving them the right to cancel if he doesn't perform."

Nora's anger grew with every word. Roley's toothless, thin-lipped mouth made a whistling sound when he exhaled. "Nora when are you going to stop this bullshit charade?"

Roley's question was met with laughter. The skin on Nora's cheeks started to burn. "Chief, Roley's comments are out of order!" Nora said, her voice booming throughout the room.

Jeremiah refused to be drawn into a fight. He had heard enough, and his patience was finished. "I'll entertain a motion."

"I'll make a motion to approve Mr. Lanigan's proposal." Juanita glanced over at Nikki, "and instruct our lawyers to put something in the agreement that protects the tribe's property."

"Second," Roley said before shoving more chew into his mouth.

Nora snarled. "Chief, I'm not done."

Roley glared at Nora, "Chief, we have a motion and a second. Call the question."

Jeremiah motioned for silence. The murmurs in the crowd subsided.

"All in favor?" Jeremiah counted four hands including his own.

"All opposed?"

Nora was the sole dissenting vote.

*****

An hour after the meeting ended, Pierce and Jeremiah walked out of the tribal headquarters. Jeremiah lit a cigarette, exhaled a cloud of smoke and shook his head.

"You okay representing Lanigan?"

"It's the only way the tribe gets the money they need so I have to be okay with it."

Jeremiah took a pull on his cigarette. "I would have done the same thing if I was in his shoes. You're a good lawyer," Jeremiah said, cigarette smoke rolling from his mouth as he spoke.

Payton was waiting outside next to Jeremiah's truck. There were traces of dark bluish color still visible on her face.

"Your face is looking better," Jeremiah said as they closed the gap between them.

Payton rolled her eyes. "Thanks pops."

Jeremiah looked at Pierce. "Couple of weeks ago she looked like an extra in one of my favorite shows. The one with all the zombies."

"Hey Clark" Payton said, lifting her hand in the air waiting for a high five.

Pierce smiled at Payton. "So, how are you doing?"

"I'm good. The painkillers helped a lot. When are you heading back?"

"Tomorrow."

"Can you push it back a day? There's something I want to show you?" She asked.

Pierce had been meaning to catch up with Payton. They seemed to be tangled together ever since she started helping him with the casino project.

Pierce nodded. "I think I can swing that."

"Great. I'll swing by your hotel in the morning around eight. And lose the suit," she grinned.

Chapter Forty-Three

At 8:15 Payton pulled up to the hotel. Pierce was standing by the entrance wearing a T-shirt and a pair of grimy jeans. She fixed her almond shaped eyes on him in a way that suggested that she approved of the look. Pierce slid into the passenger seat and handed her a cup of coffee. He had barely finished putting on his seatbelt when the jeep sped up abruptly.

"So, where are we headed to?"

"Bentonville, Arkansas. It's about a two-hour drive from here. When you described the different businesses centered around a green space, it made me think of it. Lots of shops and people just milling around shopping and eating in the square. It's a cool place. It has a coffee shop I like. I thought you should see it."

Pierce took a big sip of coffee. "Sounds interesting."

Payton gave him a sideways glance. "Relax Clark. Let's have some fun today. Do you think you can do that?"

He fought back a grin. "Okay. I think I can manage that."

"Fun fact about Bentonville," she said, turning onto Interstate 44. "It's the birthplace of Walmart. Sam Walton opened his first store on the Bentonville town square and called it "Walton's 5 and 10. It's still there by the way."

Pierce nodded thoughtfully and looked at Payton.

When he got into the jeep, his only thoughts were spending a pleasant day with a pretty lady, but it was hard for him to ignore what she'd been through.

"I'd understand if you don't want to talk about it. But I'd like to know what happened to you on the night of the raid."

Payton frowned but otherwise did not respond. She pressed down on the accelerator. After a short moment of silence, she said, "Here's a not so fun fact about Bentonville. Thousands of Creeks and Cherokee passed through there. It was part of the Trail of Tears when they were forced to leave their homes in Georgia."

They drove in silence for a while before Payton spoke again. Finally, she said, "There really isn't much to say. The MCN raided us and one officer pulled me into a back room and tried to rape me. When I resisted, he hit me with his gun and broke my jaw." Payton avoided eye contact. Her mind was elsewhere. She gripped the wheel tightly and stared straight ahead. Whatever she was thinking, she revealed nothing.

"Did anything else happen?"

Payton glanced over. "He didn't rape me. If that's what you're asking?"

Pierce sat up and stared out the window.

Payton seemed to read his mind. "There's nothing anyone could have done. So, don't blame yourself. I need you to let this go." Her eyes narrowed slightly. "Can you do that for me?"

His blue eyes flashed almost imperceptibly at her words. "I suppose so."

Pierce's voice had an undertone that seemed to suggest that as long as the MCN continued to prosecute Payton, he would not let it go.

✳✳✳✳✳

Payton pulled into the 21c parking structure next to the Museum Hotel Bentonville. She couldn't resist walking through the hotel, which seamlessly integrated works of art throughout the space featuring large-scale sculptures such as a Fleetwood Cadillac limousine covered in thousands of coins to a renowned collection of American artists. Art aficionados referred to the small museum in Northwest Arkansas as a countrified Guggenheim.

They wandered through the town square, which had turned into a popular destination featuring trendy restaurants and specialty shops all encircling a park in the center. The benches and tables in the park were all filled with mothers chatting away while children chased each other around water-spewing fountains. The confederate soldier statue encircled by seasonal flowers had been a source of conflict in the small city. Some argued that the statue commemorated a part of the city's history while the majority contended that it served as a stark reminder of the city's pro-slavery and hate filled past.

They stopped for lunch, and afterwards strolled without purpose, visiting the different shops and occasionally engaging in small talk with the various shop owners and employees. When they passed Onyx Coffee Lab Payton's eyes brightened. "We have to go in here," she said, dragging Pierce by the arm through the door. "This is one of my favorites. You should bring them to Broken Arrow. This place would be perfect."

The barista said their coffee was ready, and Payton grabbed the two cups. She sat in a chair across from Pierce.

Pierce stared at her intently. "So, can we discuss the criminal charges filed against you by the MCN?"

Payton's spine stiffened, and she pulled back. She shot him a hard look like she wanted to lash out. "Nikki is handling it. No need for you to get involved," she said plainly, not wanting to start a tense conversation.

Pierce reached across the table and touched her hand. She instantly felt a confusing combination of adrenaline and peace.

"Payton, I'm not trying to interfere. I'm very good at what I do. I'm just trying to help," he said trying to sound reassuring.

Payton let out a long wavering breath, "I know." She gazed out the window, lost in a world of jumbled thoughts. Finally, she said, "I don't want to talk about my case. I asked you to come here so you could see some possibilities for our site. I wanted to leave all the other stuff behind me. At least for today." Her voice cracked slightly.

"I'm having fun. Thank you for that." Pierce said, changing the subject and trying to lighten the mood.

"Me too," Payton said, and managed a quick smile, a forced one that lasted only a second.

The sun was setting on the afternoon. Pierce was almost done with his coffee. "We probably should head back."

Payton shook her head. "A few more minutes." She sat silently but kept looking directly at Pierce. "Can I ask you a personal question?" She kept her gaze fixed on him. Her expression open and warm.

He was relieved that the tension had eased slightly. "If I say no, you're going to ask me anyway."

She smiled. "You get me, Clark. So, are you seeing anyone?" Payton asked, eyebrows arched, radar suddenly on high alert. There had been signs, furtive glances and an instant connection that had her silently wondering. Ever since their chance meeting at the bar when Pierce drove Payton home, she felt as though they were just a step or two from getting undressed. But she also had an inkling where his boundaries were. Despite their mutual attraction, Pierce was there to help her tribe secure their treaty rights and build a casino not help himself to the Chief's daughter.

He considered his response for a moment. He took a deep breath and thought of ways to artfully dodge the question. When he could think of none, he said, "Not really."

Payton remained silent, wanting him to say more.

It was hard for Pierce to reflect on relationships with women without using the words heartache and devastation. He took a slow sip of coffee while he calculated how much to say.

Finally, he admitted that his first love abruptly ended their marriage. Years later, he gave love a second chance and the woman he began to build a life with was murdered by a drug dealer he had helped extradite to the United States. To protect everyone he cared for, Pierce jettisoned his friends and family and pursued an empty and untethered existence. "Flying solo just seems to suit me."

Payton gave an innocent shrug. "I'm sorry Pierce. I had no idea."

The memory brought a slightly embarrassed frown to Pierce's face. "No need to be sorry. That was a long time ago. I was just explaining why I don't have serious relationships."

"Don't be so provincial."

After Payton left Los Angeles, she didn't trust men. The few relationships she had were brief and barely rose above the level of one-night stands. But that all stopped when she met Pierce. He felt different and the sense of possibility was a small part of the reason she became invested in the casino project. It gave her an excuse to stay close to him.

"What do you mean?"

"What I mean is that there's more than just one type of relationship." Payton's unblinking eyes were suddenly filled with amusement. She leaned in and lowered her voice, "Do I really have to spell it out for you?" She left this rich little nugget hang in the air for a moment as she sauntered over and got a refill.

Payton was twenty-four, but the disparity in their ages looked much less. A lifetime of training and healthy eating habits made Pierce look much younger than thirty-eight.

Payton suppressed a smile because it would be inappropriate given the fact that Pierce had just shared the details of his past relationships with her. At least he was finally talking to her. That was a big step.

The way Pierce's eyes shifted suggested that he was feeling increasingly uncomfortable with the topic of conversation.

Pierce's phone chimed and he glanced down and read the text. Changing the topic, he said, "It's getting late. We should head back."

"Fine, but this conversation isn't over," Payton said, feeling a little selfish.

*****

The sun had slipped away along with the afternoon. The temperature dropped, and the wind nipped at their faces. Payton reached out and grabbed Pierce's arm and nuzzled up against him for warmth as they hurried towards the car.

When they got back to Broken Arrow, they pulled over on the shoulder of the Creek Turnpike. They were standing by the jeep overlooking the Kialegee property and exchanging ideas, when an SUV with Muscogee Nation plates and flashing lights raced towards them and came to a screeching stop just behind them. Payton stiffened. Then she turned away, as if the sight of him made her uneasy. "We should get in the car," her voice was quick and nervous.

A uniformed officer wearing a scowl walked towards them. "License and registration."

Pierce shook his head. "Do you mind telling me why you rolled up on us demanding that I give you my license?"

His question was met with a blank, hollow stare. "License and registration."

The officer recognized Payton and glared at her like he might erupt at any moment. "If I have to ask a third time, I'll arrest the both of you."

Pierce dismissed the comment with a doubtful expression but could see that the situation was unravelling and remembered the illegal raid. Reaching into his pocket, Pierce pulled the license from his wallet and handed it to him.

The officer glared at Payton. "Yours too."

Payton gritted her teeth, determined not to show the least bit of fear.

"She wasn't driving officer. Unless you have probable cause, you have no authority to require her to give you her license."

The officer stepped closer to Pierce as if he might throw a punch. "You're trespassing on Indian land and this badge gives me all the probable cause I need."

Pierce managed a smile, but it was clear his patience was being put to the test. Reaching into his wallet, he handed the officer a second license. "This is my Oklahoma license to carry a concealed weapon. The turnpike is state land and we're standing on it." Pierce pointed to the fence post about fifty yards downhill from where they were standing. "The Kialegee's land starts down there. So, you're mistaken."

Pierce smiled slightly. It was more of a reflex than a sign of deference. "I'm not Indian which means you have no legal authority to arrest or detain me."

The officer sneered. "Not true. You made an illegal turn back there, so I'm allowed to stop you and call for backup from the highway patrol."

"You will have a problem proving that."

"And why is that?"

"You have a body cam which has been recording this entire incident. You not only have no evidence of an illegal turn. Your cam footage will show that we weren't moving and already outside of the car when you approached us. If you turn it off or the footage disappears, you're going to have even a bigger problem."

Pierce stared at the officer with a confidence bordering on insolence. The officer started to speak but Pierce cut him off. "You have my license. If you don't recognize my name your attorney general will. I suggest you call him and listen carefully because you will want to get this right. If you detain me fifteen more minutes, I will file a §1983 claim against the tribe in federal court. The tribe has no sovereign immunity from violations of constitutionally protected rights and they're liable for your misconduct. I'm the lawyer that just beat the state of Oklahoma on behalf of the Kialegee and sued the United States. Suing the MCN would be just another day at the office for me. You're not scared of me because you don't know better, but if your AG has any sense, he'll tell you to cut us loose," Pierce said, barely holding his anger back.

The officer took the license and stared at Pierce for a few seconds before walking back to his vehicle and making a phone call.

A second SUV swerved in front of Payton's jeep with its overhead lights flashing. The officer jumped out of the vehicle pointing his firearm at Pierce. Pierce's eyes flashed with anger, but he bit his tongue and smiled.

Minutes later, the first officer walked back and handed Pierce his license. "You can go," he snapped at Pierce.

Pierce glanced at his watch and then looked at the officer with an expression of vague disappointment. "You made it with two minutes to spare."

Payton was already in the car anxious to leave by the time Pierce slid into the driver's seat. At that moment he caught her looking at him. She watched as his eyes locked on her.

"Are you okay?" He asked.

She had never seen eyes as intense as his and they caused her to momentarily forget his question.

Payton smiled warmly. "Yeah, and thanks for what you did back there."

Pierce shifted the car into drive. "Sure."

"I didn't know you carried a gun."

"I don't. I just have a license to carry one."

Payton gave him a confused look.

"I just wanted him to think I might have one."

Payton reached out and nudged his shoulder. "You're something else."

As Payton looked at Pierce, she decided right then and there that she was going to sleep with him, and she would not take no for an answer. She'd never seen anyone take command of a situation like he did. He exuded a calm confidence that made her insides quiver. The fact that he was her father's lawyer and older than her didn't bother her in the slightest. In certain ways it made it even more exciting.

"I admit the timing isn't the best, but since I rarely get to see you, I'm just going to put it out there. I think you should ask me out on a real date," she said.

Pierce let out a long breath. "I'm not sure that would be smart."

Payton leaned back against the car door, placed a hand under her chin and gave Pierce an appraising look. "Why not?"

Pierce shrugged. "It's not that simple. There are rules that prohibit lawyers from dating clients."

Payton actually laughed at that. "I'm not your client. The Kialegee Tribe is. Besides, Nikki and Noah both seem to think that you have feelings for me," Payton smiled.

Pierce did, but he wasn't ready to say it.

Chapter Forty-Four

UNITED STATES DISTRICT COURT FOR
THE DISTRICT OF COLUMBIA

Senior U.S. District Judge Dorothy M. Hogan's clerk issued an order setting the hearing date for the Kialegee's motion for summary judgement in the case to decide the tribe's treaty rights. When Mo saw that the scheduling order setting the hearing date was only four weeks away, he was mildly surprised since it usually took months to get one.

"My, my," Mo said as he dialed Pierce's phone. When Pierce answered, Mo didn't bother to say hello or ask how the meeting went with the Tribal Business Committee.

"We got Judge Hogan, he said. "Hearings in four weeks."

"Four weeks? That's fast," Pierce said.

"We've done some research on Judge Hogan. She's a good judge. Doesn't cut the government any slack. She put a stop to National Security Agency domestic internet metadata collection by the Attorney General and blocked the enforcement of President Donald Trump's ban on transgender individuals from serving in the military."

"From the looks of it, she doesn't want to sit on this case," Pierce said.

Mo agreed. "Four weeks will be here before you know it. We need to get busy if we're going to be ready," Mo said.

*****

At 10 AM the courtroom came to order. Judge Hogan picked up some notes and adjusted her reading glasses. "Okay. Kialegee Tribal Town versus Secretary Zinke."

Moses stood to address the court. "Good morning, Your Honor. Moses Black for the Kialegee Tribal Town, the Plaintiff. With me is Mr. Pierce Evangelista."

"Good morning your Honor. I'm Kathleen McDonough for the United States."

"Good morning. Well, there's a lot here. I guess the question I have which may help me think about these important issues is this: Does the United States dispute the content of the historical documents, letters, legislation, and cases cited and attached as exhibits by the Plaintiff?"

Kathleen McDonough smiled. "No, your Honor. We do not dispute the authenticity or relevance of the documents."

"Then I guess my follow-up question to defense counsel is why are the parties unable to resolve Plaintiff's claims?"

"Well, Your Honor, we disagree on the interpretation of the documents, not their authenticity which dictates the fundamental nature of the dispute," Kathleen said.

"You're talking about the meaning of the term 'Muscogee' in the treaties?"

"Yes."

"All right," Judge Hogan turned to Moses. "Mr. Black, you may proceed."

"Thank you, your Honor. This case centers on whether the Kialegee Tribal Town, a member of the historic Creek Nation is a party under the treaties. We contend that, the Kialegee Tribal Town, a federally recognized Indian Tribe and member of the historic Creek Nation has equal rights and shares jurisdiction over all lands within the Creek Reservation."

Mo walked the Court through the history and treaties signed by the Creek Confederacy, pointing out that in each instance leaders for all the tribal towns were not only present but also signatories.

Mo was smooth. There were no wasted words, no hyperbole. Nothing but a carefully nuanced argument.

Pierce followed Mo by illustrating to the court three specific instances where the United States breached the treaties. He argued that the Department of Interior's refusal to recognize the Kialegee's treaty rights was economically motivated to protect both the Cherokee and Creek casinos which are located within 10 miles from the Kialegee's land.

Kathleen rose and said, "Your Honor the government's position is that the Muscogee Tribe alone exercises jurisdiction over the entirety of those lands that were explicitly reserved for the whole Creek Nation. The treaty language is clear. Since the removal of the Creeks in 1832 to Oklahoma the Creek's reservation lands was exclusively reserved to and under the sole jurisdiction of the Muscogee Creek Nation, not the tribal towns."

Judge Hogan interrupted Kathleen. "But the Muscogee Creek Nation referred to in the 1832 treaty is not the present Muscogee Nation."

"We contend that it is your honor. Plaintiff's argument that it is a different tribe because the United States legislatively terminated the tribe is incongruent and unpersuasive. The Muscogee Nation never actually ceased to exist or operate as a government."

Kathleen did a skillful job in presenting the government's legal position and articulately detailed the rules for interpreting Indian treaties. She argued that as far as the Muscogee Indians were concerned, they never ceased to exist as a tribal government and understood the treaty to mean that the land was reserved to the nation as a whole. "Therefore, the term had a simple and clear meeting to them, and the treaties have to be resolved in favor of the Indians as they understood them. The Muscogee

Indians understood the language in the treaties to set the land aside to be governed by them as one nation. Thank you, your Honor," Kathleen said, and took her seat.

"Does the Plaintiff have a response?"

"A brief one," Pierce glanced over at Kathleen and gave a subtle nod. "The controlling canon of construction raised by Ms. McDonough solidifies this point. Specifically, the Indian Canon of Construction establishes that treaties and statutes are meant to be understood as the Indian signatories understood them at the time. No evidence has been proffered that the tribal towns, signatories to the treaties understood them to mean that they were giving up rights to govern their land. The whole Creek Nation means all. Merriam Webster's dictionary defines the term 'whole' to mean 'undiminished.' The exact opposite of what the defendant proposes. Thank you, your Honor."

Judge Hogan nodded at both counsel. "Well, counsel, you've done a great job of pointing out how complicated this case is and it's going to take me some time to write a careful decision and I just ask you to bear with me. I'll try to get something back to you in a month or two."

Chapter Forty-Five

OKMULGEE, OKLAHOMA

Travis Alexander's phone rang, and after a quick look at the screen he picked up.

"Good morning, Lyman. So, how did the argument go this morning?"

"Decent. The U.S. attorney did a good job. But the Kialegee's attorneys were every bit as good as advertised. Hard to say which way the judge will rule. I couldn't read her, but I think we have better than a fifty-fifty chance." His tone suggested that he wasn't convinced.

Travis thought about the possibility that the Kialegee might get a favorable decision while Lyman continued to drone on about the particulars of the hearing.

"When do you expect the judge to rule?" Travis asked.

"She said in a couple of months."

"Okay thanks. Anything else?"

"Do you want me to call the Chief?"

Travis thought about it for a few beats before answering the question. "No, thanks. This is something better handled in person. But try to be available in case the Chief has questions."

"You got it."

*****

The knock on the Chief's door was hesitant but insistent.

"Yes, what is it?"

Mary opened the door just wide enough to poke her head in. "Chief, I know you asked not to be disturbed this morning, but the Attorney General is here, and he says its important."

"What's so important that it can't wait a couple of hours?"

"It has to do with the Kialegee lawsuit Chief."

The Chief's eyes narrowed. "Tell him to come in and ask Police Chief Hawkins to join us."

Travis Alexander spoke for a few minutes without interruption before the Chief felt his mouth go dry.

"Overall, Lyman said that the U.S. attorney did a good job. He was troubled, however, by the judge's comment that the historic Muscogee Creek Nation mentioned in the treaties is not the same tribe as the MCN. In fact, Lyman said that the judge commented that they're different tribes."

The Chief pressed his palms against his temples, feeling them begin to throb. He had allowed his personal feelings about the tribal towns force an obvious error. While a small isolated casino in Broken Arrow would have siphoned off some of the River Spirit casino's business now they were facing something much worse. There had been a fundamental shift. The Kialegee Tribal Town had since partnered with one of the wealthiest and most powerful gaming families in Las Vegas. Lanigan's involvement had dramatically altered the chessboard. Michael Lanigan was a ruthless casino operator, fanatical about vanquishing his competition.

The Chief let out a long breath. "We need a sit down with Jeremiah before it's too late."

Hawkins disagreed. "Chief, the court could still rule in our favor."

"That's the only card we have left to play," the Chief said. "But we're running out of time to play it." His expression was serious, but something in it hinted at fear.

"If the judge rules against the Kialegee, they get nothing."

The Chief's eyes opened wide. "Are you willing to play Russian Roulette? Because that's what we're doing if we sit back and do nothing."

Hawkins was silent.

"Chief. Lyman thinks we have a good chance of getting a favorable ruling," Travis offered.

The Chief shook his head. "We need more than speculation. If the judge rules for Kialegee, we're in deep trouble," he said, calculating the blowback from the new partnership with Michael Lanigan. "They'd have no reason to come to the table."

The Chief couldn't hide his increased apprehension. "We have a small window while there's still uncertainty and there's a chance that they can end up with nothing."

Hawkins's jaw clenched. "Chief, I think this might be premature."

Turning his gaze to Travis, "Even if the judge rules against us, can't we appeal and tie them up? At that point we would have a reason to negotiate," Hawkins said, trying to get control of the conversation.

Travis chewed his lower lip. "We could argue that the MCN was an indispensable party on appeal. But there's no guarantee that we would be successful. Even if we have standing to appeal the appellate court may not stay the judge's order. Meaning the Kialegee would be free to move forward."

Hawkins cut in. "But Lanigan might not be willing to take the risk."

Travis disagreed.

The Chief looked past Hawkins. "Travis, I want you to reach out to Jeremiah and arrange a meeting."

Travis looked almost instantly uncomfortable. "What if he doesn't want to meet?" It wasn't a question that he wanted to ask, but there was no getting around it.

The Chief thought about it for a second. "Jeremiah has always been reasonable and a big believer that tribal leaders should resolve their differences without outside interference."

Travis let out a deep sigh. "Normally, I would agree but one of our officers tried to rape his daughter and we've done nothing about it."

Hawkins went rigid. "You're still whining about that? Your office cleared Officer Huft of all wrongdoing."

Travis shook his head. "My office did what was necessary so the feds would stop asking questions. The point I'm trying to make is that Jeremiah's probably holding a grudge."

The implication was clear but instead of recoiling, Hawkins smiled. "If he doesn't come voluntarily, the Lighthorse will pick him up."

Travis laughed. "Yeah right. That will definitely set the tone for a productive meeting."

The Chief clapped his hands together. "Enough. I'll call Jeremiah myself and offer an apology and tell him that we've disciplined Officer Huft. I'll suggest that we meet at a neutral site," the Chief said, in a tone that left no doubt that he was in charge.

*****

Jeremiah reluctantly agreed to the meeting. With many of his Kialegee tribal members related to MCN tribal members, Jeremiah knew not listening to what the MCN had to say would be criticized. Jeremiah had no choice but to swallow his anger and play the game that politics required.

Chief Yahola, Travis Alexander and Police Chief Hawkins were already waiting in the conference room when Jeremiah entered the room followed by Juanita and Pierce. Chief Yahola stood up to shake Jeremi-

269

ah's hand, and after some strained pleasantries he said, "I thought we agreed on no lawyers."

Jeremiah nodded in Travis's direction. "He's your Attorney General, ain't he?"

"He's also a tribal member."

Jeremiah's expression hardened. "Still a lawyer."

Chief Yahola smiled easily, hiding his anger at Jeremiah's audacity. "Fine. Travis do you mind stepping outside?"

Jeremiah cut in. "It doesn't matter if he leaves. My lawyer stays or there's no meeting."

Chief Yahola wanted no part of Pierce, knowing that with him sitting by Jeremiah's side it would be that much harder to convince him to walk away from the lawsuit.

Not having any choice Chief Yahola smiled and said, "Why don't we take our seats and get started?"

They all settled into chairs around the conference table. There was an awkward silence before Jeremiah addressed Chief Yahola by his first name. "Randall, neither one of us has any interest in wasting time, so why don't you start since you asked for the meeting."

Hawkins eyed Jeremiah disbelievingly. "He's your chief. Show some respect," Hawkins barked.

Jeremiah leaned forward in his chair and stared directly into Randall's eyes. "He's not my chief."

Chief Yahola waved his hand at Hawkins to silence him. "Jeremiah and I go back a long time."

Looking at Hawkins he asked, "Why don't we dispense with formalities?" Even though Randall put his words in the form of a question, his tone made it obvious that it was an order. He shared Jeremiah's sentiment. Neither had any interest in meeting longer than necessary. They both understood the purpose of the meeting and there was no point in pretending that they liked each other. "Jeremiah, we have a few things to work out and one to rectify. There has been a breakdown in communication, and I believe that led to misunderstandings and transgressions by both sides."

A look of annoyance passed across Jeremiah's face. "Transgressions? What transgressions did the Kialegee commit against the MCN?"

"You didn't come to us and ask for permission to develop your casino. If . . ." Chief Yahola's voice faded for a moment as he chose his next words. "If you had, we would have worked something out. Which is what we're here to do."

Jeremiah glared at Randall. "We don't need your permission to develop our land."

A frown formed on Randell's lips. "The MCN has jurisdiction over the treaty lands including the lands owned by the Kialegee."

"It's always been that way." Hawkins chimed in.

"That don't make it right," Juanita said.

Jeremiah nodded in agreement. "This bureaucratic amnesia has to end. The Kialegee signed the treaties and are federally recognized same as the MCN."

"Are you saying you believe the Kialegee are on equal footing with the MCN?" Hawkins asked in an openly disrespectful tone.

Jeremiah pulled out his phone just for show. "We're both federally recognized tribes. I wasn't aware that the MCN has a superior designation. Let me google it." After a quick look at his screen, he said, "Nope, can't find anything."

Randall's agitation appeared to be growing. "Jeremiah, what we want is to work something out tribe-to-tribe. We both believe that outsiders shouldn't resolve tribal differences."

Jeremiah suspected he wouldn't be interested in anything Randall offered, but let it play out. "What are you proposing?"

Randall smiled. "There's no reason that both tribes can't prosper. If you agree to dismiss your lawsuit, we'll give you 1000 acres of land in McIntosh County. You could develop your casino there."

"You're talking about the Hanna Project. That land should already be ours," Juanita said.

Randall's smile faded. "The Bureau of Indian Affairs doesn't see it that way. But we're prepared to relinquish the MCN's claim and support your claim," Randall said, the anger starting to creep into his voice.

Hawkins bristled with a warning and dire prediction of what lay ahead. "You are going to lose and you'll be left with nothing."

Jeremiah considered the offer to be an insult. McIntosh county was sparsely populated, and the land was in a remote part of the county making a casino unfeasible. Randall Yahola was quick to criticize white people for trying to take advantage of Indians, but his actions were no better. The MCN looked down on the Kialegee and this half-assed offer solidified what Jeremiah already knew, that nothing had changed. The MCN expected him to show gratitude for whatever crumbs they tossed them. Jeremiah smiled at Hawkins, hiding his anger for what his officers did to Payton. "If we lose the lawsuit, we'll be no worse off than we are now. From where I'm sitting, I think we're going to win."

Travis swallowed dryly. "I don't think so Jeremiah. The Chairman of the NIGC was at the hearing as were several other legal experts, and the consensus is the court is going to rule in favor of the United States," Travis said in a voice devoid of conviction.

Jeremiah was understandably skeptical. "My lawyer wasn't only at the hearing, he argued the motion. So, I'm more comfortable with his opinion than a bunch of Monday morning quarterbacks."

Randall groaned theatrically. "What is it that you want?" His question reeked of desperation.

Jeremiah turned to Pierce, but his mind was already made up. "What do you think?"

Pierce looked across the room assessing all three faces and their body language. Travis's nervousness seemed to grow as was Hawkins's agitation. And something in Randall's expression hinted at fear. Pierce always found the actions of desperate men to be extremely illuminating.

"Chief, I'm not in the business of making predictions," he began. "But if I was playing poker, and they dealt a hand as strong as the Kialegee lawsuit, I wouldn't fold." He looked directly at Randall. His blue eyes cold as a glacier. "If you accept this offer, it's the same as folding."

Pierce laid his palms flat on the table and spoke in a calm, almost flirtatious voice. "In fact, I'd raise."

Jeremiah nodded. He and Pierce were united in a common cause and seemed to speak the same language and the proverbial stack of chips to be won was too big to walk away from. They had arrived at a juncture where there was only one move. Jeremiah shrugged his shoulders as if to say you have your answer and motioned with his head in the general direction of the door.

"We're going to wait for the court's decision."

*****

Jeremiah reached into his truck and pulled three beers out of the cooler he had tucked away in the back seat. Popping the top of one of the unopened beers he said, "We started this together, and we'll see it through to the end. Juanita and Pierce lifted their beers and nodded in agreement.

"To finishing what we started," Juanita toasted, and they all took a sip.

273

Chapter Forty-Six

WETUMKA, OKLAHOMA

At seven thirty in the morning Jeremiah pulled into the parking lot and lumbered slowly up the wooden steps to the tribal headquarters. He turned on the electric heater in his office to burn the chill from the air and poured himself a cup of black coffee. For nearly an hour he would have the building to himself. When finally, he was ready, he put his phone on silent, put on his reading glasses, picked up the newspaper and began his morning ritual. As he poured a second cup of coffee, he caught sight of Payton's car speeding into the parking lot with Juanita's car close behind. Jeremiah watched intently as Juanita pulled into the lot and jumped out of her car and hugged Payton.

Payton burst into the tribal headquarters, "We won," her voice echoed through the hallway.

"What?" Jeremiah said, caught off-guard trying to process Payton's excited babbling.

Catching her breath, Payton grinned and leapt towards her dad, wrapping her arms around him with enthusiasm. "Dad, we won. The judge ruled for the Kialegee," she said and tenderly kissed his cheek.

Juanita giggled girlishly and turned it into a group hug. "You did it, you old coot. We've been trying to call you."

Jeremiah took a step back and dug into his jacket for his phone. When he looked at his screen, he saw he had several missed calls, three from Pierce. He nodded to himself and took a deep breath. He needed to read the order. Until he could read the judge's words for himself, a sliver of doubt would continue to exist.

"I'll be back," he said, trying to keep his voice even despite the excitement he felt. He grabbed a copy of the order, his cup of coffee and strode purposefully across the parking lot towards his truck. Minutes later, Jeremiah turned right into the Wetumka Baptist Church Cemetery. He stepped through the wooden gate and walked past familiar headstones bearing the names of family members and friends. Eight rows down on the left, Jeremiah knelt next to Samuel's grave. He rubbed the headstone and fought back tears.

"Sammy, today is a good day."

Jeremiah read Judge Hogan's order out loud. The order was 48-pages long and granted the Kialegee's Motion for Summary Judgement.

"The Muscogee Creek Nation can continue to define itself as it sees fit but must do so equally and evenhandedly with respect to the Tribal Towns," Jeremiah read to his grandson. "The 1833 and 1866 Treaties convey rights to all Creek citizens, neither of the four federally recognized Creek Tribes has rights either superior or, importantly, inferior to the other. All four tribes are successors in interest to the historic Creek Nation and all four share jurisdiction over Creek lands."

*****

Jeremiah sat alone with his thoughts and his tears. A tall figure stood by a row of headstones a few feet away.

"I thought I might find you here," he said as he reached down and touched Samuel's headstone.

It had been a year since Jeremiah had seen his uncle. Joshua Tiger had grown visibly older since that day. His cheeks had hollowed, and the dark brown eyes that once commanded respect were clouded and wet. He had more cracks and wrinkles on his face than Jeremiah remembered.

But his long, thick and gray hair swept back in a ponytail was still the same. Joshua Tiger had been Chief of the Kialegee for almost twenty years and fought for his tribe every day. He'd lost count of how many times he travelled to Washington to meet with the Bureau of Indian Affairs to plead for help. Each time they glad-handed him, ushering him out the door. Nothing ever changed, Joshua loathed the circular logic and duplicity but never stopped fighting. The alarmingly high rate of tribal diabetes and unemployment and his inability to make things better weighed heavily on him.

Joshua took a seat on the ground next to his nephew. News of the judge's order made him restless. He seemed like a man eager to settle accounts. The order made it unmistakably clear that the Bureau's and Muscogee Nation's shameful treatment of the Kialegee had come to an end.

Jeremiah knew that Joshua would have no peace until the tribe could take care of its seniors and build a youth center so that the children would have a place to play. When Joshua raised the cigarette to his lips, his right hand trembled. "You look tired," Joshua said.

"I am tired."

Joshua leaned over and rested his hand on his nephew's shoulder. "I'm proud of you."

Jeremiah thought about Samuel and shook it off. "We still have a lot of work to do."

Joshua's face broke into a genuine smile. "What I wouldn't give to see the look on old Randall's face when he gets the news."

Jeremiah nodded, a tight smile barely visible. "Yeah, that'd be a sight."

Without warning Joshua coughed violently into a handkerchief. He drew a few deep breaths then said, "When do you go back to work on the casino?"

Jeremiah wondered himself. "I'm not sure. I'll give our lawyer a call. I don't know if there are things for him to sort out before we can go back to work."

Joshua looked over his shoulder in the direction of the tribal headquarters. "There's a lot of folks back at the headquarters anxious to hear from you," he said.

Jeremiah nodded. He was tired of the case, tired of the pressure and tired of the anger he felt every day.

Jeremiah stood up and held out his hand. "Let's go. You started this fight. I'm just finishing it."

Joshua slowly crushed out his cigarette, grabbed Jeremiah's hand and pulled himself up. He continued to lean on Jeremiah for support as they walked. When they got to his truck, Joshua squeezed Jeremiah's arm. He had a permanent smile plastered across his face. "Finally, we have good news," he said.

*****

JUDGE HOGAN'S clerk emailed the order to all counsel at 10:45 p.m. Pierce thought he would sleep well after getting a favorable ruling. After tossing and turning for most of the short night, he gave up on sleep and got out of bed at 4:00 a.m. His mind wouldn't shut down, so he went downstairs to the gym and started training. Jumping on the rowing machine, he maintained a rigorous pace, his thoughts on the order, and the next steps that needed to be taken. He wasn't sure if the MCN would comply with the judge's order or resist it. After the MCN's illegal siege at gunpoint of the Kialegee's casino, Pierce could not underestimate the lengths they would go to protect their interests. The idea of Lighthorse with automatic weapons in a standoff flashed through his mind. The MCN's lenders had hundreds of millions in loans tied up in the River

Spirit casino. If the casino failed, the ripple effect on Tulsa's economy would be profound. The Kialegee did not have the men to forcibly take back their land, nor would Pierce want it to come to a firefight. He was certain that the state and local police would claim that they did not have the jurisdiction to enforce a federal judge's order involving Indian land.

While Pierce had won a decisive victory for the Kialegee, it didn't mean that there would be a surrender or détente. The conflict still existed and the State of Oklahoma and the MCN he knew they would still oppose the casino.

*****

It was late morning when Mo called Pierce and asked him to meet at Starbucks. He was tucked away in a corner scribbling in the margins of a document when Pierce arrived.

Pierce slid a cup of coffee across the table to Mo and took the seat directly across from him.

"This is a strong order. The judge did a lot of research independent of the material we provided. She made a few observations that we didn't raise in our memo," Mo started.

Pierce stirred his cappuccino with a spoon. Noah slogged in and plopped into the chair next to Pierce. His eyes cried out for sleep and the smell of coffee made his stomach flutter.

Pierce could smell the liquor on him. He looked at Mo and grinned. "Our boy has been doing a little celebrating."

Noah's puffy eyes blinked groggily. "A little too much."

"Get yourself a cup of coffee, better yet, get a double shot of espresso and join us," Pierce said. "We have a lot of ground to cover."

Moses spent the next twenty minutes sharing his opinion of the judge's ruling.

Pierce bided his time, nodding sagely at appropriate moments.

"You know she didn't give the DOJ anything to appeal," Mo said.

"Have you thought about how we enforce the order?"

Mo frowned over the rim of his coffee cup. Deep in thought, Pierce could tell he had not considered the possibility that the MCN might not go quietly. His gaze lingered on Pierce. "Do you think that's going to be a problem?"

Pierce made it his business to anticipate problems before they happened. "I think it would be a mistake not to put together an action plan for regaining control of the property." He slid a sheet of paper out of a manila envelope. "Read this, it was posted on the Muscogee Website this morning. It's a statement from the Muscogee Attorney General."

"While the U.S. District Court in granting the Kialegee's motion essentially ruled against the Muscogee Creek Nation's interests, I do not see it as a defeat. As the Attorney General, I see this as an opportunity to resolve our issues with the tribal towns. My office will work tirelessly to thoroughly review this decision and its legal ramifications and will move forward in a way that best serves the interests of the Muscogee Creek Nation and its citizens."

The statement elicited a flicker of a grimace from Mo. "Do you really think they're capable of disobeying a federal judge's order?"

"No doubt," Noah muttered.

Pierce took a sip, staring into space distracted by a thought. "They wouldn't be disobeying the order if they could convince the BIA to put everything on hold until they could work through how to handle four tribes sharing jurisdiction over the same reservation land."

Mo considered the possibility then shook his head, "This isn't the first case where Indian tribes share jurisdiction over the same land."

"You're missing my point. They can always engineer a reason to keep things status quo until they can put in place procedures to ensure a smooth and safe transition."

"Why would the BIA do that here?"

"They've been complicit all these years and the Kialegee will be taking millions of dollars from both the MCN and the Cherokee."

Mo's eyes opened wide. "A federal agency conspiring with Indian tribes to circumvent a federal judge's order sounds a little farfetched."

Pierce gave him a small, disbelieving frown. "We just sued the United States for violating a treaty by giving the MCN sole jurisdiction over treaty land to the detriment of the tribal towns. It's the same thing."

Mo unconsciously smoothed his hair. It was a habit when he was thinking. "So, what do you propose?"

"We have a small window. I think we need to get out in front of it."

"How do you suggest that we do that?

"We call the Department of Justice and explain that the Kialegee intend to reclaim their property. Since the property was taken illegally at gunpoint and is occupied by the MCN we should ask that the U.S Marshall's office accompany the Kialegee leaders to minimize the threat of an altercation. I spoke to Jeremiah this morning. Rumors are flying. It's safe to assume that the Kialegee are going to show up armed."

"Or I can ask Kathleen McDonough to contact the AG for the MCN," Mo said.

"To what point?"

"To ask her to advise the MCN that the DOJ expects them to abide by the order and not impede the Kialegee from going back on their property."

"I wouldn't trust anything they tell her. To them she's a lawyer a thousand miles away. One way to avoid a standoff is for the U.S. Marshalls to escort the Kialegee onto the property. The Lighthorse are bullies, but they're not stupid."

Mo lowered his chin and peered at Pierce. "Nothing about what you're saying sounds over the top to you?"

"You know the expression, fool me once shame on you fool me twice . . ."

"Shame on me. I know, I know." Moses finished Pierce's sentence for him.

Pierce shrugged. "I would rather take precautions and wind up not needing them than be facing a situation where I wish the U.S. Marshals were there to keep the peace. But with or without them the Kialegee or going to take control of their property tomorrow."

Mo picked up on Pierce's use of the pronoun I. "What do you mean you would rather not face?"

"I'm leaving for Tulsa tonight."

Mo fixed a melancholy gaze on his protégé. "You're a lawyer Pierce. Stay in your lane."   Pierce took note of Mo's critical tone. "When have you ever known me to half-ass a case?"

Mo's face reddened. "For Christ's sake," Mo swore. "This has nothing to do with half-assing anything. We fight our battles in the courtroom."

The expression on Pierce's face seems to say, "Are you kidding me?" The difference between a talented trial attorney and a great fixer is what they did next. The matters Pierce worked on taught him many things over the years, but two of the most important were to be thorough and to be extremely cautious when dealing with powerful, well-funded people. They played by a different set of rules. He stood, patted Mo on the shoulder and said, "I'll let you know how it goes."

Mo hesitated, like he was thinking long and hard about another reason for Pierce to stay, and then threw his hands up in a helpless gesture. "I'll make sure I get a hold of Kathleen."

Noah drained what was left of his espresso. "I can be ready to go in about an hour."

"You're not coming," Pierce nodded thoughtfully. "Go home and get a couple of hours of sleep. Then, get to the office and prepare a Writ of Mandamus that we can file with Judge Hogan. If Mo doesn't have any luck with the Justice Department, we need to be ready with a court order that the U.S Marshal's office will have no choice but to enforce," Pierce said in a tone that said he wasn't leaving anything to chance.

Chapter Forty-Seven

BROKEN ARROW

A white van carrying Jeremiah, Pierce and the Business Committee rolled onto the property with four pick-up trucks following close behind. Pierce spotted five men in the parking lot standing between two vehicles engaged in conversation. Two of the men were wearing Navy blue FBI jackets. Two men were U.S. Marshals, and the fifth was a Lighthorse officer.

Jeremiah jumped out and motioned to the others to stay in their vehicles. He and Pierce started across the parking lot directly towards the men. The officers began walking towards Jeremiah and Pierce. They appraised each other like captains of opposing football teams meeting at midfield. Pierce flashed a television smile. "Gentlemen. Pierce Evangelista, legal counsel to the Kialegee Tribe and this is Jeremiah Tiger, the Chief."

The men exchanged quick, uneasy handshakes.

A squat, powerfully built man with a thick face set in a furrowed scowl handed Jeremiah a set of keys and rushed towards his Lighthorse vehicle before anyone said a word. Five minutes later the black SUV was on the Creek Turnpike headed back to Okmulgee.

"The MCN have cleared out. If there's nothing else Chief, we're going to be heading out," Special Agent Mayfield said on behalf of the federal agents. None of them wanted to be there any longer than they needed to be.

Jeremiah shook his head. "Thank you all for coming."

A sense of relief spread across Jeremiah's face. "That went a lot better than I expected."

Pierce squinted as he watched the cars bearing the insignias of the FBI and U.S. Marshal leave the casino property. He had a hunch that if not for Kathleen McDonough, the transition from the MCN to the Kialegee tribe would not have gone smoothly.

Jeremiah waved at the van and the pickup trucks to pull up in front of the casino entrance. The power to the building had been shut off, so Jeremiah reached into the glove compartment and pulled out a flashlight. When he got within ten feet of the front door, the rancid smell of rotting food hit him like a left cross from a heavyweight contender. Jeremiah's eyes watered and he bent over retching.

*****

Juanita drove to the Walmart about two miles away on Elm and bought twenty bandanas and several flashlights. She sprayed the bandanas with a floral scent before handing them out to the tribal members as face coverings. "Breathe through your mouth," she told them.

Jeremiah was not prepared for what he saw when he walked through the casino entrance. As the tribal members walked through the building, their shock was nearly absolute. Derogatory epithets were spray painted on the walls. The native wood carvings and artwork commissioned to display the proud history of the Creeks were hacked to pieces. All the cameras and video surveillance equipment were missing. The touch screens on most of the slot machines were cracked or kicked in. The rotting food in the coolers emitted a vile smell like that of rotting corpses. Its putrefying vapor had seeped into the carpets and coated the floors. The stairwells reeked of moldering wood and rat droppings. Even with the bandanas, the stench was unbearable and numbing and several of the members had to escape to the parking lot after only a few minutes.

Juanita bolted past Jeremiah, out the front door and just made it outside before she was violently sick. Jeremiah closed his eyes and fought off another wave of nausea. He knew the MCN actions were calculated to produce the most damage possible to delay the opening.

Pierce's eyes were damp and raw as he made mental notes walking through the casino while formulating a plan. He waved at Jeremiah to follow him outside so they could talk.

Jeremiah looked defeated. "We'll never get rid of that smell."

Pierce winced. "It won't be easy, but we'll get it done. The coolers have to go, and I suspect all the flooring and wall treatments as well."

Pierce forced a smile. "We've been through worse. I'll call David and ask him to get his team out here to start assessing the damage."

Jeremiah was quietly fuming and smoking nervously.

"Chief, I think you should talk to your tribal members and keep their spirits up."

Jeremiah shook his head tensely.

Pierce's logical and disciplined mind was working at an accelerated speed. He pulled out his phone and tapped on the surface scrolling for a name.

"Who are you calling?"

Pierce knew the questions running through Jeremiah's mind. "Michael Lanigan's people. You're going to need slot machines, a new security system and a bunch of gaming equipment."

Jeremiah's vanquished eyes came to life.

Pierce spent the next twenty minutes giving Audrey a detailed accounting of the damage to the casino.

"I had a hunch something like this might happen," Audrey said. "Can you stand the smell enough to take pictures?"

"No electricity and bottles filled with kerosene and rags took out the backup generators."

"Okay, we do business with several suppliers in Texas. We'll have a couple of generators up there today. I'll arrange to have a security team there in a few hours."

"I was going to take care of that."

"No, we'll handle it." Audrey cut him off. "No one local."

There was a brief silence on the call. Pierce got the impression Audrey was going through her own mental checklist. "Where are you staying in town?"

"At the Doubletree on Yale."

"I'll book us a conference room there and meet you at 8 am. Now, I have to go. I have a lot of calls to make."

*****

Five hours later a flatbed truck carrying two generators followed by two vans ambled onto the property. Two men holding hardhats, masks and clipboards met Pierce and Jeremiah at the entrance to the building. They were with Lonestar Electric and explained that they were there to get the generators working so the general contractor could get a cleanup crew started. Over the course of the next few hours work crews were busy emptying the contents of the casino into waiting dump trucks.

Before sunset two SUVs turned right and rolled into the parking lot. Jeremiah was standing outside with a cigarette between his lips when he spotted eight men in total climb out of the vehicles and fan out in a synchronized fashion. They were armed and wearing earpieces, looking and moving more like secret service agents than security guards. Jeremiah waved at them and one of the men broke off and started in his direction. A tall linebacker sized man handed Jeremiah his card and explained that they were hired by Michael Lanigan.

*****

Audrey and Monica Malone marched into the lobby of the Double-tree hotel a few minutes before eight. Monica was one of Michael Lanigan's favorite interior designers. He hoped to convince Monica to lend her considerable talents to the interior design of the smaller casino by promising her she would do the interior design for the boutique hotel and the larger casino.

Monica wore a well-cut black suit, and at forty-four, she was as slim as she had been when she graduated from the Parsons School of Design.

Audrey ducked into the Starbucks kiosk in the lobby to buy a Macchiato. There was coffee in the conference room, but Audrey knew from experience that most hotel coffee was flavorless.

There was a knock on the door. Before Pierce could respond it opened. Audrey walked in. She smiled at Pierce and strode purposefully towards Jeremiah with her hand extended. "Chief, I'm sorry we're seeing each other under these circumstances, but we will get this worked out," she said in a confident tone. Everyone took a seat. Audrey walked everyone through the steps that needed to be taken before the casino could open. She was always of two minds, the hopeful half versus the skeptic, optimist against pessimist. She could tell from Jeremiah's grim expression that she didn't need to point out the potential landmines, but Audrey wasn't one to sugarcoat anything.

"Chief, I know you were hoping to open in six weeks. By now, you know that isn't going to happen. It could take us six weeks just to get rid of the odor. We can't bring anything into the

building until the odor is completely gone. You have very high ceilings and a good smoke eating system so that should help."

Audrey continued focusing on the timeline to get the casino open.

Jeremiah seemed to accept the explanation but had a look of pure loathing on his face.

"Your men made a lot of progress yesterday. The coolers and refrigerators as well as the rest of the kitchen equipment is gone, and all the flooring is out," Pierce said.

Audrey had two instantaneous thoughts: the first, that while it looked like they were moving quickly it would be months before the casino could open, second the finished product would be much better.

The door flung open and Payton waltzed in like a guest late for a dinner party.

Jeremiah looked at his watch. "You're late."

"I know, sorry pops."

"Everyone this is my daughter Payton."

Payton swatted Pierce's arm as she breezed by him. Her lips looked like they were attempting to suppress a smile.

Audrey turned the meeting over to Monica. Monica touched on color palettes, motifs, lighting, symmetry to maximize functionality and clear sight lines for easy navigation of the gaming floor. Her questions were calculated to elicit responses that would help formulate a concept that incorporated a mix of the Kialegee culture and the glamor and rich opulence of a Las Vegas casino. The challenge and where she excelled was in making the two work together seamlessly and create a mood that made people feel comfortable and encouraged to give the slot machines a try. She explained the science behind casino design.

When she was done, Jeremiah stepped outside to have a cigarette. He and Pierce rode the escalator and headed out the back entrance into LaFortune Park. They walked along the jogging trail, Pierce and Jeremiah side by side. It would take some time for Jeremiah to process all the information he had just been given. Jeremiah was smart and shrewd when it came to Indian politics but this situation confronting him now was beyond anything he had ever encountered.

Jeremiah drew a deep breath and let it out slowly as a foreboding premonition hijacked his thoughts. "The MCN won't stop trying to sabotage us."

"They probably won't," Pierce agreed.

Jeremiah managed a fatigued smile. "I remember when I was a boy, we didn't think in terms of MCN and tribal towns. We were all Creek." Jeremiah's eyes were fixed on Pierce, but his thoughts were somewhere else. "When the MCN opened their first casino, everything changed overnight, and they started treating the tribal towns like Indians."

"What do you mean?"

"White people look at us like we're second class citizens. Let's just say the MCN started looking at us the same way."

Pierce frowned thoughtfully.

Jeremiah shrugged his shoulders, stopped walking and turned and faced Pierce. Frustration showed on his face. "The MCN will try and get their people hired by us, so they can get information. We can't hire any MCN or any Indians unless they're Kialegee. We also can't hire anyone that worked for any MCN or Cherokee casinos."

Pierce was silent for a moment as he thought of the long road he and Jeremiah had recently travelled; the lawsuits, the raid, Michael Lanigan, and the team of professionals committed to rebuilding and opening the casino before he said with unblemished certainty, "They won't be able to stop you this time."

Epilogue

EIGHTEEN MONTHS LATER

Jeremiah made good on his promise to build a community center and swimming pool for the children. He named the center after his grandson Samuel. He also built a senior center and a medical facility was already under construction. The Kialegee Tribe purchased C.C. pond and the surrounding two hundred acres. They cleaned out all the abandoned vehicles, drained the dirty pond and demolished the buildings. The land was going to be used for tribal housing.

On the three-year anniversary of Samuel's death, two hundred members of the Kialegee Tribal Town gathered at the hole where the C.C. pond once existed. Jeremiah and his two daughters stood at the edge. Dump trucks filled with soil lined up on the opposite side were waiting for the Chief to give the order.

Jeremiah turned around and faced his members. The Business Committee and the Tribal Elders were gathered just behind him. Nora chose to fade into the crowd. Her support for the MCN had been badly undermined by Jeremiah's determination and the success of the casino. For the first time, there was no one who would listen to her rants about the need for having a strong alliance with the MCN. She was cast adrift.

Like Nora, Scott Masters suffered a similar fate. He was no longer the front runner for the Governor's office. The ideological fervor and negativity he used to fuel his popularity faltered. Jeremiah had not forgotten Pierce's advice about retaining well paid lobbyists and public relations firms. The Governor withdrew her endorsement the instant the media broke the story about Scott Masters' lavish expenditures that went beyond the Kialegee trial. And Scott Masters never recovered.

Nikki gestured to Jeremiah that it was time. She was still adjusting to her full-time role as the Kialegee's legal counsel. She accepted the position on the condition that she could still represent poor Indian tribes. Jeremiah nodded and waved at the foreman. "Fill it in."

*****

The boutique hotel, entertainment and eating venues anchored by a Kialegee casino were all open and very profitable. Michael Lanigan's team exceeded expectations by integrating incompatible and distinct themes. The Red Creek Casino fused together beautiful Native American themes with modern design concepts using metal, glass and steel to inspire and awe casino visitors. The marketing team was aggressive and creative making sure the Red Creek Casino was the most popular destination for gambling and entertainment in Tulsa.

The Hard Rock Casino was a distant second, and the MCN River Spirit casino was forced to renegotiate their loans to stay in business. Construction of the second phase of Michael Lanigan's vision was moving at a brisk pace. Payton went to work for Michael Lanigan and was being groomed to one day run the casino.

Pierce successfully restructured the bank financing for the Apache casino project that Audrey mentioned during their first meeting. With Pierce busy flying around the country overseeing Michael Lanigan's projects, Audrey settled into the position of President, allowing Michael to spend more time on his new estate in Ireland.

Noah struggled with the idea of not working with Pierce but eventually left the firm with his blessing to pursue his true calling, a position with Earthjustice, a nonprofit environmental organization dedicated to fighting corporate abuses on behalf of impoverished communities.

*****

Nikki glanced at her watch. "Payton, we should go if you're going to make your flight."

Payton kissed her dad on the cheek. "I gotta go. My flight for Miami leaves in three hours."

"Tell Pierce, he's not getting any younger. He needs to think about settling down," Jeremiah said jokingly.

Payton smiled. "Not yet but soon."

A broad grin spread across Jeremiah's face.

About the Author

Luis Figueredo was born and raised in the Bronx, New York. He completed his undergraduate degree in History from Brandeis University in Massachusetts and earned his law degree from Harvard Law School. He is currently the City Attorney for the City of Doral.

During his legal profession, Luis developed a nationwide practice representing a diverse group of clients that include municipalities, national trade associations, corporations, real estate developers, and Indian Tribes.

Coming Soon!

WHEN CANARIES DIE
BY
LUIS FIGUEREDO

When Canaries Die is a legal thriller involving a deadly pandemic that originates in the Brazilian rainforest. While the pharmaceutical companies race to develop a vaccine for the highly contagious virus, the only thing keeping patients alive are blood transfusions. Blood supplies around the world run dangerously low. The push for the human race to survive the pandemic becomes the only concern, and blood becomes the most valuable commodity. Criminal organizations prey on vulnerable men and women as a major source of trafficked blood. The U.S. border has been shut down by the government to stop the spread of the virus. People fleeing the executions are trapped at the border. With thousands of lives at stake, Pierce Evangelista must convince a federal judge to reopen the border.

For more information
visit: www.SpeakingVolumes.us

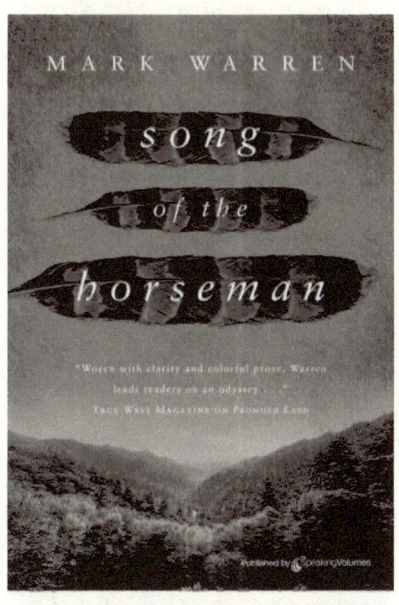